A FATAL AFFAIR

S. F. WILLIAMS

INTRIGUE PRESS

For my Nyes Landing Sleuths

"There is an alchemy of quiet malice by which women can concoct a subtle poison from ordinary trifles."

— NATHANIEL HAWTHORNE

CHAPTER ONE

WHILE PATROLLING the streets of Nyes Landing a little after two o'clock on a drizzly morning in June, wondering whatever possessed me to leave New York City for this snooze of a township nestled in the Catskill Mountains, Suki from dispatch radios that a situation has erupted at the Bear Claw Tavern. No doubt, Oliver Crispin has picked a fight again. I must have responded to at least a dozen incidents involving the volatile actor since he arrived in town last month. With the squad car's lights flashing but the sirens off so as not to disturb any sleeping residents, I make a sharp U-turn and speed toward the scene.

Soon after I accepted a position on the Nyes Landing police force last spring, Daphne Levine, the drama queen from our high school class of 1988, moved home from the city with her several-decades-older husband, Bill Sinclair. He purchased her a mountaintop mansion on the outskirts of town and leased the art deco movie theater in our historic downtown, which offered second-run movies for a dollar when I was a boy. Daphne wholeheartedly threw herself into renovating the dilapidated movie theater into a viable playhouse. Their first production opens tonight.

When I reach the Bear Claw Tavern, Ike—the tavern's burly owner—has Oliver Crispin clenched in a headlock. Crispin stomps on Ike's foot. Ike curses and tightens his grip. Despite being half Ike's size, Crispin refuses to surrender.

Ernest Drucker, a scrawny guy whose wire-rimmed eyeglasses make him look more like a lab scientist than my idea of an actor, cowers behind Terrell Robinson, a gentle giant of a baritone who's also in the show.

"Good luck with this jerk," Ike says. He shoves Crispin toward me and retreats inside his tavern.

"I want one more drink for the road," Oliver Crispin whines. "That's all."

"Bar's closed," I say.

Oliver Crispin rattles the handle of the tavern's door so hard the window shakes.

"Open up, you son-of-a-bitch of a bartender!"

"Move along," I say.

"It's a free country."

"You're creating a disturbance."

"Ollie assaulted me," Ernest Drucker says.

"I never laid a hand on you, Fruit Loops."

"I am not gay!"

"Enough!" I shout. "Go home. All of you. Before you wake up the whole town."

"You're not going to arrest Ollie?" Ernest Drucker says. "He punched me. My nose is bleeding."

"Give me a break," Oliver Crispin says. "That's ketchup from that basket of fries you inhaled."

"You're a menace, Ollie," Ernest Drucker says. "He should be locked up."

"Do you want to press charges?"

"Heck, yeah," Ernest Drucker says.

"He may be behind bars tonight and miss the show," I say, "but that's your call."

"Otherwise, you'll do nothing?"

"I can cite him for drunk and disorderly."

"The hell you will!"

Oliver Crispin stumbles off the curb and falls on his face. I maintain a professional demeanor but am laughing my ass off inside. The inebriated stooge stumbles two more times before he clambers onto his feet and staggers off down the middle of the street.

"Are we really doing this again, Crispin?"

"You told me to leave, so I'm leaving."

If I could trust Crispin to return to the inn and stay out of trouble, I'd let him go. But I can't. He's too intoxicated.

"Place your hands behind your back."

"Don't touch me, faggot!"

Crispin shakes me off.

"You're testing my patience, Crispin."

"I didn't do anything wrong."

"Quit pulling your arms away," I say.

"Get off of me!"

Oliver Crispin and I tussle. I take him to the ground. He tucks his hands under his chest. "Is this how you get your rocks off, Officer Nowak?" He snickers. I wrestle his right arm loose and cuff that wrist. He hurls a stream of lewd curses at me. Nothing I haven't heard before. I wrestle his left arm behind his back, cuff that wrist, and haul him onto his feet. He rubs against me and whispers, "Maybe we can work something out."

Crispin thinks he can seduce his way out of any mess. His magnetic sensuality both attracts and repels me. I open the rear door of the squad car.

"Even if I found you attractive—which I don't—that shit doesn't fly with me. Now, get inside."

Oliver Crispin plops down on the backseat. I tuck his feet inside the vehicle, buckle his seat belt, and slam the door.

"Show's over, boys," I say. "Go home."

Ernest Drucker and Terrell Robinson shuffle down the sidewalk toward the Stone Witch Inn, which is where they're staying while they're in town. The inn's proprietor, Frieda Gladstone, must look forward to the show closing and the actors checking out. Especially Crispin.

Once we're on the road, Crispin suggests we pull over and let him settle his ticket, and his tone makes it clear he's not talking about a cash bribe. I ignore his suggestive comments. He accuses me of police brutality and swears he's going to sue the whole town. We go through this same rigmarole every time I pick him up. The guy's a head case. I ignore his drunken ravings. By the time we reach the station, he's passed out. I shake his shoulders. He bolts awake. I haul his ass inside.

While I'm filling out Crispin's paperwork, he nods off again. I kick the leg of his metal folding chair. He sits up. I issue his citation.

Bill Sinclair strides into the station wearing a black satin bathrobe over matching pajamas, which probably cost more than I earn in a week. Tall and lean, with a thick head of wavy silver-gray hair, intense hazel eyes, and the complexion of a much younger man, he exudes privilege. Even his cologne smells expensive. I release Oliver Crispin into his custody. He does not look pleased, and who can blame him? This is not the first time he's gotten dragged out of bed in the middle of the night because of Crispin's shenanigans, and it won't likely be the last.

By the time I clock out and drive home, Annie is rushing out the door. She teaches second grade at the local elementary school. We dated in high school before I came out as gay. Last year, her husband and my chief high school rival, Kit, died in my arms of a gunshot wound. Watching him bleed out and not being able to do anything to save his life was one of the worst moments of mine. Only topped by witnessing my mother's murder when I was thirteen years old. After I apprehended Kit's killer, who was the town's former chief of police, his successor offered me a position on the local force, and Annie invited me to move in.

Falling into bed, I toss and turn for a few hours before giving up and taking a shower, hoping the steamy spray will wake me up. I need caffeine. Slipping on a sweatshirt and sweatpants, I pad through the living and dining rooms, stepping around the area rug that hides the faint brownish-red stains from where Kit bled out, which no amount of scrubbing will ever remove. Grabbing a carafe of iced coffee from the refrigerator, I chug several gulps of the bitter brew. My stomach rumbles. I need sustenance. Annie baked a lasagna last night. There must be leftovers.

Even after all that coffee, I can't stop yawning. But I promised I'd run errands for the theater this afternoon. I need to learn to say no and not feel like I'm letting everyone down.

After I finish my lasagna, I put my dishes in the dishwasher, brush my teeth, and put on my sneakers. Their rubber soles are coming loose. I need a new pair, but I hate shopping for clothes. Our mom bought our shoes at the thrift store when we were kids, and we wore them until they fell apart.

Hopping behind the wheel of my chili-pepper red Ford F-150 pickup, which I purchased with cash last summer from a former high school buddy of mine, Joe Farley, who works for a dealership in Kingston, I cruise through town. Downstaters waiting for tables crowd the sidewalk outside the Nyes Landing Diner. Summer has arrived with a vengeance.

Turning left onto Birch Lane, I cruise past The Sisters of Mercy Catholic Church with its Gothic steeple, which was constructed in the 1800s from locally quarried bluestone, and Turtle Park with its rainbow-colored playground and kidney-shaped swimming pool. Victorian mansions give way to ranch-style homes interspersed with clapboard farmhouses. Leaving the town limits, I cross over the Esopus Creek bridge and pass through a heavily wooded area.

Mama Libby's farmhouse tops the hill ahead. Had she and

Papa Frank not taken me and my younger sister, Mary Catherine, into their home after our mother's death, I might have ended up on the other side of the law. Last fall, Demetrius and I painted the siding and rebuilt the front porch, and I hired a buddy of his to replace the roof. I park behind Moses's beat-up Chevy Impala. The old guy rents the apartment over the garage.

"Wipe your shoes off before you come inside," Mama Libby says. "I just swept and mopped the floors."

I stomp my feet on the mat and step through the door. A massive green and orange puppet that's shaped like a plant with teeth takes up half of the room.

"I can't wait to get this monstrosity out of my house," Mama Libby says. "It took me two weeks to stitch together those roots or limbs or tentacles or whatever they're called. Sparky chewed a hole in one of its leaves this morning. That's why I locked her in the mudroom."

Sparky barks. She must've heard her name. The golden retriever-border collie mix could give the Energizer Bunny a run for his money, but she's smart. Last spring, she helped me find a missing boy.

"Would you like coffee?" Mama Libby asks. "Or a sandwich? I have some leftover smoked ham from the Memorial Day picnic last weekend."

"I should go. Bo Satterlee asked me to pick up some supplies from the hardware store. What time should we swing by for you tonight?"

"Gladys Crabtree offered me a ride to the theater. She must have a juicy piece of gossip she can't wait to share."

"Are you sure?"

"Gladys may be an old fool, but we grew up together. She's practically family."

"I'll see you at the show, then."

"With Demetrius, right?"

"That's the plan."

"How's he doing?"

"Okay, I suppose."

"What do you mean 'you suppose'?" Mama Libby says. "Don't the two of you talk?"

"Sure, we talk."

"Do you listen?"

"I need to go."

"Callum Nowak, that man is the best thing that ever happened to you."

"So everyone keeps telling me."

Mama Libby follows me outside.

"I love you, son, but you push people away."

"I'll see you tonight."

I load the giant puppet into the bed of my pickup and drive away, wondering why everyone expects so much from me.

CHAPTER TWO

DEMETRIUS CARRIES a bundle of two-by-fours out of his hardware store and slides the boards into the bed of my pickup. I add a bucket of paint and a shopping bag full of brushes, drop cloths, and other supplies to the load.

"That's everything," Demetrius says. "I'll close up shop early tonight so we can grab dinner before the show."

"Where should we meet?"

"I'll pick you up."

If Demetrius expects to spend the night, he's going to be disappointed because I'm running on fumes and need sleep. We've dated—a word that still sounds foreign coming out of my mouth—for the past year. Before that, I'd seldom slept with the same guy twice. Demetrius has an ex-wife and a little girl and had never slept with a man before me. Being a mixed-race, same-sex couple in small-town Americana, we've had our share of altercations with the local bigots, but most folks have accepted, if not embraced, us.

Demetrius backs me against the pickup's grille and kisses my mouth. Slipping out of his embrace, I mumble, "I'll see you later."

Cops probably shouldn't be in relationships. We've seen too

much of the dark side of humanity. On top of the stresses of the job, gay cops must cope with homophobia. A buddy of mine in the city who got outed by a jealous ex-lover couldn't handle the ridicule he faced from his own squad and ate his gun.

A few blocks further down Main Street, I pass through the town's two-block-long historic district and make a left onto Pine Grove Road. Turning into the alley that runs behind the Nyes Landing Playhouse, I back my pickup into the loading dock.

Bo Satterlee greets me dressed in his signature flannel shirt, blue jeans, and hiking boots, with his walnut-brown hair tied back in a ponytail. When Bo wasn't chasing skirts in high school, he discovered he had a talent for carpentry. He now runs his own furniture design studio and volunteered to build the sets for the show. He and I unload the supplies.

"How's the show going?" I ask.

"I don't see how I'm going to build this set by tonight."

"If you need a spare set of hands, put me to work."

"You failed shop class, dude."

"My lamp's electrical wiring shorted out," I say as I follow Bo inside the theater. "That wasn't my fault."

When I worked for the NYPD, I often got dispatched to theaters on and off Broadway, usually for petty thefts that didn't require venturing further than the lobby. The few shows I've attended as an audience member looked so polished. Nothing like the chaos that prevails backstage here. Volunteers rush back and forth like they're prepping to perform brain surgery, not producing a play—a word that implies fun.

Howie Fowler hoists a cumbersome lighting instrument up a ladder. The husky local mechanic and I played football together in high school. He, Sergeant Oakley Reeves, and Annie's deceased husband, Kit—the Grunt Squad—gave me and everyone else in our class hell. But we're civil now.

While clamping the lighting instrument onto the metal pipe mounted into the ceiling, Howie drops his wrench. In his attempt to catch the falling tool, he loses his grip and shouts. "Heads up!"

Stanley yanks Annie's mom, Nadine, to safety seconds before the lighting instrument crashes against the floor. Nadine stares at the mangled mess, her mouth agape. Dust and paint streak her bedazzled pink sweatsuit. Stanley hugs Nadine against his chest. The couple met at a realtor convention a few months back. When he landed a role in the show, she volunteered to manage the production.

"Sorry about that, Mrs. Leighton," Howie says, scrambling down the ladder, which creaks under his bulk.

"She could've been seriously injured," Stanley says. "You should be more careful."

"I'm really sorry," Howie says. He looks like he might cry.

"No harm done, Howie," Nadine says. She sees me and smiles. "Did you pick up Bo's supplies?"

"They're in his more than capable hands."

"You're the best."

Nadine crosses the item off her task list.

"Washington's family is coming tonight," I say. "She is so excited."

Officer Shirisha Washington fancies herself the next Whitney Houston, but she's built like a linebacker. The rest of us officers worked overtime for the past couple of weeks so that she could rehearse. Washington's a stand-up gal. She'll make it up to us.

"Shirisha is . . . enthusiastic," Nadine says. "I'll say that much."

"I should run my lines," Stanley says. He kisses Nadine on the cheek and goes to his dressing room.

"You really like Stanley, don't you?"

"He's a good man," Nadine says. "And he makes me laugh."

"Who do I talk to about getting tickets for tonight?" I ask.

"Demetrius already reserved your seats."

"Of course he did."

"You won the lottery when you met that man."

I'm tired of hearing how wonderful my boyfriend is, but I must agree. Demetrius is handsome and kind. He's a good father to Cora. He treats me better than I deserve. But in my experience, the good times never last.

A heavyset young woman dressed in a hoodie and blue jeans rushes through the loading dock entrance. She brushes her dull-brown curls out of her eyes. Her fingers look purple. "Excuse me," she says. "I'm Vona Thomas. The Sinclairs's housekeeper."

"I'm Nadine, the show's production manager. How can I help you?"

"Mrs. Sinclair asked me to bring her a bottle of elderberry syrup."

Vona holds up a small tote bag.

"I'll take that," Nadine says.

"No offense, ma'am," Vona says, "but I would prefer to give Mrs. Sinclair the package myself. It's not that I don't trust you. It's just that, well, she can be . . . trying. I'm sure you understand."

"Do I ever," Nadine says. "Down the hall on your left. The dressing room with the giant gold star on the door."

A circular saw screeches.

Ernest Drucker rushes up and sticks his fingers in his ears. "I can't work under these conditions!" He removes his wire-rimmed eyeglasses and dabs the sweat off his brow with a handkerchief. "You promised I could rehearse on the stage this afternoon."

"How much longer are you going to be, Howie?" Nadine asks.

"Maybe half an hour or so," Howie shouts down from atop his ladder.

"Tell you what, Ernie," Nadine says. "In an hour, I'll clear the stage and let you rehearse for thirty minutes."

"This company is so unprofessional," Ernest Drucker says, and he stomps off.

Oliver Crispin swaggers out of his dressing room. Ernest Drucker tries to step around Crispin, but Crispin blocks his path.

"What's the matter, Ernie?" Crispin asks. "Did you and Bert break up?"

"I'm not gay."

"Methinks the faggot doth protest too much."

"That's not funny, Ollie."

"Neither is your performance," Oliver Crispin says. "You do realize this show is a comedy?"

"Bite me, butthead!"

Ernest Drucker shoves past Oliver Crispin and ducks inside his dressing room. Crispin laughs and returns to his dressing room.

Bill Sinclair ambles through the open roll-up door from the loading dock. He looks like a million bucks in a crisply tailored suit and tie. His black oxfords shine. He knocks and enters his wife's dressing room. Vona scurries out and departs the theater in haste.

"Before you go, Cal, I want to give you this." Nadine hands me a tote bag. "For your weekend away."

Demetrius and I are going camping this weekend, a prospect that gives me the willies. Nothing good ever happens in the woods.

Helena Potter, another former classmate, rolls a wardrobe rack loaded with costumes through the door. She wears layers of lacy black clothes and heavy dark makeup and sports a spider tattoo crawling up her neck that she has had for as long as I can remember. She runs her own ceramics gallery. Downstaters pay exorbitant prices for her pieces.

"Cal, am I glad to see you," Helena says. "Did you pick up the puppet from Mama Libby?"

"Yes, m'lady. It's right over here." I show Helena where I piled the green and orange monstrosity and ask, "If it's a plant, why does it have teeth?"

"Come see the show and find out."

"Demetrius and I will be here tonight. How's Washington doing?"

"She's loud," Helena says. "Which would be okay if she hit the right notes."

"Ouch."

"Don't tell Shirisha I said that," Helena says. "She's a sweetheart." She rolls her eyes. "I wish I could say the same for Daphne. I should never have offered to help with the costumes for her stupid show. If that bitch doesn't like any of these dresses, she can go on stage in her birthday suit."

Oliver Crispin sneaks up behind Helena and grabs her ass.

Helena whips around. "What the—?" Her face lights up. "I might've known."

"After the show tonight," Oliver Crispin says, kissing her neck, "let's—." He whispers in her ear. Helena giggles, a sound I've never heard her make.

Daphne strides out of her dressing room wearing a red silk kimono and slippers. A wig cap covers her blond curls. "There you are, Helen. I thought you would never arrive."

"Helena."

"What?"

"My name is Helena."

"That's what I said."

"You called me Helen, not Helena."

Daphne rummages through the clothes on the rack.

"Helen, did you bring me anything that isn't hideous?"

"There are several cute dresses here you might squeeze into," Helena says, "assuming you haven't gained any more weight."

Crispin chuckles.

"Ollie, go run lines," Daphne says.

"Don't be jealous, baby." Crispin wraps his arms around Daphne. "There's more than enough of me to go around." He swaggers off.

"I realize you're not a theatrical professional, Helen, but you mustn't distract Ollie. He needs to focus on his performance."

"I'll leave this rack in your dressing room," Helena says. "Along with some lard and fishing line that you can use to squeeze your fat ass into whatever dress you decide to wear."

"You can't talk to me that way."

"What are you going to do?" Helena says as she rolls the rack away. "Fire me?"

"You always look stunning, darling, no matter what you wear," Bill Sinclair says. He kisses his wife's cheek. "Break a leg tonight."

"Why would you say something so awful?" Nadine asks.

"'Break a leg' is how actors wish each other good luck," Daphne says.

"That makes no sense," Nadine says with a shake of her head.

"Did you need something, Nadine?"

"This nice young man delivered the rental tables and chairs for tonight's after-party."

A lanky kid in his late teens or early twenties steps forward and flashes a crooked grin. He's missing a front tooth.

"Tell him he can leave the rental furniture in the lobby," Daphne says. "I would've thought that was obvious."

"That's where he put everything," Nadine says. "He needs to get paid."

"Tell him to send me an invoice."

"No can do, ma'am." The guy hands Daphne the invoice for payment. "C.O.D."

"Cash on delivery," Nadine says.

"I know what C.O.D. means," Daphne says. "Bill, darling—"

"How much this time?" Bill asks.

"Only a measly two hundred and fifty-two dollars."

"You're fifteen thousand dollars over budget, hon."

"Fine," Daphne says. "Send the tables and chairs away. Our guests can sit on the floor."

"Don't be ridiculous." Bill pulls out his checkbook and a pen and fills out and signs a check. "Here you go."

Daphne snatches the check with a smile. "Thank you, darling. Now go fix a martini with that elderberry syrup you like. It'll soothe your nerves."

The Wholesome Table van backs up to the loading dock. Short, stout Rose Ryland and her willowy partner, Trixie Sylvester, climb out and open the rear doors. Catering equipment and foodstuffs for tonight fill the cargo hold. I help the couple unload. Their effusive graciousness envelops me like a warm hug.

"I hope we have enough sauce for the meatballs," Rose said.

"I wish you'd relax, Rose," Trixie says. "Everything will be fine."

"That's what you said the last time. Then, an hour before the event started, I had to drive all over town searching for pomegranate syrup."

"You're never going to let me live that down, are you?"

"Where's the prosciutto?"

"It's in the cooler."

"No, it's not."

"I'll see you gals tonight," I say, and I beat a hasty retreat before they rope me into running any more errands.

CHAPTER THREE

ANNIE SHAKES my shoulders and whispers, "Demetrius is here."

I sit up in my bed and rub my eyes. "Oh, shit!" I'd only meant to rest for a few minutes. "What time is it?"

"Five-fifteen."

"Give me five minutes."

Annie steps out of my room and shuts the door. I sniff a tee shirt I find wadded up on the floor and, deciding it smells clean enough, wear it with faded blue jeans and my tactical boots. I splash cold water on my face and fuss with my cowlick for a few minutes before accepting that the only thing that will tame this unruly mess is the haircut I've been putting off.

"Hey, baby," Demetrius says. He leaps up when I step out of my room, which is situated off the living room and was probably a front parlor in the original house.

"Sorry, I overslept."

"We have a six-thirty dinner reservation for three at the Stone Witch Inn."

"Annie's coming with us?"

"Is that a problem?"

"Of course not."

Since Demetrius and I both own pickup trucks, Annie insists we take her Honda. She tosses me the keys and slides into the back seat. Demetrius climbs into the passenger seat. As I pull out of the driveway, they debate which of the fictional doctors on the television show *ER* is the hottest. Demetrius prefers Dr. Greene, which Annie says is silly because anyone can see that Dr. Ross is hands down the handsomest. I do not know who they're talking about, nor do I care.

At the Stone Witch Inn, Frieda Gladstone greets us with a warm smile and leads us to a table by the fireplace, which isn't lit in the summer. She and her husband, Morris, bought the old Victorian mansion years ago and converted it into an inn, naming it after a woman from the 1700s who was banished to the wilderness for practicing witchcraft. Locals claim her ghost still haunts the surrounding mountains. As if I needed another reason to dread going camping.

"It seems like everyone is on their way to the theater tonight," Frieda says. "Don't get me wrong. I'm grateful for the business." She leans in and whispers, "But I can't wait until that Oliver Crispin checks out. He might be the most disruptive guest who's ever stayed at the inn."

"Drunk and disorderly rates will plummet, that's for sure. I picked up the guy again last night."

"That explains why he didn't come in until after dawn," Frieda says. She passes us menus. "Enjoy your meal."

"Kit and I celebrated our last anniversary here," Annie says.

"If I'd known," Demetrius says, "I would never have—"

"If I avoided every place that Kit and I went," Annie says, "I'd never go anywhere." She opens her menu. "They serve an amazing smoked trout dip. I tried to replicate the recipe once and didn't come close."

A young server with ginger hair and freckles approaches our table. "Would you like to hear our specials?"

"I would," Annie says.

"For an appetizer, we have a polenta topped with an asparagus relish. The chef's specialty is a roasted duck breast with a raspberry glaze. Our pasta is a fettuccine with smoked trout, shaved fennel, and tarragon. And for dessert, we're serving a mixed berry cobbler that's topped with a Chambord-infused whipped cream."

"Everything sounds yummy," Annie says.

"We'll start with the trout dip," I say. I don't like smoked fish, but Demetrius and Annie do. "And an order of the sticky chicken wings."

"I've had those before, too," Annie says. "They're good."

"Certainly," our server says. He scribbles on his order pad.

"I'll have a glass of rosé while I decide," Annie says.

"A double Jameson on the rocks for me," I say.

"I'll have a cognac," Demetrius says. "And water for the table."

A lanky busboy with shaggy hair and a goatee brings us three glasses of water.

"Ask and you shall receive," our server says.

From the snippets of conversations I overhear, the surrounding diners look forward to seeing the show tonight. I stifle a yawn. I hope I can stay awake.

"This weekend, Cal and I are going camping," Demetrius says. "He can hardly wait."

My jaw tightens.

"I can only imagine what you had to do to convince him to go," Annie says.

"I don't kiss and tell," Demetrius says.

"You two aren't as funny as you think," I say.

I find the men's room and splash some cold water on my face. As a cop, I must stand strong. But whenever I venture into the woods for more than a few minutes, I can't help but relive those five awful days and nights I spent hiding from my mother's killer in the old paper mill when I was thirteen years old.

"Are you all right?" Demetrius asks. I didn't hear him come in. He brushes my hair out of my eyes and hugs me.

"Fine." I wash my hands. "Let's eat."

Our server brings our drinks and takes our order.

"I saw Evan Langford in the hallway today," Annie says. "That little boy is growing like a weed."

Evan Langford, the little boy I rescued from a pedophile last year, must be eight years old by now. To have gone through something that awful at such a young age puts my adolescent trauma in perspective.

"He's staying with a nice foster family in Wuduland," Annie says.

Wuduland—a small hamlet of Nyes Landing with a population of a little over three hundred people—lies about six miles northwest of town.

"If his parents don't clean up their act," Annie says, "they're going to lose custody."

"I know it sounds harsh," I say. "But that might be for the best."

"If a pedophile ever laid a finger on Cora," Demetrius says. "I'd beat him bloody."

Although Demetrius is one of the chillest guys I've ever met, when his papa bear side rears its ugly head, look out. I spotted a guy one time I thought might be watching his daughter. He came unglued and would've seriously injured the guy had I not intervened.

Our appetizers arrive. Annie and Demetrius scoop pita chips into the cheesy trout dip. I gnaw the meat off a sticky chicken wing.

"I have a garage full of Kit's old camping equipment that I'll never use," Annie says. "If you guys need anything for your trip, help yourselves."

"Nadine gave me a bear horn today," I say, "and a first aid kit."

"That's my mom. She's always taking care of everybody but herself."

"If what I saw her dealing with this afternoon is any indication," I say, "she has her hands full at the theater."

"I spoke to Mom earlier," Annie says. "She warned me not to expect too much tonight."

Our server removes our appetizer plates and sets our entrees before us.

"Would anybody like to try the roast duck?" Demetrius asks.

I shake my head.

"I would," Annie says.

Demetrius feeds Annie a bite. She offers him a forkful of her salad, which he declines. I slice off a hearty bite of my strip steak and savor its juicy tenderness.

While we eat, Demetrius prattles on about all the errands he must do before our camping trip. I can't bail on the guy again. I'm out of excuses. But I do not look forward to spending the night in a tent in the woods, surrounded by whatever lurks out there in the darkness. I wipe my clammy palms on my jeans.

On our way to the theater, we pass the drugstore. Ernest Drucker rushes out the door, clutching a small white shopping bag. He waves. I nod back.

"Who's that?" Demetrius asks.

"My new boyfriend."

Demetrius slouches against the passenger door. Surely, he doesn't think I'd cheat on the hottest guy in town with that little dweeb. I reach across the seat and squeeze his hand. "His name's Ernest Drucker. He's in the show tonight."

From three blocks away, the bright lights of the theater marquee sparkle. We park in the lot across the street.

Ernestine Middleton—the editor-in-chief of the Nyes Landing Gazette—stands on the sidewalk outside the theater, holding interviews. Her cat-eye eyeglasses dangle on a rhinestone chain around her neck. She fluffs her platinum-blond curls and extends a microphone toward Mayor Lucille Miller. Dressed in her signature navy-blue suit, with her auburn hair teased into the shape of a football helmet, the mayor sings the Sinclairs's praises and smiles and poses for the camera. The woman never misses a chance to seize the spotlight.

Inside the restored art deco lobby, an ornate chandelier dripping in crystals and a dozen geometric-shaped chrome wall sconces cast a warm glow over the copper and light green wallpaper and polished marble floors.

Brandy Speedman offers everyone glasses of her spring rosé. She owns a winery in the valley west of town. Her royal blue cocktail dress highlights her ivory complexion and ebony hair, which she wears swept atop her head. Annie and Demetrius accept wine and chat with Brandy about her different grape varietals. I sneak a sip from the flask of whiskey I keep stashed in the pocket of my windbreaker and pretend like I know the difference between a Grenache and a Mourvèdre.

Nadine rushes through the lobby wearing a fuzzy pink sweater and slacks with sneakers and clutching a three-ring binder against her ample chest. She sweeps her white-blond bangs out of her eyes and chatters into her headset. I recognize that look. She's at the end of her tether. An explosion of shattering glass, followed by a shrill scream that sounds more like a toddler throwing a tantrum than a woman in distress, startles the crowd. Nadine shakes her head and disappears inside the auditorium.

A red-faced Bill Sinclair strides through the lobby wearing a spiffy black tuxedo and shiny patent leather Derby shoes. I found out that's what that style of shoes with the open laces is called when I worked security for a charity event in the city. Bill clenches his fists. He looks like he wants to punch someone.

Mama Libby arrives wearing a simple housedress and orthopedic shoes. Gladys Crabtree follows, dressed in her usual tracksuit and sneakers.

"It's shameful, I tell you," Gladys Crabtree whispers louder than most people speak. "And Daphne is not the only gal in town making a fool of herself over that gigolo. I spotted Helena with him at the diner, and they looked like they'd stayed up all night. What is the world coming to?"

"Helena must be getting something in return," Mama Libby says.

"We all know what that is, too."

"Lord, give me the strength not to choke this old nincompoop."

"You're terrible, Becky Goodman."

Nadine rushes through the lobby and confers with Jenny Miller, Mayor Miller's teenage daughter, who's working the box office.

A striking young woman with long, sleek black hair and a complexion the color of dried wheat strolls through the door dressed in an emerald-green cape embroidered in gold over a matching tunic and pants. Her poise turns heads. She acknowledges everyone with a polite nod.

Demetrius leans in and whispers, "Isn't Padma beautiful?"

"How do you know her?"

"I met her at the town council meeting for small business owners this past spring."

"That gorgeous woman lives in Nyes Landing?"

"She owns the Sacred Roots Apothecary."

"That yellow and blue candle shop on Warbler Lane?"

"Padma sells candles and other gift items, but she's also an apothecary."

"An apothe—what?"

"A person who's knowledgeable about herbs and natural health remedies. She taught me that echinacea bolsters the immune system."

"Does it?"

"I haven't caught a cold since I started taking the tablets."

Chief Jimenez arrives dressed in a white suit and tie, with her buzzcut slicked with gel. Her girlfriend, Marta, wears a yellow sundress with high heels and has her sleek mahogany hair twisted up in a spiky bun. A study in contrasts, the couple celebrated their tenth anniversary together last fall.

Sergeant Reeves swaggers through the door with his arm around the waist of a leggy redhead. Given the sergeant's record for playing the field, I'll likely never see the woman again, so I don't bother learning her name when we're introduced.

Annie's former mother-in-law, Bonnie Nye, meanders through the lobby, her face a mask of scorn. When Kit died last year, Bonnie blamed Annie for her son's death and frequently attacked Annie in public. Horace Nye shuffles along behind his wife, a giant of a man crushed by the loss of his son.

"Annabelle," Bonnie says. "You look healthy. Have you put on weight?"

Annie smiles at her mother-in-law, but her shoulders slouch.

Nadine rushes over. "I swear, Bonnie, you look younger every time I see you." She leans in and whispers conspiratorially. "I guess that new Botox stuff really works, huh?"

Bonnie Nye stiffens. "I would never." She leads her husband away in a huff.

Demetrius and I stifle our laughter.

Locals and downstaters fill the lobby. From the snippets of conversations I overhear, everyone seems impressed with the restoration of the old movie house. I must agree. It feels like we've stepped back in time.

A boisterous group of three women and two men bustles inside the lobby. Their towering height and prominent facial features leave no doubt that they're Officer Washington's family members.

"This play better be good," Gladys says. "I'm missing *ER*."

"That show is too bloody for me," Annie says.

"Every week," Demetrius says, "she makes some lame excuse

to step away during the final ten minutes when all hell breaks loose in the emergency room."

When Demetrius and I began dating, he'd resented how much time I spent with Annie. Now, those two often hang out while I'm on night patrol. I'm glad they're friends, but I don't appreciate when they gang up on me.

"I need more wine," Annie says.

"Did I hear someone say more wine?" Brandy tops off Annie and Demetrius's glasses. I sneak a shot of whiskey from my flask.

Nadine opens the doors that lead into the auditorium. "Ladies and gentlemen, the house is open." She flashes the lights in the lobby. "Please take your seats."

Demetrius excuses himself and goes to the men's room. I went before we left the restaurant, so I'm good. Annie and I glance over our programs. Daphne looks like she's still in high school in her headshot. The hyperbole in her biography gives me a chuckle.

"I realize you're tired," Annie says, "but be nice to Demetrius."

I sigh.

"In ten years of marriage, Kit never once looked at me the way Demetrius looks at you."

"I'm a mess."

"Horse hooey! You're just afraid you'll get your heart broken." Annie hugs me. "Give love a chance."

"What are we talking about?" Demetrius asks when he returns.

"Me being an asshole." I smile and take his hand. "Shall we find our seats?"

CHAPTER FOUR

Following a smattering of applause, we file out of the theater. No one seems to know what to say. Except for Gladys Crabtree, who never met a silence she couldn't fill.

"If that wasn't the silliest play I have ever seen," Gladys Crabtree says. "A man-eating plant from outer space." She scoffs. "That sings, no less."

It's rare that I agree with Gladys.

"When was the last time you went to the theater, Gladys?" Mama Libby asks.

"My daughter, Clarissa, took me to see *Beauty and the Beast* on Broadway."

"That was ten years ago."

"I know what I like, don't I?"

"I don't know, do you?"

"Yes, Betty, dear, I do."

"Drive me home, Gladys," Mama Libby says. "I've had about all of your nonsense I can stand for one night."

"Fine," Gladys says. "They're not serving gin at the bar anyhow."

Padma Patel glides past us.

"That woman is hiding something," Gladys Crabtree whispers. "Mark my words."

"Give it a rest, Gladys," Mama Libby says. She kisses Demetrius and me on our cheeks and hugs Annie. On her way out the door, she wishes Nadine a good night.

Stanley strolls into the lobby, having changed out of his costume into a golf shirt and chinos. He slips his arm around Nadine's waist and says, "We made it all the way through the show without stopping."

"Hallelujah and pass the wine," Nadine says.

"You cracked me up, Stanley," Annie says.

"Me, too," Demetrius says. "I don't understand what women see in Oliver Crispin, though. He's a maniac."

"Some women find that sort of manic energy exhilarating," Annie says. "I should know. I was married to Kit for ten years."

"Ollie is a mess, but he's incredibly talented," Stanley says. "He'd be on Broadway if he weren't so strung out on booze and drugs."

"Say what you will about the guy," Nadine says. "He was always on time. He knew his lines and his music. He never gave me any grief."

"Unlike Daphne?" Stanley says.

"Don't get me started," Nadine says.

"I almost stood up and applauded when that alien plant thing finally ate Daphne," I say. "But I was afraid she might take that as a compliment and return for an encore."

"You're terrible, Cal," Annie says, and she gives my arm a playful slap.

"Daphne doesn't sing so much as screech," Demetrius says. "Like an owl." He leans in and whispers, "And I don't think your cop buddy is going to be cutting any recording deals."

I wish I could defend Sharisha, but I can't. She drowned out Kiki from the diner and the other woman she shared the stage with. Turned their trio into her personal solo, which even to my untrained ear sounded off-key.

"I have no idea what I'm going to say when Sharisha asks me what I thought of the show."

"You're going to lie, Cal," Annie says, "like the rest of us."

On a banquet table along the wall, Trixie and Rose have arranged a steaming hot pot of meatballs swimming in marinara sauce surrounded by an impressive spread of locally sourced meats and cheeses and bowls of grilled and raw vegetables. Rose stands behind the table, with her bushy salt-and-pepper curls tucked under a hairnet, serving guests in her Save the Peregrine Falcons apron.

Trixie offers guests shots of locally distilled whiskeys and bottles of ale. A hairnet covers her spiked silver pixie cut. She wears a Save the Bog Turtles tee shirt. I have no clue what a bog turtle is, but I'm sure Demetrius does. I don't ask because I'm not in the mood to listen to a lecture on the wonders of nature. Trixie passes me a shot of honey rye whiskey. Its smooth sweetness slides down my throat like liquid candy.

Daphne sails into the lobby wearing a flowing green gown. She swirls through the crowd, greeting her guests from the city with kisses on their cheeks. The women ooh and ah over her dress. Bill lurks in the shadows. He does not look pleased.

"We're going to head out," Chief Jimenez says. "I have an early day tomorrow."

Rose steps away from her station. Ernest helps himself to a bowl of meatballs. He glances over his shoulder and stirs the pot. Rose returns with a stack of paper bowls and resumes her post.

Oliver Crispin swaggers into the lobby with his arm around Helena Potter. Bo Satterlee follows the couple. Based upon their bloodshot eyes and unsteady gait, they're high. So long as they don't get behind the wheel of a car, I'm off duty.

"Let's get this party started!" Crispin shouts. He waltzes Daphne around the lobby. She laughs through feeble protests.

The guy may be an asshole, but he's a good-looking asshole, and his devil-may-care approach toward life looks fun until someone gets hurt.

"You look so serious." Demetrius slips his arm around my waist. "What's on your mind?"

"Should I try another shot of that honey rye whiskey or switch to beer?"

"Are you all right?"

"Why wouldn't I be?"

Sergeant Reeves sidles up beside me. "What do you think of Roxie?"

"She looks like a stripper."

"I know, right? And she's going to dance all over my you-know-what tonight."

"Oakley!" Annie says. "You're not in a locker room."

"Lighten up, Annie."

"I thought we were leaving, babe," Roxie says.

"Keep your tits on, woman."

"Let's grab some fresh air," Demetrius says. He leads me outside. We weave through the crowd of smokers gathered on the sidewalk and slip around the corner. He shoves me against the wall and kisses me hard. I kiss back. He whispers in my ear, "I love you."

Those three little words shouldn't freak me out. Demetrius and I have been dating for over a year now. He's almost too good to be true. Eventually, I'll mess up, though, and he'll move on to someone more deserving of his affections.

"We should go back inside," I say.

As we round the corner, Bonnie Nye shouts, "Oh, gross!" Assuming she's seen us kiss, I'm prepared to give her a piece of my mind when several audience members rush out of the theater. A man in a suit and a woman in a gown double over and puke on the sidewalk.

"What the—?" I rush inside the lobby.

A dozen people tussle over access to the bathrooms. The chief and the sergeant have left, so I take charge of the situation.

"Everyone! Stay put until we figure out what's going on here!"

"I'll alert the chief," Officer Washington says. Dressed in her uniform but still wearing her stage makeup, she resembles a television cop.

"Tell her to call the health department," I say. "We're probably looking at an outbreak of food poisoning here."

Daphne charges toward Rose and Trixie, shouting, "You did this on purpose!"

"You're out of your mind, woman," Rose says.

"Calm down, Daphne," I say, hoping I can diffuse the situation.

"Those nasty women poisoned my audience on purpose."

"That's slanderous!" Rose steps between Trixie and Daphne. "The Wholesome Table has an A-plus rating from the health department."

"What possible reason would Rose and Trixie have for poisoning your audience?" I ask.

"They've held a grudge ever since—"

"If anyone holds a grudge, it's you, lady," Trixie says.

"We sued her and her husband in court," Rose says, "and we won."

"The chief is on her way," Officer Washington says.

"We should quarantine the theater."

"I'll lock the doors," Nadine says.

"Let's gather everyone's information," I say.

"This is not how I imagined my opening night going," Officer Washington says. "At least nobody died."

"Yet."

"Way to look on the bright side, Nowak."

"Excuse me, officers," Ernest Drucker says. "I think Ollie might have put something in the food."

"What makes you say that?"

"Ollie pulls pranks all the time."

"Did he say or do anything that made you suspicious?"

"No, but you should search his dressing room."

"What will we find if we do?"

"I don't know. But I'll bet he's behind this."

Ernest Drucker has issues with Oliver Crispin, so I don't take his accusation seriously.

Officer Washington and I gather the names and contact information from the ailing audience members. Their breathing is shallow, and they're sweating profusely. Rose and Trixie pass around bottles of water and tell everyone to hydrate.

"They're witches!" Daphne shouts at Rose and Trixie.

"If I were a witch, lady," Rose says. "I'd have—"

"Calm down, Rose," Trixie says. "Your blood pressure's high enough."

"Why would we deliberately make anyone sick?" Rose stammers.

"It wouldn't be the first time," Daphne says.

Rose looks like someone slapped her in the face.

Officer Washington catches my eye. I give her the nod. She confronts Daphne.

"If you don't control yourself, ma'am, I'll detain you."

"How dare you threaten my wife?" Bill Sinclair says. "We're the victims here."

"Are you sick, sir?" Officer Washington asks.

"Certainly not."

"Is your wife ill?"

"She's upset. Her opening night is ruined."

"But is she sick?"

"Not yet."

"Be thankful, then, and let us do our job."

"If you have questions for my wife and me, officers," Bill Sinclair says, slipping his arm around Daphne's waist. "You may speak to our attorney." He passes me a business card embossed in gold, which I pocket, and leaves with his wife.

"Help! Somebody help!" Helena Potter screams. "He can't breathe!"

Officer Washington and I rush over beside Oliver Crispin, who lies sprawled on his back, twitching and gasping for breath. His dilated pupils make me suspect an overdose. I've dealt with my fair share of those in the city. I need to find out what he's on.

Daphne shoves Helena aside and cradles Oliver Crispin in her arms. Bill drags his wife off the guy. "Calm down, darling." He hugs her against his chest. "You're making a scene."

"What did he drink tonight?" I eye Helena and Bo. "Did he do drugs, legal or otherwise?"

"We smoked a joint," Bo says. He twists his ponytail into a topknot. "And knocked back a few shots of vodka."

"We drank some wine, too," Helena says.

"How many drinks did Crispin have?"

"Quite a few."

"The paramedics are on their way," Nadine reports.

"Stay with me, Crispin." I check the guy's pulse. His skin feels hot to the touch, yet he's not sweating. His heart rate is quite erratic. "Calm down, buddy," I say. "Breathe." I sit Crispin up and tilt his head backward so he won't choke if he throws up. He's not salivating, which is odd. "Talk to me, Crispin. Come on, buddy." I stick my fingers down his throat and open his airway. "Breathe, dammit!"

"Spiders!" Oliver Crispin claws at his arms. "They're crawling all over me! Brush them off! Brush them off!"

"I don't see any spiders, Crispin," I say. "Do you see any spiders, Annie?"

Annie cups her hand over her mouth and shakes her head. I imagine she's recalling the night Kit bled out in my arms. I know I certainly am.

"The spiders are eating me alive!"

"What's happening, Cal?" Annie asks.

I don't know what to say. This is unlike any overdose I've ever dealt with.

"Crispin, listen. There are no spiders."

Crispin's eyes widen in horror. He points at me. "They're crawling out of your nose and mouth!"

"You're seeing things, buddy."

Crispin locks eyes with me and mumbles, "I'm scared."

"Hang in there. Help is on the way."

Crispin seizes. His eyes roll backward, and he gags. I tilt his head to the side. He dry heaves.

"Where the hell are those medics?"

CHAPTER FIVE

Two medics rush inside the lobby of the theater. Nadine points them in our direction.

"We'll take things from here, officers," the portly medic says. Beads of sweat dot his shiny bald scalp. He shoves me aside. The younger medic follows her partner's lead. I step back and let the pair do their job.

"Whose drink was this?" Officer Washington asks. She holds up a red plastic cup.

"Probably Ollie's," Helena says.

Officer Washington sniffs the red plastic cup. "Gin."

"I thought you said Crispin was drinking vodka."

"He was," Bo says. "And whiskey. Maybe gin."

"Trixie served whiskeys and ales," I say. "And Brandy offered glasses of her wine. Nobody served gin."

"Ollie probably raided Mr. Sinclair's stash," Bo says. "The dude's a party animal."

"You said you smoked a joint. What other drugs did you do?"

Bo eyes Helena. She shrugs and says, "Ollie brought a gram of coke to the theater tonight."

"I didn't partake," Bo says.

"Me either." Helena adds.

I don't believe that for a moment.

Chief Jimenez bangs on the door. Nadine lets her inside.

"Where's Lecoq?" I ask.

Officer Lecoq may be slight of stature, but his keen eye for spotting details less meticulous officers like me might miss makes him an indispensable member of our team.

"Someone has to keep an eye on the town," Chief Jimenez says, "while we're sorting out this mess."

"What about Reeves?"

"The sergeant didn't answer his phone when I called. And his radio must be off."

"He's probably giving Roxie a cavity search."

"I can't believe that jerk brought a stripper to my show," Officer Washington says.

"Roxie's not a stripper," Chief Jimenez says. "She's an exotic dancer."

Officer Washington and I choke down our laughter.

Nadine opens the door for a nurse from the county health department. I catch the woman up to speed. She checks the vital signs of our victims and assesses their condition. "They're dehydrated," she shares, "but their bouts of nausea seem to have passed."

"They all ate the meatballs," Officer Washington says.

"Did you have the meatballs?" I ask.

Chief Jimenez and Officer Washington shake their heads.

"Neither did I."

Officer Washington's mother and sister stagger out of the ladies's room. Officer Washington grabs two folding chairs so the women can sit down. Washington's mother leans forward and hangs her head between her knees.

"Did you eat the meatballs?" Officer Washington asks. Her mother and sister nod.

"I can't imagine what could've gone wrong," Trixie says.

Despite the best efforts of the medics, Crispin remains in crisis. They hoist the spastic guy onto a gurney. A sobbing Daphne attempts to follow them outside, but Bill holds her back. I catch up with the medics and ask Crispin if he ate the meatballs tonight. He shakes his head, which surprises me. I repeat the question in case he didn't understand and receive the same response. The portly medic crawls inside the box with Crispin and slams the doors in my face. His young partner climbs behind the wheel. The ambulance speeds away, sirens blaring.

It's going to be a long night, and I am running on fumes. I kiss Demetrius, give Annie a hug, and send the pair home.

Officer Washington retrieves plastic gloves and a box of evidence bags, and we gather samples for the health department to analyze. In the city, specialists would've done this work.

A half-hour later, Demetrius knocks on the door and holds up two Gas & Go shopping bags. Nadine lets him inside. "I brought sustenance," he says with a smile.

Several pastries and cups of coffee stuff the bags.

"I was on my way home and figured you could use a pick-me-up."

Demetrius means well, but right now he's a distraction.

"I'm working a crime scene."

"I just thought—"

"You should go."

"I didn't mean—"

"Don't mind me," I say. "I'm tired and cranky."

"Call me," Demetrius says. He ducks out the door. I've hurt his feelings—again.

"Nowak," Chief Jimenez says. "Help Washington search backstage."

"Gather up the trash," the nurse from the health department says, "and anything else that might have made these people sick. We may not need it, but better safe than sorry."

Backstage, I run into Ernest Drucker coming out of Oliver Crispin's room.

"I'm going to take Terrell home," Ernest says.

"How is Terrell feeling?" I ask.

"Weak, but his stomach has settled."

"Do you have your I.D. on you?"

"Sure. Why?"

"We need to identify everyone here tonight."

Ernest pulls out his wallet and hands me his driver's license.

"You're from Columbus?"

"I graduated from Ohio University with my master's degree in classical acting last year," Ernest says. "I'd be performing on Broadway if I weren't wasting my talents in this podunk town."

I jot down Ernest's information and return his driver's license.

"You're free to go. I know where to find you."

In the green room, I find Officer Washington photographing the contents of the refrigerator. To prevent cutting myself on anything sharp, I sift through the trash using my baton and find nothing but empty cups, dirty napkins, and food scraps. I confiscate the plastic liner and tie the flaps shut.

We search through the cast's dressing rooms. A smattering of white powder dusts Crispin's makeup table. My best guess is that's cocaine. I sweep the dust into a bag, which I seal, and I collect his trash, which contains an empty bottle of eye drops, an empty vodka bottle, and several cotton balls smeared with makeup. We collect an empty bottle of gin and a bottle of elderberry syrup from Daphne's dressing room, both of which bear Bill Sinclair's initials.

A play script lies open on the chair before the vanity table.

"The Mirror Crack'd."

"It's an Agatha Christie play that Daphne's thinking about producing next season," Officer Washington says. "I asked her if there were any roles for a talented Black queen. She said maybe. That's better than a no, right?"

The play script isn't likely significant, but I bag it all the same. We load the samples of fluids that we collected from the sick guests into a portable cooler, which I hand over to the nurse from the health department. She suggests we hold onto the rest of the evidence we gathered. If the laboratory needs it for testing, she'll let us know. We exchange business cards, and she drives away.

Officer Washington loads the evidence from backstage into the trunk of the chief's squad car. Nadine tapes the health department notice the nurse gave us over the box office window.

"It's late," Chief Jimenez says. "Everyone, go home. We'll pick up where we left off in the morning."

CHAPTER SIX

F RIDAY MORNING, I reach the station a little before eight o'clock and find Rose and Trixie waiting in the reception area. I acknowledge the couple with a nod. Suki is seated behind the front desk. She and my old high school buddy, Joe Farley, who sold me my pickup, are married and have a six-month-old son.

"How's Daisuke?" I ask.

"He slept through the night."

"I envy the boy."

"I heard you had quite the evening."

"I wouldn't want to be on the clean-up crew for the theater today," I say. "Where's everybody else?"

"Lecoq clocked out and went home to grab a few hours of sleep. The chief drove up to the Sinclairs's house. Reeves is responding to a domestic abuse call."

"Has he requested backup?"

"Nope."

"What are those two doing here?" I nod toward Rose and Trixie.

"They claim they're being set up."

"How so?"

"You'll have to ask them," Suki says. She answers the phone when it rings. "What's your emergency?" After listening for a moment, she says, "Sure, he's here." She passes me the receiver and whispers, "It's the chief."

"What's up, Chief?"

Chief Jimenez fills me in on her meeting with the Sinclairs. They're upset but cooperating with the investigation. I share that Trixie and Rose are waiting at the station. She suggests I hear them out. I invite the couple into the interview room and offer them seats on metal folding chairs.

"What brings you in, ladies?"

"Whatever happened last night was Daphne's doing," Rose said.

"Why do you say that?"

Trixie's cheeks flush. She opens her mouth to speak and stops herself. Her chin quivers. She looks like she might burst into tears.

"That bitch wanted a pond on her property," Rose says, "so she and her husband diverted the stream."

"Is that a problem?"

"Cutting off the water supply for those of us who live further down the mountain? Damn straight it's a problem."

"We could've lost everything," Trixie says.

"We sued and won," Rose says. "Out of spite, those awful people tainted the water supply, killing several of our goats."

"Poor Buddy," Trixie says. "And Lorelei."

"We lost several chickens, too."

"How did they contaminate the stream?" I ask.

"They submerged a deer carcass in the bend upstream of our farm."

"I don't recall hearing about that."

"A deputy from the sheriff's office who had a shitty attitude came out and wrote up a report," Rose says. "He told us that unless we actually saw the couple dump the carcass in the stream, there wasn't much he could do."

"Yet Daphne hired you to cater her opening night party?"

"That surprised us, too," Trixie says.

"We wouldn't have taken the job," Rose says, "but we need to pay our property taxes, which get more expensive every year thanks to our mayor. That woman couldn't balance a budget to save her life."

"Something made those people sick?"

"Maybe Daphne poisoned our food."

"Perhaps you used tainted ingredients."

"We grow all our own vegetables," Trixie says, "and can our own pickles and jams."

"Smoke our own meats," Rose says. "I even grind the chicken we use for our meatballs."

"I appreciate that," I say, "and I'm sure you're careful. But accidents happen."

"I can't imagine how—"

"When we receive the results from the health department, we'll know more."

I show Rose and Trixie out.

Finding myself with a few minutes alone, I pull out the file box I withdrew from the cold case evidence locker several months ago but never sorted through and read my mother's name scrawled across the label. I hope I'm ready for this. I lift the lid.

"There you are, Nowak." Chief Jimenez says.

I fumble around and shove the box under my desk.

"Am I interrupting something?"

"It can wait."

"The Sinclairs seem convinced that Rose and Trixie sabotaged their party."

"Rose and Trixie accused the Sinclairs, and Daphne in particular, of poisoning their food."

"Things could get nasty."

"They already have," I say.

"There might be lawsuits."

"There already have been."

I explain about the deer carcass left in the stream and the subsequent court case.

"We need to smooth over this situation before anyone else gets hurt."

"Have you heard from the lab yet?"

"I spoke with the technician earlier," Chief Jimenez says. "He promised he'd have something for us by the end of the day. The Sinclairs hired a professional cleaning crew to sanitize the theater."

"That seems fast."

"The mayor fears we might be dealing with a viral outbreak."

"That woman watches too many science fiction movies."

"I tried reasoning with her, but you can imagine how that went."

"Any word on Crispin?"

"As of this morning, he's in serious but stable condition."

"What about our other victims?"

"Marta woke up feeling all kinds of queasy—not surprising, considering she put away a lot of vino last night and didn't bother to eat a damn thing. But once she got some food in her, she was good to go."

"I need coffee."

"Me too."

"Black with two sugars, right?"

Chief Jimenez nods.

"Be right back."

It's a beautiful day. I should go for more walks. In the city, I walked everywhere. When I pass the theater, I notice a cleaning crew scrubbing the lobby floor. An announcement posted on the box office window alongside the notice from the health department states that anyone who bought tickets for this weekend can receive a full refund by calling the number below.

At the Nyes Landing Diner, I encounter Ernest Drucker and Terrell Robinson having lunch. Terrell slurps up a bowl of chicken noodle soup.

"How's your stomach, Terrell?" I ask.

"It's been better."

"I feel awful that you got sick," Ernest says.

"Why?" I say. "You didn't poison him."

"Of course not! Why would you say that?"

"Relax, buddy," I say, taken aback by Drucker's fervor. "We'll know more when we receive the results from the toxicology lab."

The two tables of downstaters I recognize from last night appear to be fine. Based upon their conversations, though, they won't be visiting our little town again anytime soon.

At the counter, I order two large coffees from a young guy with a pimply face and crooked teeth. He refuses to take my money. I slip a couple of bucks into his tip jar.

Back at the station, Chief Jimenez shares she received a call from the toxicology laboratory. Preliminary tests found no traces of suspicious bacteria in the samples we gathered.

"Interesting," I say.

"So what made all those people sick?"

"That's what I intend to find out."

CHAPTER SEVEN

OFFICER WASHINGTON and I sit around a folding table, cataloging the evidence we collected from the theater. The smell of the barbecue sauce from the baby back ribs she ate for lunch makes me wish I'd eaten those rather than my Caesar salad. But I need to get in shape.

"Where is the trash we collected from the dressing rooms?" I ask.

Since the food samples and bodily fluids that the health department tested came back negative for bacteria, the laboratory wants to see all the evidence we collected.

Officer Washington plops several small plastic bags on the table. "This one is from the green room." She indicates the largest of the lot. "I labeled the others with the name of the actor whose dressing room they were collected from."

Candy and gum wrappers, soiled make-up sponges, vodka and wine bottles, an empty bottle of toothpaste, and a used disposable razor. A receipt from the drugstore for eye drops from Ernest Drucker's trash and an empty bottle of eye drops from Oliver Crispin's trash.

Officer Washington bags the empty bottles of eye drops, elderberry syrup, and booze.

"This play script that Daphne is reading," I say. "What's it about?"

"I have no clue. Why? Are you thinking about auditioning?"

"Not on your life," I say. "Let's hope the lab can figure out this mess."

"You think the solution is in this pile of trash?"

"Something made those people sick."

"It still might be food poisoning," Officer Washington says.

"Crispin's condition has worsened."

"Where did you hear that?"

"The chief told me."

"Poor Ollie."

"Not everyone who ate the meatballs got sick," I say. "But everyone who became sick ate the meatballs. Except for Crispin."

"What are we missing here?"

"I don't know," I say, rising and slipping on my jacket, "but I know who might."

———

ROSE ANSWERS the door when I knock. Her brow furrows. "I have a few more questions," I say. She invites me inside.

"Would you like coffee?"

"I'll pass, thanks. I need to get some sleep tonight."

Trixie joins us in the cozy living room of their renovated clapboard farmhouse.

"I have good news and bad news."

"Hit us with the bad news first," Rose says.

"Oliver Crispin is in serious but stable condition."

"That poor young man," Trixie says. "I hope he feels better soon."

"You'll be relieved to hear that preliminary lab results found no evidence of food poisoning."

"If we'd made all those people sick," Trixie says. "I'd never have forgiven myself."

"Everyone who fell ill ate your meatballs."

"But some guests tried our meatballs and didn't get sick, right?"

I acknowledge that's true and ask if they'd mind sharing their recipe. Perhaps there's a clue in the ingredients. Rose takes a pen and paper and writes down a few basic ingredients and a handful of steps that even I could follow.

"Would you like a tour of our farm?" Trixie asks.

"I've bothered you enough for one day."

"It's no bother."

"Trixie adores showing off our little slice of heaven."

"I'm proud, sure, but I'm not boastful. Come see."

I follow Trixie outside.

"You have every right to brag," I say. "Your farm is beautiful."

"You're too kind," Trixie says. We pass a large chicken coop. "Our Rhode Island Red gals. They lay the most delicious brown eggs."

"They make for good eating, too," Rose adds. "That old rooster has outlived his usefulness. He'll be chicken stew soon."

When I was a little boy, a rooster chased me up a tree, so I maintain a safe distance.

We stroll through a grove of budding fruit trees.

"In August, we'll harvest the juiciest peaches, plums, and cherries you've ever had," Trixie says, "and three varieties of apples in the fall."

Beyond the orchard, we come across a row of beehives. I prepare to bolt from the buzzing insects should they swarm. Further up the mountainside, we encounter four goats grazing in a fenced meadow.

"The rest of our herd died after drinking contaminated water from the stream last year," Rose says. She leads me upstream a ways and points out where the deer carcass decomposed.

"It took the county weeks to clean up the mess."

"Do you have any proof that Bill Sinclair dumped the deer there?"

"Who else would have done something so vile, huh?" Rose asks. "Tell me that."

I step back and throw up my hands. "I didn't mean to upset you."

"I'm not upset. I'm pissed off. That son-of-a-bitch could shoot someone in the middle of Main Street and get off with a slap on the wrist."

"That's what happens when a person has more money than heart," Trixie says.

"I realize how much you love your animals," I say. "But in the eyes of the law, they're property."

"The law is not always right," Rose says. "I'm sure you know that . . . Lost Boy."

Upon hearing the nickname the press saddled me with after I spent five days and nights hiding out from my mother's killer in the old mill, I flinch.

"Officer Nowak," Trixie says. "Come see."

A small tributary from the stream flows down a steep ravine into a watery marsh.

"A bale of bog turtles lives down there," Trixie says. "One of a handful left in the region."

"We do our best to protect their habitat from predators," Rose says, "and punk kids who steal the baby turtles for pets."

We trudge back down the mountainside. I bid Rose and Trixie goodbye in their driveway and climb behind the wheel of my pickup. The NLPD leases two squad cars. Chief Jimenez drives one. The rest of us share the other, which Sergeant Reeves has this morning.

CHAPTER EIGHT

DRIVING HOME AFTER MY SHIFT, I remember that I'm supposed to pick up something from the grocery store, but I can't recall what. Annie planned a small dinner party for tonight. Her first since Kit was killed. I find a parking place near the entrance and call home on my way inside.

Annie answers the phone on the fifth ring. "A bunch of basil, a can of whole tomatoes, not crushed or pureed." She sounds out of breath. "And two bags of—"

"Ice," I say, remembering what she told me this morning. "How did you know it was me?"

"A woman's intuition."

"Give me a break."

"We have caller ID, silly."

Technology has come a long way from the dial-up days of my childhood, when we had to answer the phone if we wanted to know who was on the other end of the line. Like the song says, the times, they are a-changin'.

"I can't find the basil, so I grab a bag of spinach. Based upon the pictures on the signs overhead, the two ingredients look similar. I find a can of whole tomatoes and head to the cash register, where I order two bags of ice, which I pick up from the freezer on my way out the door.

Rose and Trixie strike me as sincere, but they're hiding something, and I can't ignore the fact that they catered the opening night party. I should investigate their backgrounds. See if anything turns up. That Bill Sinclair might dump a deer carcass in the stream out of spite strikes me as possible, but Rose and Trixie have no witnesses to corroborate their accusation. This case baffles me.

Caught up in my thoughts, I miss my turn and must double back. By the time I reach home, it's after seven o'clock. Annie greets me at the door and takes the shopping bags.

"Go change. Our guests will be here soon."

After I take a quick shower, I put on the white dress shirt and khaki chinos that Annie gave me for my thirty-third birthday last April and follow an enticing array of smells into the kitchen. Annie removes a roasted chicken from the oven.

"What is this, Cal?"

"I couldn't find the basil, so I grabbed a bag of spinach. They look the same."

"Well, they're not." Annie sighs. "I was going to make a Caprese salad. I guess we'll have a spinach salad instead."

I have no clue what a Caprese salad is, but I like spinach.

"Make yourself useful, Cal, and set up the bar."

I open a bag of ice, fill the bucket on the bar, and slice the lime that Annie tosses me into wedges. When I'm done, I pour myself a whiskey.

"Can you set the table, Cal?"

I grab a handful of paper napkins from the counter and open the utensil drawer.

"Use the good flatware and china from the hutch in the dining room," Annie says. "You'll find a tablecloth and napkins in the middle drawer."

The tablecloth won't lie flat because of all the creases in the fabric. I'm not sure which plates I should use or what spoon goes where, nor do I understand why it matters what we eat on and with. If it had been up to me, we'd be eating out at that new steakhouse in Capachick that I've heard grills an amazing ribeye. But Annie wanted to entertain.

Annie snatches the napkins out of my hand. "I'll finish setting the table," she says. "Is your bathroom clean?"

"Yes."

At least, it will be by the time everyone arrives.

"Did you put out fresh towels?"

"I'll check."

As I finish wiping down the counter around my sink, the bell rings.

"Cal, get the door, please."

"Sure thing."

I wonder who the first guest will be.

"Howie, come in."

"I hope I'm not too early. I don't go to dinner parties much."

"Take a load off."

"I brought a bottle of wine." Howie holds up a bag from the liquor store. "Sauvignon Blanc. I think that's the kind Annie likes."

"Would you like a drink? Or a brewski? I think we have a few IPAs."

"Where's Annie? In the kitchen?"

I nod, knock back my whiskey, and pour myself another.

Howie goes into the kitchen. It's obvious the guy has a crush on Annie. I don't think she feels the same way, but we haven't discussed the matter. Howie and his brothers spent time in foster care with Mama Libby and Papa Frank when we were in high school, but he and I never became friends because he hung out with Kit and Oakley.

Demetrius arrives, and we share a kiss.

"Would you like a drink?" I ask.

"Let me give Annie my artichoke dip." Demetrius grabs my ass on his way into the kitchen. "Be right back, sexy."

Chief Jimenez and her girlfriend, Marta, knock and enter.

"Annie said to bring an appetizer," Marta says, "so I baked empanadillas. They're like empanadas, only lighter."

On her way into the kitchen, Marta passes Demetrius, and the pair hug. Demetrius joins me and the chief in the living room.

"We need music," Demetrius says.

"I'll play DJ," Chief Jimenez says. She looks through Annie's CD collection. "J. Lo! This is a great album!"

Nadine and Stanley bumble through the door, loaded with packages. Nadine heads straight for the kitchen. Stanley nods toward our drinks. "Mind if I help myself?"

"You know where the bar is," I say.

Demetrius slips his arms around me. "I'm looking forward to this weekend."

"Me too."

"No, you're not."

"No, I'm not."

Demetrius nuzzles against me and says, "I won't let a bear eat you."

"If this case at the theater blows up, I may have to work."

"Nice try, Nowak," Chief Jimenez says. "Unless the health department finds something their preliminary tests missed, we have no case."

"Where are you fellows going camping?" Stanley asks.

"The Devil's Tombstone," Demetrius says.

"Are you serious?" I say. "I feel so much better."

"It's beautiful there," Stanley says.

"Where?" Nadine asks. She slips her arm around Stanley.

"The Devil's Tombstone."

"Patrick and I took Annie hiking at Devil's Tombstone when she was a little girl," Nadine says. "We saw some breathtaking views."

When Annie and I were sophomores in high school, her father, Patrick Leighton, died suddenly of a brain aneurysm.

Annie carries a plate of Marta's empanadillas into the living room and sets them on the coffee table. Howie follows with Demetrius's dip on a platter accompanied by bread and carrot sticks. Everyone digs in.

"Any word from the health department?" Nadine asks.

Chief Jimenez shares what we know so far, which isn't much.

"I hope Oliver Crispin feels better soon," Annie says. "But I hated the sadistic dentist he played in the show."

"Am I the only one who thought that show was silly?" I ask. "No offense, Stanley. You were funny. But a man-eating plant from outer space that sings? Seriously?"

"The show is based on a 1960s sci-fi movie," Stanley says. "I saw the off-Broadway production with the original cast. It was a ton of fun."

While Nadine and Annie finish cooking dinner, Howie and Stanley debate whether dirt or asphalt tracks are better. I know nothing about race cars.

"Should we take a look at that camping equipment Annie offered us?" Demetrius asks.

"Might as well," I say.

Demetrius follows me out to the garage. Annie was not kidding. Kit owned more camping equipment than one man could ever use. Quality items, of course, because he only bought the best.

"You're the expert," I say. "See anything we need?"

"We'll borrow this sweet cooler," Demetrius says. He checks out the rods and reels leaning against the wall. "We won't have time to go fishing."

That's a relief. Sitting around waiting for the fish to bite is not my idea of a good time.

"How about this tent?" I ask.

"It's nice, but I prefer mine. We'll borrow these sleeping bags, though, and this lantern."

Demetrius and I load the items we're borrowing into the bed of his pickup. By the time we finish, Annie calls us inside for dinner. Demetrius and I wash our hands and join everyone at the dining table. Nadine offers me a glass of wine. I decline and top off my whiskey.

Over dinner, Nadine and Stanley tell funny stories about entitled downstaters looking to buy vacation homes and the impossible requests they make. Demetrius shares some of the ridiculous orders he receives from customers at his hardware store. His anecdotes spark a larger debate over the state of the economy. Everyone agrees the terrorist attacks last year shook the world. I hope no one asks about my experiences from that awful day or the weeks that turned into months afterward that I spent sifting through rumble from the fallen World Trade Center towers. Forensics only identified a handful of the remains we uncovered.

"On a happier note," Demetrius says. "The Yankees look good this season."

"They're about to get their asses handed to them by the Sox," Chief Jimenez says.

"In your dreams," Stanley says.

All my life, I've avoided taking a side in that infamous rivalry. Until I met Demetrius. Now I'm a closeted Yankees fan.

After dinner, everyone gathers in the living room for drinks and dessert. Annie baked a strawberry rhubarb crisp—which I mistakenly call a cobbler—that's delicious. Stanley tells a joke about a priest, a rabbi, and a monk, but I doze off for a second and miss the punchline. I stifle a yawn.

"We should go, Stanley," Nadine says.

"Are you driving back to Kingston, Mom?"

"Yes, sweetheart. Since the theater is closed this weekend, Stanley is staying with me."

I give Nadine a hug and shake Stanley's hand. "I hope you weren't offended by my comment about the play. You were great."

"Be thankful you only had to suffer through Daphne's performance once," Stanley says with a smile. "In rehearsals, I wore earplugs during her numbers."

"Daphne can't carry a tune to save her life," Nadine says.

"Mom, that isn't nice."

"Neither is Daphne, sweetheart." Nadine gives Annie a hug. "I'll call you tomorrow."

Chief Jimenez and Marta help Annie clear the table and wash the dishes. Howie offers to take out the garbage.

Demetrius hugs me.

"You look tired."

"I'm beat."

"We're off," Chief Jimenez says. "I'll see you on Monday, Nowak. Try to have fun this weekend. I realize that's hard for you."

"Thank you for the wine, Howie," Annie says. "Be careful driving home."

"Um, yeah, okay," Howie stammers. "See you around." He shuffles out the door.

"I'm off to bed, boys," Annie says. She hugs us and goes upstairs.

I need a good night's sleep, but I don't want to offend Demetrius, so I plop down on the couch and close my eyes.

"I can take a hint," Demetrius says.

"I'll be more fun after I get some sleep."

"I hope so."

We share a kiss. Our eyes meet. He opens his mouth to speak but stops himself.

"Penny for your thoughts," I say.

Tears pool in the corners of Demetrius's violet eyes. He hesitates for a second, then walks away, leaving me standing on the porch, watching his taillights disappear up the street, wondering what I've done wrong this time.

CHAPTER NINE

Saturday morning, I pace the living room floor. My palms sweat over the thought of spending the night in a tent in the woods. I take several deep breaths and don't feel any better.

"You need to sit down," Annie says. "You're wearing a hole in my rug."

"I think I have a fever," I say. "Feel my forehead."

"You are not getting sick, you big baby."

I take a swig of whiskey from my flask. I packed a bottle in the fancy orange and green backpack I borrowed from Kit, which sits packed and ready to go by the door.

"What if there's a major crime this weekend?"

"This town survived for centuries without your law enforcement expertise."

"Like when that pedophile, Harris, ran the department?"

"Don't spoil this trip for Demetrius," Annie says. "He's been looking forward to going away with you for weeks."

"If a bear mauls me to death, bury me next to my mother."

"You're ridiculous," Annie says. She passes me a small tote bag. "Mom said to give you this. She forgot last night."

I peek inside the bag and find a can of insecticide spray, a tube of itch cream, a bottle of ibuprofen, half a dozen energy bars, a box of bandages, and a tube of antiseptic ointment. I shove the bag inside the backpack with the bear horn and first aid kit that Nadine gave me earlier.

Demetrius pulls into the driveway. Flower leaps out of the pickup and bounds across the lawn. Demetrius follows his dog, grinning from ear to ear.

"Looks like I'm really doing this," I say.

"You'll be fine." Annie straightens the collar of my flannel shirt, which I picked up from the local thrift store for the occasion.

Demetrius knocks and opens the front door. Flower races past. His nails clatter across the hardwood floors. He was only a puppy when Demetrius and I met last spring. He must weigh fifty pounds now.

Flower leaps on Annie. She pets him. He never stops wiggling.

"Thanks for dog-sitting," Demetrius says.

"We're going to have fun this weekend," Annie says. "Aren't we, Flower?"

"See you, buddy," Demetrius says. He pats Flower on the head and faces me. "Are you ready to hit the road?"

"Let's do this," I say, "before I change my mind."

Annie hugs me and whispers in my ear, "Behave."

Demetrius and I pile inside his dark blue Dodge Ram quad-cab pickup, which he purchased when the dealership in Kingston closed out their 2002 models this past winter. It still smells new. We drive north out of town.

"I'm sorry," I say.

"For what?"

"Being such a little bitch."

"I realize this isn't easy for you."

"I'm fine."

"I won't let anything happen to you."

"I can protect myself."

"I realize that," Demetrius says. "I was trying . . . oh, never mind."

We drive in silence for about thirty minutes until we reach the Devil's Tombstone. I didn't realize we'd be staying this close to home. Demetrius made a reservation, so our check-in goes smoothly. Now, joy of joys, we must hike to our campsite.

Demetrius hugs me and asks, "Are you okay?"

"Let the good times roll."

Demetrius kisses me. I pull away.

"We can fool around after we settle in."

Demetrius shrugs and strides up the trail with the ice chest in one hand and the tent bag in the other. I trudge after him, scanning the woods for signs of danger. Before I realize it, I've fallen behind. I catch up as fast as I can manage without falling on my ass. "How much longer?" I ask between gasps for breath.

"Maybe ten miles."

"What?"

"I'm joking."

Perhaps it's best I'm kept in the dark about how far we must hike because I may not like the answer. I steel my nerves and forge ahead. My feet ache. My lungs burn. This is worse than chasing criminals through the back alleyways of the city. I don't complain, though, because I don't want Demetrius to think I'm a wuss.

At last, we reach the top of the mountain. I marvel at the vastness of the rolling green slopes that surround our overlook and the secrets they must hold. "Why is this place called the Devil's Tombstone?"

"Legend has it that centuries ago the devil passed through this land, and many people have claimed they've experienced frightening or supernatural occurrences here."

"I had to ask."

"I won't let the stone witch curse you."

"She's real?" I ask. "Never mind. I'd rather not know."

"Don't tell me that a big, strong cop like you fears ghosts."

"Ghosts, no. But the jury's still out on witches."

Demetrius slips his arm around my waist and says, "I realize you'd rather be anywhere but here." He leans against me. I draw him close and wonder why this isn't enough for me. "Are you hungry?" he asks.

"Yep," I say, "and thirsty."

Demetrius pitches me a bottle of water, which I gulp down.

"I made sandwiches," Demetrius says. "Do you want ham or turkey?"

"Both."

We eat a late lunch while seated on a boulder overlooking the sprawling mountains. It's peaceful, which is a feeling I never thought I'd experience in the woods.

"Did you get enough to eat?" Demetrius asks.

I nod.

"Let's pitch our tent, then."

Demetrius takes charge, which is best. I have no clue how to put up a tent. He lays out the footprint and assembles the poles. I'm impressed by his nimbleness. I help slide the poles into their grommets. We attach the tent's body and stake down the ropes. By the time we finish, it's late afternoon.

"That wasn't as hard as I thought it would be," I say, wiping the sweat from my brow.

"There may be hope for you after all."

Demetrius shucks off his shirt and dabs the sweat from his too-handsome-for-his-own-good face. In the glow of the setting sun, he looks like an angel. I trace my fingers over his smooth mahogany chest. He may be the most beautiful man I've ever met.

"Now, we can fool around," Demetrius says. He shoves me inside the tent and tugs off my shirt. I lie back and pull him down on top of me. He kisses his way down my torso and yanks off my jeans. I close my eyes. His hands rove over my body while his tongue teases my most sensitive spots. I shudder and lift my legs.

He rolls on a condom and slips inside me. I gasp. He eases in and out until I relax and picks up the pace. Entwined in one another's arms, we lose ourselves and explode together.

Once we catch our breath, we share a slow kiss and get dressed. I never imagined I'd find a guy I'd desire to the exclusion of all others. The good times never last, though.

"We should gather firewood before the sun goes down," Demetrius says. He laces up his hiking boots and crawls out of the tent. I finish buttoning my shirt and follow him. We wander through the shadowy woods, gathering dried branches and twigs, which he uses to build a fire. I'm amazed. Were it left to me, we'd be sitting in the dark tonight, freezing our asses off. I lie back, propped up on my elbows, and stare at the dancing blue and white flames.

"Why do you put up with me?" I ask.

"Somebody has to." Demetrius gives me a playful shove. I shove back. We wrestle around on the ground. He pins my arms and says, "Seriously, though. You're one of the good guys."

"I'm a mess."

"I wish you'd stop saying that."

"You deserve better."

"Even if that were true—which it's not—I love you."

My shoulders stiffen.

"Don't freak out," Demetrius says. "I don't expect you to say the words back."

"You should be with some nice guy—"

Demetrius shuts me up with a kiss. "I am." His violet eyes and dazzling smile make me forget where I am for a moment.

CHAPTER TEN

Sunday morning, I wake up and reach for Demetrius, but he's not there. It's still dark outside, and someone is moving around behind our tent. I whisper Demetrius's name. He doesn't answer. Blinking the sweat from my eyes, I reach for my weapon, then remember I left it in his pickup because the park service forbids firearms inside state campgrounds. The bottom of the tent flaps. Whoever is out there wants inside. "I'm a police officer!" I shout, hoping I sound intimidating. "Step back or I'll shoot!" The sniffing snout of a skunk pokes under the rear of the tent. Relieved but fearful of getting sprayed, I back out of the tent and zip the flap shut.

Demetrius lopes out of the woods. "I didn't expect you up this early." He holds out a paper plate. "Wild strawberries."

I point toward the tent and stammer, "Skunk."

Demetrius laughs and motions for me to scoot back. He opens the tent flap. "Hey, little fellow. Are you hungry?" He tosses a strawberry inside the tent. "You like that, do you? Want another?" He places a berry outside the entrance. "Come and get it." He coaxes the skunk out of the tent and sets a trail of berries on the ground leading away from our campsite. The skunk eats its way into the woods.

"Crisis averted," Demetrius says. He brews a pot of coffee over the campfire and fries a pan of eggs and sausages. He feeds me a strawberry that tastes sweeter than the berries from the store.

After breakfast, Demetrius and I take a hike through the woods. No bears cross our path, but we encounter a bobcat that runs off when we approach. We trek down a steep embankment and stumble upon a waterfall, which feeds into a stream that cascades down the mountainside.

"Watch out!" Demetrius shouts. He grabs my arm and guides me around several large bushes covered in clusters of tiny, umbrella-shaped yellow flowers. "Those wild parsnips are toxic, particularly when they're in bloom. Their sap will blister your skin."

"Sounds nasty."

"It is," Demetrius says. "As I learned the hard way when I was a kid."

"Look at those huge mushrooms." I point toward a patch of tall, white fungi sprouting through a pile of pine needles and twigs.

"Amanita bisporigera," Demetrius says.

"I should pick some for Annie. She makes the best mushroom gravy I've ever eaten."

"I wouldn't if I were you. They'll make you sick."

"You're kidding?"

"Dozens of toxic plants thrive in these woods, including several species of mushrooms. Those bushy plants you're standing next to with the clusters of little white flowers are water hemlock, the deadliest plant in all North America."

"Now you tell me."

I step away from the questionable bushes.

"Water hemlock is only lethal when it's ingested."

"Remind me again why camping is fun."

Demetrius leaps on me. We tumble to the ground. He tickles my ribs.

"Get off me!" I shriek. "Cut it out!"

"Not until you lighten up."

"Okay! Okay! Okay!" I shove his hands aside. "Stop tickling me!"

Demetrius backs off. I clutch my side and catch my breath.

"Ever since humans emerged from the primordial slime," Demetrius says. "Plants have both sustained and poisoned us."

"You sound like a human encyclopedia."

"My grandmother taught me to respect the wilderness," Demetrius says. "Remember, we're invading their world, not the other way around."

I sigh.

"Would you rush into a dangerous crime scene unarmed?" Demetrius asks.

"Point taken."

Demetrius shucks off his hiking boots and socks, rolls his pants halfway up his shins, and wades into the stream. I struggle with untying my tangled bootlace. Demetrius shoves my hands aside, loosens the knot, and tugs off my boots and socks. I stand. The cool water swirls around my ankles. Demetrius splashes water in my face. I recoil. His next slosh drenches my furry chest. I tackle him, and we roll around in the stream until we're soaked and share a kiss. He crawls out onto the bank and strips off his wet clothes. Since we're alone in the middle of nowhere, I do the same. We lay our clothes on a rock to dry and lie back on the bank.

A robin harmonizes with a flock of sparrows in the treetops. A trio of squabbling squirrels leaps through the branches. The startled sparrows take flight, but the robin stands his ground. I close my eyes and enjoy the peace and quiet. I'm on the verge of dozing off when I hear voices.

"We're almost there, Harry," a woman says.

"That's what you said ten minutes ago, Alice," a man responds.

"Oh, shit," Demetrius says. "Someone's coming." He takes my hand and leads me behind a dense thicket of shrubs. We crouch and peer through the leafy branches. An elderly couple hikes into view, using walking sticks for balance.

"Look at that waterfall, Harry. Isn't it beautiful?"

"You dragged my arthritic ass all the way up this God-forsaken mountain to look at water? I swear, woman, sometimes I think you've got a screw loose."

"I think I'll get a better shot from this angle. No, maybe over here. What do you think, Harry? Is the light better on this side or this side? Harry?"

"Oh, for God's sake, Alice, shut your yap and take your dang pictures. My bunions are killing me."

The old woman snaps off several shots. Neither she nor her husband appears to notice our damp clothes. The bickering couple leave.

Demetrius nudges me and points at the ground. "We're standing in poison ivy." We leap into the stream and scrub our legs and feet, get dressed, and hike up to our campsite. My ankles and feet itch like crazy.

"Have you figured out what made those people at the theater sick yet?"

"We're waiting for the final toxicology report from the health department."

Demetrius laughs.

"What's so funny?" I ask.

"When I was in high school," Demetrius says, "our class prankster put eye drops in the Sloppy Joes. Dozens of kids puked all over the cafeteria. Some even shit their pants. It was so gross."

"You're kidding me."

"You don't think—?"

"We need to go."

CHAPTER ELEVEN

DEMETRIUS GIVES me the silent treatment on the drive back to town. I refuse to apologize. I'm on a case. He should understand that. He careens around several Sunday drivers who are departing their church parking lots following their services and slams on the brakes. We screech to a stop in front of the station. I leap out and have barely shut the door when he speeds away.

"I thought this was your day off," Suki says when I walk through the door.

"Something came up."

Retrieving the evidence box, I dig out the receipt for eye drops we found in Ernest Drucker's dressing room and the empty bottle. I locate the business card for the nurse from the health department and dial her number.

"What can I do for you, Officer Nowak?"

"If someone put eye drops into the meatball sauce at the theater that night, could that have made everyone sick?"

"Tetrahydrozoline—one of the key ingredients in eye drops—is toxic if ingested. Why do you ask?"

I share what I've discovered.

"I'll alert the lab," she says.

Demetrius and I saw Ernest Drucker coming out of the drugstore around the same time that's printed on the receipt we found in his trash can. But we found the empty bottle of eye drops in Oliver Crispin's dressing room. I ran into Drucker coming out of Crispin's dressing room when I was collecting evidence that night. He insisted that Crispin had poisoned the food. But if that's true, why is Crispin hospitalized?

"I didn't expect to see you this weekend," Chief Jimenez says.

I explain why I cut my camping trip short and what I've learned.

"I hope it's not too late," Chief Jimenez says. "Oliver Crispin has slipped into a coma."

"He's the only victim who ended up hospitalized. Why?"

"Figuring that out could save his life."

Demetrius drove this weekend, so my pickup is at home, and both squad cars are in use. I start out on foot for the Stone Witch Inn. Along the way, I bump into Jewel Nye, pushing a stroller down the sidewalk. She hooked up with a pallbearer at her brother Kit's funeral last May and has a baby now.

"Are you keeping your nose clean, Jewel?"

"And my veins," Jewel says. "Want to see?" She rolls up the sleeves of her blouse and shows me faded scar tissue but no fresh needle marks.

"Who's this little angel?" I crouch before the stroller.

"This is Pearl."

"Hello, Pearl."

Pearl screws up her face and cries at what I hope is the top of her lungs because if she wails any louder, she's going to blow out my eardrums. I beat a hasty retreat before I upset her any further.

At the Stone Witch Inn, I find Ernest seated on the rustic wooden porch bench, reading a book about acting.

"Mind if I sit down, Ernest?"

"It's a free country, more or less."

"Nice afternoon."

"What brings you by, officer?"

"We found this in your dressing room."

I show Ernest the receipt for eye drops from the drugstore. He blanches for a second, and the color returns to his cheeks.

"I needed eye drops. So what?"

"We found the receipt but not the bottle."

"It's probably in my room upstairs."

"May I see it?" I ask. "If you don't mind."

"I'm not sure where I put it."

"Let's see if we can find it, shall we?" I say, and I stand.

Ernest rises with an exasperated sigh. I follow the guy inside the inn. Frieda Gladstone stands behind the reception desk, appeasing a disgruntled customer over the phone. She waves. I acknowledge her with a nod and follow Ernest up the stairs.

"Now, where did I put that bottle?" Ernest rifles through his backpack. "Maybe I left it in the bathroom, which is down the hall."

"The eye drops aren't here, are they, Ernest?"

"Maybe they fell out of my backpack."

"Perhaps we should chat down at the station."

"No, wait—"

"We found a bottle of eye drops at the theater."

"I must've left it there."

"You said you took the bottle back to your room."

"I thought I did."

"The bottle we found was empty."

"Everyone uses my stuff."

"You expect me to believe your fellow cast members used an entire bottle of eye drops on opening night?"

"It's possible."

"But not likely." I take a seat on the bed beside him. "Listen, Ernest, I can see you want to tell me the truth."

"I am telling you the truth."

"We have a witness who saw what you did."

"No way! Who? I mean . . . I didn't do anything."

"Why don't you tell me how all those people got sick, Ernest?"

"Perhaps someone put something in their food?"

"Like eye drops?"

"Ollie did it!"

"Why would Crispin poison himself?"

"Why does Ollie do anything?"

"If you put eye drops in the food and he dies, you could face manslaughter charges. Or worse, if the prosecutor determines you intended harm."

"You don't understand."

"You better hope he makes a full recovery."

———

When I reach home, Annie asks me what's going on. I apprise her of Crispin's condition.

"That's awful," Annie says, "but that's not what I'm talking about. Demetrius is afraid you're dumping him."

"He called you?"

"He dropped off your things when he picked up Flower."

The backpack I borrowed for the trip sits by the front door.

"He's one of the good ones, Cal."

"He's not as perfect as everyone thinks."

Snatching Kit's backpack, I retreat into my room, pull out my bottle of whiskey, and take a swig. I toss my dirty clothes into the laundry basket and step into the shower. The hot water soothes my aching muscles. As I scrub the dirt and grime off my body, I can't stop scratching my itchy soles. I blame Demetrius for dragging me into the woods. How can he be so sure about us? I'm the first man he's ever had sex with. That's like deciding you only like vanilla ice cream when you've never tried any other flavors.

After I get dressed, I join Annie on the couch. She's curled up with a glass of wine, engrossed in a British murder mystery. From what I gather after a few minutes, a woman at this posh party died, but she wasn't the intended victim, or so the old lady sleuth thinks.

"What are we watching?" I ask.

"*The Mirror Crack'd*," Annie says. "It's based upon an Agatha Christie novel. The beautiful woman with the violet eyes is Elizabeth Taylor, the hunk playing her husband is Rock Hudson, and that's the lady from *Murder, She Wrote*."

"We found a play script in Daphne's dressing room with that title."

"Daphne could play the Elizabeth Taylor part," Annie says. "If she were a better actress."

My stomach grumbles.

"There's meatloaf on the stove," Annie says.

"Are you hungry?"

"I ate earlier."

I make myself a meatloaf sandwich, grab a bag of potato chips, and return to the living room in time to learn that the actress in the movie poisoned a woman's drink because she contracted German measles from the woman years earlier and can't conceive children as a result. But another woman drank the poisoned drink by mistake and died.

Annie turns off the television and tops off her wine glass. "So?" She leans back on the couch.

"What?"

Annie cocks her head and stares at me.

"I don't know why Demetrius thinks I'm breaking up with him."

"You're thick-headed, Cal." Annie hits me playfully with an occasional pillow. "But you're not stupid."

"What are you saying?"

"You're afraid of commitment."

"I don't need this right now."

I take my whiskey and retreat into my room.

"If you keep running away from your feelings, Cal, you're going to end up a sad, bitter old queen."

"Too late."

CHAPTER TWELVE

WHEN I DRIVE past the Nyes Landing Playhouse on Monday morning, Bill Sinclair stands on the sidewalk outside, consoling Daphne. Padma Patel watches from across the street. She slips on her sunglasses and walks away. I double-park the squad car and leap out.

"I can't believe Ollie is dead." Daphne sobs into Bill's chest.

"Crispin died?"

"He went into cardiac arrest this morning," Bill says.

My cellular phone rings. It's the nurse from the health department. I step away and take the call.

"Our lab technicians found traces of tetrahydrozoline in the samples you sent us."

"Are you sure?"

"They tested the samples twice."

I radio the chief and fill her in.

"I'll pick up Drucker."

"Slow your roll, Nowak."

"He poisoned all those people."

"Let's wait for the medical examiner's report before we draw any conclusions."

"What if he skips town?"

"I'm not going to argue with you, Nowak."

"How about charging Drucker with reckless endangerment?"

Chief Jimenez considers my suggestion and says, "Pick the guy up."

———

INSIDE THE STONE WITCH INN, I find Ernest Drucker standing in front of the registration desk with his suitcase. It's a good thing I got here when I did.

"Going somewhere, Ernest?"

"Ollie passed away," Ernest says. "But I suppose you know that." He shuffles his feet. I don't say anything. After a moment, he continues. "I'm going home to the city." He passes Frieda Gladstone his credit card. "My agent called, and I've been cast in the lead in a new musical that's headed for Broadway."

"That was fast."

"My agent called last week."

"Before the show opened?"

"I tried to get out of my contract, but Bill Sinclair wouldn't budge."

"But now that the show has closed, your contract is null and void."

Ernest Drucker stammers for a moment and says, "I might have the timing wrong."

"Ernest Drucker, you're under arrest for reckless endangerment."

"No, wait—"

"Don't make this harder than it needs to be."

"It was an accident."

"You accidentally spilled eye drops into the sauce?"

"I didn't think anyone would get seriously hurt."

"Turn around."

"I start rehearsals tomorrow."

"That's not happening."

"But—"

"Place your hands behind your back."

Ernest groans and turns around. I handcuff his wrists and march him outside. He slides into the rear of the squad car. I buckle his seat belt and shut the door.

After I book Ernest, he calls Bill Sinclair.

"I'll handle Sinclair when he arrives," Chief Jimenez says.

"You want me to transport Drucker to Kingston?"

"Finish your shift and go home."

"You don't have to tell me twice, ma'am."

"What's with the ma'am shit?"

"Sorry, Chief."

———

AFTER LEAVING THE STATION, I stop by the hardware store. That annoying bell over the door announces my arrival. Demetrius emerges from the back room. When he sees me, his smile fades. He steps behind the counter and sorts through a stack of receipts.

"What brings you by?"

"Do I need a reason?" I ask.

"I'm about to close up shop.'

"Would you like to grab dinner?"

"I have to drive to New Paltz for Cora's parent-teacher conference. I told you this weekend."

Although I can't remember now, I'm sure he did.

"Would you like company?" I ask. "We could grab dinner after you finish."

"Keisha and I will probably take Cora out for pizza after we meet with her teachers."

"Right, well . . . call me later."

As I drive away from the hardware store, I roll down the

windows of my pickup, hoping the fresh air will clear my head. I wish I wasn't always letting Demetrius down.

Finding myself with a night off, I stop by the Roadhouse—the local queer bar on the edge of town. "Love Shack" by the B-52s plays on the jukebox. I belly up to the bar.

Gunner slaps a cocktail napkin on the bar. "Your usual?" A bandage covers his forehead.

"What happened?"

"Nothing I can't handle."

"Are you sure about that?"

"You should see the other guy."

Gunner sets a pint of Guinness stout and a shot of Irish whiskey before me. I sip my beer. He washes glasses in the sink behind the bar.

"I got jumped while I was locking up last night."

"Did you see who attacked you?"

"It was dark," Gunner says. "He came at me from behind."

"It was a guy, then?"

"I don't know any gals who can punch with that much force."

"I work with a couple."

"Jimenez and Washington are not most women."

"That's for sure," I say. I knock back my shot. "Why didn't you call us?"

"Over a simple assault?"

"What did he steal?"

"Not a damn thing."

"Who'd you piss off?"

"Probably some redneck who doesn't like queers."

"If they come back, you better call me."

"I can handle my own business."

"Don't do anything stupid."

"What's up with you?" Gunner asks.

"Keeping busy."

"Where's your boyfriend?"

"Not you, too."

"Me, too, what?"

"Everyone keeps telling me how great Demetrius is."

"I prefer the strong, silent type." Gunner winks. "If you ever get bored."

Gunner and I had a quickie once before I met Demetrius.

"How's Tanner?"

Gunner and his long-time boyfriend, Tanner, have an open relationship. Demetrius would never go for that. He and I haven't said out loud that we're exclusive, but after dating for a year, that's implied. Sometimes I miss being able to do whatever I wanted, with whoever I wanted, whenever I wanted.

"From Charlie," Gunner says. He sets another round in front of me and nods toward the opposite end of the bar. A bald guy with a paunch who could be anywhere from fifty to seventy raises his highball glass and winks at me. Gunner leans in and whispers, "Charlie has a thing for men in uniform."

I chuckle. When I lived in the city, guys with cop fetishes often cruised me.

"Go say hello," Gunner says. "Give the old guy a thrill."

I knock back my whiskey, grab my beer, and introduce myself.

"You don't remember me, do you?" Charlie says.

"We never...did we?"

"Oh, my lord, no." Charlie chuckles. "Your mom and I, we used to hang out."

"You knew my mom?"

"Dede and I helped each other through some dark times."

"You two were friends?"

"The best."

"Where'd you meet?"

"In foster care."

"What was my mom like?"

"Funny," Charlie says. "Sweet . . . but sad." He smiles. "A little bit nuts." He lifts his glass. "To Dede." Snatching a cocktail napkin, he wipes his eyes. "I miss her."

"Me too."

Charlie slips me his phone number and gives me a hug. His hands rove. I pull away and pay my tab. I miss Demetrius when he's not around but push him away when we're together. What is my problem?

———

After leaving the Roadhouse, I cruise past Demetrius's cabin. His pickup is not in the driveway. He's probably still with Keisha and Cora. I would call him, but I don't have cellular service out here.

Meeting Charlie made me realize how much I miss my mom. I drive out to the cemetery. The full moon through the trees casts a silver haze across her headstone. The flowers I brought last time have withered and dried. I take a seat on the grass and tell my mom about running into Charlie tonight. While I'm talking, the memory of a nice guy helping me build a fortress out of Legos when I was around six or seven flashes through my mind. Charlie had been rail thin back then, with bad teeth and stringy, bleached-blond hair.

"I plan to have the evidence from your case retested, Mom. DNA analysis has advanced by leaps and bounds since nineteen eighty-three." I take a sip of whiskey from the flask in my pocket. "I'm going to find whoever hurt you. If it's the last thing I do."

CHAPTER THIRTEEN

FOLLOWING a restless night's sleep fraught with nightmares in which I'm racing through the woods, trying to save Demetrius from someone who, upon reflection, looks an awful lot like me, I crawl out of bed and take a hot shower. Ten minutes later, I'm dressed and out the door.

As soon as I reach the station, Chief Jimenez calls me into her office.

"The medical examiner has ruled Crispin's death was due to acute mixed drug and alcohol toxicity."

"What about the eye drops?"

"They found no traces of tetrahydrozoline in his system."

"I've encountered dozens of overdoses," I say. "I've never seen anyone experience the symptoms he did."

"I don't know what to tell you, Nowak. The case is closed."

"I realize that, but—"

"No buts. Our work is done. Let it go."

The chief is right. We've closed the case. Our job is done. But my spidey sense tells me there's more going on here than meets the eye.

"The judge released Ernest Drucker on bail," Chief Jimenez says. Her phone rings. She dismisses me.

While on patrol, I cruise past the Stone Witch Inn and spy Ernest Drucker seated on the porch, sifting through a stack of papers. I pull over and park.

"How are you doing, Ernest?" I shout as I rush up the walkway. Ernest shrugs.

"Beautiful day."

"You didn't come here to discuss the weather, officer."

"Too bad about your buddy, Crispin."

"Ollie died of an overdose," Ernest says.

"You didn't like the guy much, did you?"

"He was a bully."

"Maybe you decided to even the score."

"That's absurd! I made a stupid mistake by putting eye drops in the meatballs. But I'm not a murderer."

"We'll see." I rise. "Don't go anywhere."

Inside the inn, Frieda Gladstone shuffles downstairs clutching a bundle of dirty linens.

"Cal," she says. "What brings you by?"

"You heard about Oliver Crispin?"

"Such a shame," Frieda says, shaking her head. "But I can't say I'm surprised."

"Why's that?"

"Ollie drank like a fish, as you know," Frieda says. "And he indulged in other suspicious substances, too."

"Did you ever see him take illegal drugs?"

"I smelled marijuana smoke on his clothes several times," Frieda says. "And I found a light dusting of white powder on the bathroom sink once when I was cleaning that I suspect was," she touches her nose and whispers, "cocaine."

"You saw Crispin do cocaine?"

Frieda shakes her head.

"Did he have many female visitors?"

"I washed a lot of sheets."

"Have you cleared out his room yet?"

"I'm not sure what I should do with his belongings."

"Mind if I have a look around?"

"Take a right at the top of the stairs," Frieda says. "Last door on the left. The door's unlocked."

Dirty clothes lie piled around the floor of Crispin's room. I'm reminded of my old studio apartment in the city.

A pair of lacy women's panties pokes out from under the bed. I scoop them up using my baton. It's unlikely they're Crispin's, but you never know. A glint catches my eye. Slipping on a pair of nitrile gloves, I reach beneath the bed and pull out a spider-shaped silver brooch that I have seen Helena Potter wear.

A worn address book lies on top of a rustic pine chest of drawers. I flip through several pages of contacts. None bear the surname Crispin. Most are women. I pocket the book. Perhaps I can locate a sister or aunt among the entries who changed her name after she married. I find a few loose coins, a crushed pack of cigarettes, and a prescription for doxycycline, beneath which lies a credit card issued to Brandy Speedman.

A copy of the play script for *The Mirror Crack'd* rests atop the bedside table. I flip through the pages. A note falls out. *Whatever role you want to play is yours, Ollie, my love.* Ten to one, that's Daphne's handwriting.

After sorting through the pockets of Oliver's clothes and finding nothing further of interest, I bag the evidence I've gathered and return to patrolling the streets of Nyes Landing.

As soon as I turn the corner onto Main Street, a car with Connecticut license plates runs a stop sign. I flash my lights. The elderly driver pulls over and apologizes profusely. I issue him a warning and send him and his wife on their way.

Besides protecting Nyes Landing, my fellow officers and I patrol the surrounding hamlets. I merge onto the highway and travel east for ten minutes, passing through Capachick with its one stoplight. From there, I cruise down the mountain into the valley below, with its picturesque farms. I pass lush rows of green grapevines and pull into the parking lot of Stony Brook Cellars, Brandy Speedman's winery, which is located inside a renovated colonial-era barn.

Inside, I entered a vast open tasting room with a vaulted ceiling and polished oak floors, with wrought-iron tables and chairs arranged around the perimeter. An L-shaped gift shop in the corner, constructed from empty wine barrels topped by a sheet of glass, offers branded merchandise, bottled water, and locally sourced snacks.

Brandy walks my way. With her dark hair, ivory skin, and ruby lips, she resembles a sexy Snow White in a blue and yellow dress.

"Cal, to what do I owe the pleasure?"

"Oliver Crispin passed away."

"You drove all the way out here to tell me that?"

"I thought I should let you know."

"Why?"

"Weren't you and Crispin involved?"

"Whatever gave you that idea?"

I pull Brandy's credit card from my pocket.

"That little shit," Brandy says.

"How did Crispin come to be in possession of your credit card?"

Brandy invites me to step inside a private tasting room. She shuts the door and asks if I'd like a glass of wine.

"I'm more of a whiskey drinker."

"Me too."

Brandy pulls out a bottle of twenty-one-year-old single malt Scotch and pours two shots. She and her husband, Trevor, divorced shortly after they purchased the winery last spring. Trevor returned to Napa Valley, where the couple lived before moving back east, and she took over the management here.

"I'm on duty," I say.

"I'll never tell," Brandy says. She raises her glass. I join her.

"How did Crispin come to be in possession of your credit card?"

"He must've taken it from my purse."

"When did Crispin have access to your purse?"

"We hooked up a few times."

"So you were having sex with Crispin."

"I have needs, Cal," Brandy says. "You of all people can understand that." She pours herself another shot. "Ollie did things to my body that no man has ever done." She smiles. "You're blushing." She offers me a refill. I cover my glass with my hand. She swigs her drink and slams down the glass. "I don't like to share, though, so I moved on to greener pastures."

"There were other women?" I ask, even though I know the answer.

"Ollie attracted women like flies on crap," Brandy says. She raises her glass. "May the little shit rest in peace."

"How eloquent."

"I call them like I see them."

"The medical examiner ruled his death an overdose."

"I'm not surprised."

"I am," I say. "I've dealt with my share of junkies. They grow agitated, hyperactive, even combative. But I've only witnessed hallucinations like that once before, during an encounter with a schizophrenic woman who was living on the streets."

"Do you think Ollie may have been schizophrenic?"

"I don't think anything . . . yet."

"Thanks for returning my credit card," Brandy says, and she rises. "If there's nothing else . . ."

I thank Brandy for her time and take off, wondering if one of Crispin's lovers got jealous and ended his life. I need to speak with the other women he seduced and see what I can learn.

CHAPTER FOURTEEN

AFTER I TYPE up my reports for the day and clock out, I stop by the hardware store. A couple from the city who recently purchased a cabin and are planning their renovations barrage Demetrius with questions. He glances in my direction and smiles, which I take as a sign he's forgiven me for cutting our camping trip short.

I peruse a shelf of home improvement and gardening books. *Poisonous Plants of the Catskill Mountains* catches my eye. As I flip through the pages, I recognize some of the plants Demetrius told me about on our camping trip. Nature is more frightening than I'd imagined.

Demetrius ushers the young couple out the door and asks what I'm reading. I hold up the book.

"I'm never going camping again."

"I'm surprised you went once."

"What are you doing tonight?"

"Why?"

"I'd like to take my boyfriend to dinner."

"Am I your boyfriend?"

"What do you think?"

I give his ass a playful smack.

"Give me a minute." Demetrius turns the open sign around, locks his cash drawer inside the safe, and sets the security alarm. "Let's go."

I open the door of my pickup for Demetrius. He climbs inside. I hop behind the wheel and pull out onto Main Street.

"Where are we going?"

"It's a surprise."

As we drive through town, Demetrius tells me Cora's doing well in school. I merge onto the highway. I can't shake my suspicion that Crispin did not die of an overdose.

"Earth to Cal," Demetrius says.

"I'm listening."

"What did I say?"

"Something about Cora?"

"I might as well be talking to a wall."

"It's this case."

I share my suspicion that Crispin's death was a homicide.

"Can you prove that?"

"Not yet."

Exiting the highway, we cruise up the mountainside and reach the Summit Lodge and Hearth. A valet attendant rushes up, takes the keys to my pickup, and passes me my claim check. The hostess seats us at a table for two by the window. The rustic dining room overlooks the surrounding slopes.

"What a spectacular view," Demetrius says.

"I thought you'd enjoy this spot."

Demetrius reaches across the table, squeezes my hand, and mouths the words, "I love you."

Our server arrives. Early twenties, I'd guess, with blond hair and an athletic build. Too all-American boy-next-door for me. He shares the dinner specials and takes our drink order.

"Cora has a boyfriend," Demetrius says.

"She's eight years old."

"According to her, they're getting married."

"Kids grow up so fast these days."

Our server brings our drinks—a cognac for Demetrius and my usual beer with a shot of whiskey—and takes our order.

Daphne and Bill Sinclair stroll through the door. I'd heard they were regulars here. The hostess seats the couple on the far side of the room. The husky Italian chef with his thick, curly black hair—Giovanni, according to his biography on the back of the menu—rushes out of the kitchen and presents the couple with a special appetizer.

Our server brings our entrées. He sets the prime rib before Demetrius and the chicken piccata before me. We switch plates. Our server apologizes.

Demetrius shares a story about something cute that Cora did at school. I miss half of what he's saying because I'm wondering if Daphne could be capable of murder. In high school, her rival for the lead in the senior play fell down a flight of stairs and broke her ankle the day auditions took place. Some students said they saw Daphne push the girl, but that was never corroborated. If she loved Crispin, though, like the note I found suggests, I can't imagine why she'd want the guy dead.

"Way to make a man feel ignored," Demetrius says.

"I can't get this case off my mind."

"I thought the medical examiner found Oliver Crispin died of an overdose."

"I've seen many overdoses in my time," I say. "But I've never seen anyone hallucinate the way Crispin did."

"You're married to that badge."

"That's not fair."

"Some date night."

Demetrius goes to the men's room. I debate following and decide I should give him his space.

Bill Sinclair takes a call on his cellular phone and steps away. While he's gone, I approach Daphne.

"Lose something?"

I toss the lacy panties I found under Crispin's bed onto the table. Daphne's cheeks redden.

"How do you think your husband would feel if he knew you'd had an affair?"

"Humiliated, that's how I feel," Bill Sinclair says. "I trust that answers your question, officer."

"I'm sorry, I didn't—"

"My wife made a foolish mistake. She knows that now. Don't you, darling?"

Daphne nods.

"If you have any further questions, you may speak to our attorney." Bill Sinclair hands me a business card. "In case you lost his number."

Could Bill Sinclair have done away with his wife's lover? Or am I letting my imagination run wild?

By the time I return to our table, Demetrius has finished eating. I ask my server if I can take my prime rib home. He whisks my plate away.

Demetrius glances over the wine list.

"Interesting."

"What?"

"They ferment their own elderberry wine."

"I'm not much of a wine drinker."

"I'll try a glass while you finish your beer."

Our server returns with my prime rib neatly wrapped in foil and packed in a shopping bag. Demetrius orders his wine, which our server brings, and we watch the moon rise over the mountains.

"Try a sip."

Demetrius passes me his glass. My mouth puckers from the tartness of the syrupy-thick wine.

"Must be an acquired taste," I say.

Our server brings our check, which I pay, and I drive Demetrius back to the hardware store where he left his pickup.

"I need to let Flower out before he pees on my bearskin rug again," Demetrius says. "You're welcome to come over."

"I have an early morning tomorrow."

"I have Cora this weekend."

"I'll call you."

"I love you."

"Ditto."

Did I just say ditto? Is that the best I can do?

CHAPTER FIFTEEN

When I reach the station on Wednesday morning, Chief Jimenez shouts, "My office, Nowak! Pronto!" I hustle to comply. The chief leans back in her chair. "You insulted the Sinclairs? In public, no less." Her intense dark eyes narrow. "What were you thinking?" Her no-nonsense demeanor makes me reconsider cracking a joke.

"I merely returned an article of clothing to its rightful owner."

"You humiliated the Sinclairs, and they are out for blood. But they'll settle for your badge."

"Oliver Crispin did not die of a drug overdose."

"You're not a doctor, Nowak. You're a cop." Chief Jimenez sighs. "Although you won't be much longer if you keep acting the fool."

Once more, I find myself on the outside looking in.

"Apologize to the Sinclairs, Nowak."

"But—"

"Give me your word."

"You have my word."

"And let Crispin rest in peace."

I nod because I must if I want to keep my job. But I have no intention of backing off this case. Even a jerk like Oliver Crispin deserves justice.

———

As I drive up the mountainside, I pass Rose and Trixie's farm. Rose is on her hands and knees digging in her garden, while Trixie scatters feed before their flock of plump, red hens. I tap my horn and wave. The women wave back.

The Sinclairs's sprawling mountaintop mansion must have cost a fortune. I ring the doorbell, wait a moment, and ring again. I ring twice more before Vona, the housekeeper, answers, clutching the handle of a vacuum cleaner.

"I hope you haven't been standing here long, officer."

"I need to speak with the Sinclairs."

"The Sinclairs drove into the city today."

"When do you expect them back?"

"They didn't say.

"Are you all right?"

"Why wouldn't I be?"

"Your fingers look bruised."

"I made the mistake of not wearing gloves the last time I brewed elderberry syrup."

"I tried elderberry wine the other night. It's too bitter for me."

"Mrs. Sinclair swears by elderberry syrup for whatever ails a person."

"Where does she find elderberries?" I ask.

"She grows them in her garden."

"May I see?"

"Follow me."

Vona leads me around behind the house. Her flip-flops smack against the stone pathway. We walk across a vibrant, dark green carpet of neatly mowed grass and reach a garden filled with brightly colored chili peppers, tomato vines, and beanstalks. At the far end of the plot, a pair of woody shrubs with leafy branches covered in clusters of green berries towers over the other plants.

"Elderberry bushes bloom in late summer, but the berries don't ripen until the fall."

"How do you make elderberry syrup in June, then?"

"Mrs. Sinclair froze several bags of the berries she harvested last fall."

It's hard to imagine the Daphne I knew in high school gardening. But she probably never figured I'd become a cop either.

"Tell the Sinclairs I stopped by."

On my way back down the mountain, I pay Rose and Trixie a visit.

"Whatever it is," Rose says, "we didn't do it."

"Now that Ernest Drucker has confessed that he poured eye drops in your meatball sauce, you're off the hook."

"We can't afford to have anyone suggest they got sick from eating our food," Rose says. "A rumor like that could ruin our business."

"Once the truth comes out—" I say.

"Nobody cares about the truth," Rose says.

Rose is right. People often want to believe the worst.

"Do you like jam, Cal?" Trixie asks.

"Who doesn't like jam?"

"Be right back."

Trixie rushes inside the house. Rose and I contemplate the dark clouds overhead and agree that rain is coming. Trixie returns clutching two glass jars.

"Would you prefer blackberry or elderberry?"

"Elderberry jam?"

"Made from a bushel of the wild berries I picked last fall," Trixie says. "Downstaters can't buy the stuff fast enough."

"Elderberries are nutritious?"

"They're rich in antioxidants," Trixie says. "Padma taught us that when properly handled, they reduce inflammation and regulate blood sugar levels far better than traditional medicines."

"The Indian woman who sells candles and cards?"

"That's right. Padma hosts a natural harmony gathering at her shop on Wednesday nights," Rose says. "We share herbal remedies for common ailments and gab about our lives."

"I'd better play it safe and try the blackberry flavor."

"Take both."

"You should send him home with some crumpets, too," Rose says. "We'll never eat four dozen."

"Good idea." Trixie rushes back inside the house.

I have no clue what a crumpet is and say as much.

"Have you ever had an English muffin?" Rose asks.

"Sure."

"The Brits call those crumpets."

"When I was a little girl," Trixie says upon her return, "I read about tea and crumpets in my nursery rhymes." She passes me a paper bag. "That Christmas, Santa Claus brought me an Easy-Bake oven, and I haven't stopped baking since."

"Thanks for the jam," I say, and I drive back to town.

As I cruise down Main Street, I spot Chief Jimenez and Officer Lecoq arguing with a red-faced Gladys Crabtree, who is seated behind the wheel of her AMC Pacer, which, despite being well over twenty years old, looks brand new.

"I was not speeding!" Gladys shouts so loudly I can hear her from across the street.

"You can argue that in court, ma'am," Officer Lecoq says. His eyeglasses slide down. He shoves the pair back up on his nose and extends the ticket on a clipboard through the window of the Pacer. "Sign here."

"This is outrageous!" Gladys Crabtree scrawls her signature where Officer Lecoq indicates. If looks could kill, he'd be dead on arrival. "May I go now? Or do you need to strip-search me?"

Officer Lecoq's cheeks redden. With his receding hairline, he looks a decade older than his twenty-eight years. "That won't be necessary, ma'am." He hands Gladys a copy of the citation, which she wads up and tosses over her shoulder into the backseat. "Wait until the mayor hears about this." She almost runs over Lecoq's foot when she drives away.

"I didn't expect you back so soon, Nowak," Chief Jimenez asks. "Did you make peace with the Sinclairs?"

"They drove into the city for the day."

"That doesn't let you off the hook."

"I told their housekeeper I'd come back."

"We can't afford to alienate the Sinclairs."

"I hear you, chief."

"Don't make me regret taking a chance on you, Nowak."

"If it's okay with you, chief," Officer Lecoq asks. "I need to go home for lunch and feed my birds."

Officer Lecoq raises and shows bantam chickens, an unusual hobby for a grown man. Or anyone, for that matter. He invited me over once. Coops of the brightly colored game roosters and their dull-brown mates cluttered the yard of his rundown cabin.

"Have you eaten, Nowak?" Chief Jimenez asks.

"Nope."

"Lunch is on me."

CHAPTER SIXTEEN

KIKI SHOWS Chief Jimenez and me to a booth in the rear of the Nyes Landing Diner and shares the specials of the day. We place our order. Once we're alone, Chief Jimenez leans in and says, "This little stunt you pulled with the Sinclairs has the mayor's panties in a twist."

"That woman has never liked me."

"You're your own worst enemy, Nowak."

"Tell me something I don't know."

"Keep this up and you could lose your badge."

"This case—"

"We have no case, Nowak. The medical examiner ruled Crispin died from alcohol and drug toxicity."

"What about—?"

"Drop it, Nowak."

My quest for justice has upset the town leadership. Someone is covering up something. But who and what?

"I'll keep my nose clean," I say because I want to keep my job.

"You better."

Our lunch arrives. Burgers with all the fixings and a basket of fries and onion rings, which we share.

"Lecoq has his chicken show at the county fair this weekend, so we're down an officer," Chief Jimenez says. She drenches three fries in ketchup and stuffs them into her mouth. "Are you okay with covering the Pride celebration at the Roadhouse Saturday night?"

"Whatever you need me to do."

"How was your camping trip?"

"We caught poison ivy."

"How did you do that?"

I tell her. She laughs so hard she snorts.

———

AFTER LUNCH, I review the evidence that Officer Washington and I collected from the theater for the umpteenth time, searching for anything we may have missed. The red plastic cup Crispin drank from does smell of gin. Washington was right. We found an empty vodka bottle in Crispin's dressing room, but the only gin we found was in Daphne's dressing room. Frustrated, I clock out for the day.

When I reach home, I find Annie curled up on the couch, watching reruns of *Murder, She Wrote* on the television. Ever since Kit's untimely death, she has been obsessed with crime shows. The police work in most of those programs makes me cringe. I pour myself three fingers of whiskey and join her on the couch.

"What's Jessica Fletcher up to tonight?"

Without taking her eyes off the screen, Annie says, "Someone murdered her best friend's husband, and she suspects foul play." She sips her wine. "How was your date with Demetrius last night?"

"Fine," I say. I don't mention the scene I caused with the Sinclairs.

"I invited Howie over to watch a movie."

"Is there something going on between you two?"

"We're just friends."

"Does he know that?"

"You're the last person who should be giving out relationship advice, Cal."

"I'm going out."

I escape into my room. Stripping off my uniform, I climb into the shower. If Bill Sinclair drinks gin, he may have shared his bottle with Crispin. Or Crispin may have found the bottle and helped himself. Not that it matters. Gin isn't poisonous. I'm grasping at straws, but something feels off here. I'll do some digging, but I must be discreet, or I could lose my job.

When I emerge from my room, I hear Annie puttering around in the kitchen. I slip out the front door and take a drive. The streets are even quieter than usual. I pass Officer Lecoq giving directions to a lost family.

When I drive by Demetrius's cabin, he's walking Flower—and he's not alone! A lean, tan guy with blond highlights who looks familiar, but I can't place from where, follows Demetrius around the yard. I make a sharp U-turn and pull over onto the shoulder of the road. I don't like the way the blond guy touches Demetrius's arm and pats his back. Demetrius throws back his head and laughs. Has he met someone else?

Before I'm caught spying, I drive away and cruise around aimlessly until I reach the Roadhouse, which is as good a place as any to drown my sorrows. I can't believe Demetrius did this to me —to us, rather. I'm even more pissed at myself for letting this happen.

Bellying up to the bar, I order a double shot of whiskey with a pint of Guinness.

"Rough day?" Gunner asks.

"I've had better."

Gunner sets my drinks before me. He still wears a bandage on his forehead from his recent assault.

"How's your head?" I ask.

"I'll live," Gunner says.

I chug my shot and ask for another. Gunner sets me up. I tell him about the blond guy I saw hanging out with Demetrius.

"You're an idiot," Gunner says. "You know that, right?"

"You and Tanner may have an open relationship, but we don't."

"You saw Demetrius walking his dog with some guy and figured they must be having an affair?"

Suddenly, I feel stupid. They could be friends from college or high school teammates. Demetrius and I only met a year ago. There's a lot we don't know about each other.

"I'm such a doofus."

"You don't like the thought of Demetrius seeing another man," Gunner says. "That's only natural."

That Celine Dion song from the movie *Titanic* blasts from the jukebox. A cute guy in his early twenties, with jet black hair and a tawny complexion, straddles the stool beside me and orders a vodka and tonic. When his drink arrives, he raises his glass and says, "Happy Hump Day!"

I knock back my shot and signal to Gunner that I'd like another.

"I'm Kirk," the young guy says.

"Officer Nowak."

"Do you have a first name, officer?"

"Callum," I say. "But my friends call me Cal."

"What should I call you?"

"Officer Nowak."

"Are you always this charming?"

Gunner brings my shot and draws me a fresh pint of Guinness. If the guy with Demetrius is just a friend, why didn't he mention they were getting together? I check out Kirk with his sultry dark eyes and crooked smile. A few inches shorter than me, with a lean swimmer's build, he's adorable. But if I fooled around with anyone but Demetrius, Annie might never speak to me again.

Kirk rubs his knee against mine.

"I'm sorry, Kirk," I say. "You're cute. But I'm in a relationship."

"I'm not asking you to marry me."

My cellular phone rings. I glance at the screen. It's Demetrius.

"I need to take this," I say, and I step outside so I can hear better. "What's up?"

"I called the house. Annie said you went out."

"She and Howie are watching a movie tonight. I didn't want to be a third wheel."

"Are they—"

"He wishes."

"What are you doing?"

"I stopped by the Roadhouse for a drink."

"You'll never guess who I ran into."

"Who?"

"Remember Trevor Speedman?"

Relief washes over me. That's where I know the lean, tan guy with the blond highlights from. Trevor is Brandy Speedman's ex-husband. He moved back to California after the couple filed for divorce last summer.

"What's Trevor doing in town?"

"He and Brandy have some business they need to take care of, and her birthday is later this month."

"That's right. Everyone in town is talking about that party."

"Trevor dropped by the hardware store and wanted to catch up, so I invited him over. You should join us. Unless you're—"

"I'm on my way."

I buy a round for Kirk as an apology for my rudeness, pay my bar tab, and take off, grateful I didn't make a bigger fool of myself than I did. I arrive to find Demetrius sprawled back on the couch beside Trevor Speedman, who looks as handsome as ever. He and Annie's husband, Kit, had a moment of oral passion in Atlantic

City that must've rocked his world because his tee shirt reads "Out and Proud Bisexual."

"You two make a hot couple," Trevor says.

"We're lucky we found each other," Demetrius says.

I slip my arm around Demetrius. He leans against my shoulder. I should have my head examined for not appreciating this more.

"I'm screwing this accountant named Bruce," Trevor says, "who performs in drag as Netta Worth."

Trevor is a hot mess, but he seems more relaxed now that he's come to terms with his bisexuality, something he and Demetrius share. After listening to the guy talk about himself for several minutes, I've had about all his smugness I can handle for one night. My mind wanders back to the case. Tomorrow, I must call the lab and see if they've found anything.

By the time Trevor runs out of stories, we're out of booze, and he's too drunk to drive. Demetrius fetches a blanket and pillows and puts Trevor to bed on the couch, then takes Flower outside one last time before bed while I brush my teeth, and we turn in for the night.

CHAPTER SEVENTEEN

THURSDAY MORNING, I creep out of Demetrius's bedroom at the first light of dawn. Trevor Speedman lies snoring on the couch, having kicked off his blankets, leaving his lean, tan body exposed. He groans awake when I walk through the room and yawns and stretches his arms.

"Do you drink coffee?" I ask on my way into the kitchen.

Trevor follows me. He rubs his crotch against my backside. "You like what you see?" He reeks of whiskey and beer. I press the start button on the machine and take a step back. He shrugs. "Suit yourself."

Returning to the bedroom, I crawl under the covers and snuggle against Demetrius. He rolls over, facing me. We both have morning breath, but I don't mind if he doesn't. I kiss my way down his smooth torso and tease my tongue over his privates. He moans. I take him into my mouth. Within moments, his breathing quickens. I drive him to the edge several times before I finish him off.

Once Demetrius settles down, he slips on his bathrobe and goes for coffee. I dress and join him in the kitchen. Trevor has put on his clothes and folded his blankets on the couch. Demetrius pours two mugs of coffee, passes me one, and adds cream and sugar to his. I take mine black.

"I need to go home, shower, and put on my uniform for work," I say.

Demetrius draws me close and whispers, "I love you." I start to speak. He places his fingers over my lips and says, "Don't insult me by saying the words if you don't mean them."

"I don't know what you want from me. I've never—"

"You've never been in a relationship before. I know. And I've never slept with another man. Are we ever going to move past those excuses?"

"Can we talk about this later?"

I nod toward the living room where Trevor sits. Demetrius sighs.

"Fine."

Trevor's cellular phone rings. He answers and says, "I'm on my way," and grabs his jacket. "Thanks for letting me crash here, dudes."

"Next time you're in town, man," Demetrius says. "Look us up."

"I'll call you later," I tell Demetrius, and I follow Trevor out the door. Trevor hops behind the wheel of his rental car and drives away. I climb inside my pickup and follow him to the junction with the highway. He turns north, while I turn south toward town.

At the station, Officer Lecoq tosses me the keys to the squad car and clocks out. I review the night patrol log. A couple of domestic abuse complaints, neither of which were substantiated. A citation for an expired license plate. A lost dog who found its way home. Not exactly the sort of heart-pounding cases I'd imagined investigating when I entered law enforcement.

Finding myself alone at the station, I take out the box of evidence from my mother's case and lift the lid. At the sight of her blood-soaked nightgown folded inside a plastic bag, my throat tightens. I squeeze my eyes shut and take a deep breath. If Papa Frank were alive, he'd tell me to man up.

To clear my head, I jog around the block. The fresh air invigorates my senses. I purchase a honey bun from the diner for the sugar high.

Back at the station, I take a deep breath and, setting aside the plastic bag that contains my mother's blood-soaked nightgown, pull out the police report. Leaning back in my chair, I study the scant few pages. The responding officers' descriptions of the crime scene ring true with my memories from that awful night. No one in the nearby trailers they canvassed saw or heard anything suspicious, which I find hard to believe. Crime scene investigators recovered a bloody boot print and several smudged fingerprints, which weren't a match for anyone in the system.

Polaroid snapshots from the crime scene make me queasy. I'm not sure I've got the stomach for this investigation. But if I don't find my mother's killer, who will? I set aside the disturbing images and pull out a plastic bag that contains my mother's wedding ring, which she must've worn at the time of her death. She would go through periods of accepting my father had deserted us, and then she'd wear his ring for a while and insist he was coming home soon. I put everything back in the box and shut the lid.

Grabbing the keys to the squad car, I go on patrol. Vehicles crowd the parking lot of the Nyes Landing Diner. Trevor and Brandy sit at a table near the window, arguing. I continue down Main Street, past the Stone Witch Inn. Ernest Drucker sits on the front porch, reading a book. His trial will hit the docket soon, and the prosecution will probably call upon me to testify.

While patrolling an older neighborhood on the northeast side of town, I spy a gang of teenage boys loitering in a vacant lot. I pull over to the curb and park. The boys eye me from afar. I stare back. If they're up to no good, they'll betray their intentions. Boys their age always do. They stub out their cigarette butts and disperse. I wait until they turn the corner at the end of the block and move on.

As I drive past the elementary school, shrieking children race out the doors and dash around the playground. It must be time for morning recess. Annie and two other teachers whose names I can't recall right now keep an eye on their rowdy charges. I wave. They wave back.

Cruising down Creekside Drive, I pass the abandoned paper mill where I hid from my mother's killer for five days and nights when I was thirteen years old and where, last spring, I rescued a missing boy. The dilapidated structure is not only an eyesore but also dangerous and should be demolished.

Merging onto the highway, I drive for ten miles and pass through Capachick. Aside from a couple of parking summonses, which I leave on the windshields of the offending vehicles, there's not much happening in Nyes Landing's southeasternmost hamlet.

Merging onto the highway, I drive northeast for twenty miles and take the exit toward New Maastricht, the most affluent of Nye Landing's hamlets. I cruise past several expansive ranch-style houses on sprawling green lots. Brandy Speedman lives in the green and white cottage on the mountainside. I pass through downtown, keeping an eye out for suspicious activity. Most of the crimes in this hamlet involve property damage or theft. Seeing nothing amiss, I return to the highway.

As I drive back to Nyes Landing, I call Demetrius while I have cellular service and ask if he's hungry. He is, but he can't leave the hardware store right now. I pull into the drive-thru lane at the Jukebox Junction and order two cheeseburgers, a large order of fries for us to share, and a couple of shakes. I'll work off the calories later, or so I tell myself.

Demetrius stands behind the cash register when I arrive, ringing up a customer. I hold up the Jukebox Junction bag and indicate I'll take our lunch into the back room. He nods. I unpack our food on top of his workbench. He likes mayonnaise and ketchup on his burgers. I prefer mustard. I set the vanilla shake beside his burger, poke a straw through the lid of my chocolate shake, and take a long sip.

"Hey, babe," Demetrius says. He squeezes my shoulder and takes a seat on the stool across the workbench from me. "You're a lifesaver."

"Busy day, huh?"

"I've been swamped with downstaters renovating their vacation homes."

"I can't believe how fast the town has grown. The whole county, for that matter. If this continues, we're going to need more officers."

"Cora keeps asking me if you're going camping with us this weekend."

Cora is an adorable little girl, but she talks nonstop, and her constant questions can challenge my already thin patience.

"The chief assigned me to cover the PRIDE celebration at the Roadhouse Saturday night."

"I figured as much."

"Duty calls."

"Doesn't it always?"

"What's that supposed to mean?"

Demetrius shrugs. I pop the last bite of my cheeseburger into my mouth, slurp up the dregs of my chocolate shake from the bottom of my cup, and stuff my burger wrapper and dirty napkins into the bag, which I wad up and lob into the trash can across the room.

"I should go," I say. I kiss Demetrius. "I'll call you later."

CHAPTER EIGHTEEN

THURSDAY MORNING, Rose and Trixie call and report that someone has poisoned their chickens. I drive out to their farm. The distraught couple's large red hens stumble in circles, shitting watery bile down their feathery rumps. Several spastic birds flop around on the ground.

"What the hell happened?" I ask.

"We woke up and found our girls in this state." Trixie says. Tears streak her long face.

"I'd wager my bottom dollar that Bill Sinclair had a hand in this," Rose says.

Given the couple's history of conflicts with their neighbors up the mountain, I wouldn't be surprised. But suspicion and evidence of guilt are two different matters.

"Did you see Mr. Sinclair on your property?" I ask.

"We were asleep," Trixie says.

"Our security alarm went off last night," Rose says. "We thought a bear had broken into our shed again."

"What are we going to do?" Trixie sobs.

"Dr. Webb is on his way," Rose says.

Another chicken collapses and flops around on the ground,

flapping its wings. Two more chickens topple over, their beaks opening and closing, gasping for breath. I don't know what's happening, but I know someone who might. I ask Rose and Trixie if I can use their phone.

"It's in the kitchen," Trixie says. "Follow me."

Trixie leads me through the cluttered but comfortable living room. A portable phone rests in its cradle on the kitchen counter. I look up the number and dial.

"Lecoq, here." A loud thud follows. "Um, sorry. I dropped the phone."

"It's Nowak."

"What's up?"

I share what I've observed.

"I'm on my way."

"Our girls are dying," Trixie sobs. She rushes from one distressed chicken to another. "We must do something."

"I can't watch the old gals suffer this way," Rose says. She stretches the neck of the nearest chicken until it snaps. The chicken falls slack. Trixie wails and rushes inside the house. Rose euthanizes the rest of the distressed flock.

Officer Lecoq arrives in his beat-up cargo van. He leaps out and asks if he can take a closer look. Rose and Trixie shoo him through the coop's gate. He examines the first carcass he comes upon, shakes his head, and examines another. His eyes widen. He picks up a half-eaten green berry off the ground and, sifting through the grain in the flock's trough, finds more berries with holes pecked in their flesh.

"How did these wind up in their feed?" Lecoq asks.

"I have no idea," Rose says.

"What are they?" I ask.

"Some type of berry," Rose says. "Padma would know."

Slipping on a pair of gloves, I gather up several green berries with a paper towel and secure them inside a plastic evidence bag.

"Someone mixed the berries into their feed," Officer Lecoq says.

"I'll bet I know who, too," Rose says.

"I'll admit the situation looks suspicious," I say, "especially given your history with the Sinclairs."

A van with the Nyes Landing Veterinary Clinic logo printed on its side panels pulls into the driveway. Dr. Webb climbs out. With his bushy mustache and thick sideburns, he resembles the Marlboro Man whose picture was splashed all over billboards along the highway in the 1970s when I was a child. After hearing us out, he examines the dead chickens and agrees with Officer Lecoq—they likely died from eating the berries. But he has no idea what type of berries we're dealing with. He bags three of the carcasses and tosses them into his van. "I'll know more after I autopsy these specimens." He climbs behind the wheel of his van and backs out of the driveway.

"I can't imagine what I'd do if something like this happened to my flock," Officer Lecoq says. "I wish I could've done more."

After I take Rose's and Trixie's official statements, I grab the digital camera from the squad car and snap a shot of what remains of their flock. The shutter clicks, and the camera whirs as it writes the image to a floppy disk. A soft beep sound follows. I snap four more shots and sigh. The disk is full. I slide the metal catch on the side of the camera. The disk pops out with a mechanical clunk. I tuck it into my jacket pocket and pull out a fresh disk from the plastic case. It snaps into place with a familiar click. I take a few close-up shots, pack up, and go.

If Bill Sinclair contaminated the stream with a deer carcass, he's certainly capable of poisoning a few chickens. But without proof, there's not much I can do.

———

WHEN I ARRIVE HOME that evening, I find Annie curled up in her bed, clutching a framed photograph of her and Kit on their wedding day. Annie sobs into her pillow. I can't make out what she's saying. A half-empty wine bottle rests on her nightstand alongside an empty wine glass and a bottle of pills.

"Rough day?" I ask.

She nods. I rub her back and ask her if she's hungry. She shakes her head and mumbles she has a migraine. "I'll check in on you later," I whisper, and I switch off the light on my way out the door.

Pouring myself a hearty glass of whiskey, I settle onto the couch and dig the remote control out from between the cushions. After scrolling through the cable television channels twice, I land on an episode of *Forensic Files*.

Doctors admit an eleven-month-old boy to the hospital for chronic vomiting. The following day, the boy's father falls ill and ends up hospitalized as well. The boy falls into a coma and dies. His father succumbs a few days later. Investigators analyze everything the family ate and discover the lemonade the father and son drank contained toxic amounts of an herbicide. Further investigation reveals that the man's wife was having an affair that she'd broken off, and the man she'd been having the affair with poisoned the lemonade, hoping to kill her for breaking his heart.

People in love do crazy stuff, and so do feuding neighbors.

Before pouring another whiskey, I lope upstairs and check on Annie. She's sleeping.

After sitting through two episodes of *Homicide: Life on the Street*—my favorite cop show, which is in reruns on the Lifetime channel—I pour myself a shot of whiskey and turn in for the night. As I reach to turn off my bedside lamp, my cellular phone rings, which surprises me. I don't recognize the number.

"Officer Nowak?"

"Yes."

"This is Dr. Webb. I'm sorry to call so late, but I thought

you'd want to know. Those chickens consumed elderberries. At least, that's what the partially digested bits of fruit I recovered indicate."

"Aren't elderberries safe to consume?"

"Not for chickens," Dr. Webb says. "Especially in large quantities."

Someone intentionally poisoned Rose and Trixie's flock. But who? And why?

CHAPTER NINETEEN

ON MY WAY into work Friday morning, I stop by the Gas & Go, fill up the tank of my pickup, and grab a large cup of black coffee and a blueberry muffin. At the cash register, I bump into Helena Potter, who's buying a carton of half-and-half and a packet of rolling papers. She mentions there's going to be a memorial service for Oliver Crispin next week.

"I can't believe Ollie is gone," Helena says. "He was so full of life."

Helena seems to genuinely miss Crispin. Unlike Brandy, who seems unfazed, and Daphne, whose manufactured tears I don't trust.

As I pull away from the fuel pump, I slosh coffee on my shirt and blot the stain with a paper napkin while keeping an eye on the road. When I reach the station, Sergeant Reeves tosses me the keys to the squad car and pinches off a bite of my muffin, which he pops into his mouth. He flashes me a smug grin. I could tell him he has a blueberry stuck between his front teeth, but I don't.

Before I go on patrol, I take out the evidence box from my mother's cold case and lift the lid, prepared this time for what I'll find inside. I set the bag containing my mother's blood-soaked nightgown aside and open the envelope of Polaroids from the crime scene. A shot of my mother's lifeless body sprawled across her bed, drenched in blood, makes me queasy. I put my head between my knees and breathe until my stomach settles and continue. With each subsequent shot I view, my resolve for justice strengthens into a fervent desire for revenge.

At the bottom of the box, I find a small plastic evidence bag that contains a few strands of hair that couldn't have belonged to my mother. She had blond hair at the time of her death, and these samples look as black as pitch. Perhaps someone at the Forensics Investigation Center in Albany can retest their DNA. Significant advances in the technology have been made since 1983. For that matter, fingerprint recognition software has improved as well. I'll have the partial prints the investigators recovered from the scene rerun.

Before the chief arrives, I repack the evidence and slip the box under the desk. Grabbing the keys to the squad car, I go on patrol. It's a gray day outside. Clouds hang low overhead. I smell rain on the way.

Downstaters escaping the city for the weekend swarm the sidewalks, and their vehicles crowd the limited parking spaces along Main Street. Their casual sense of entitlement irritates me, but their lavish spending feeds our local economy. I double-park near the hardware store and dash inside to say hello.

"Cal!" Cora rushes up and waves a coloring book in my face. "Look what I drawed!" I crouch and admire her pictures. She grins. She's lost another tooth.

Demetrius finishes ringing up a young couple's purchases and joins us. "Hey, babe, what brings you by?"

"I had to see my best girl before you stole her away for the weekend."

"You're welcome to join us."

"I wish I could—"

"No, you don't."

Cora tugs on my pants leg. "Come with us."

"I can't, sweetie. I have to work."

"Speaking of which," Demetrius says. He approaches a pinch-faced woman with frizzy hair and asks if she needs help.

"Is the manager here?" the woman asks.

"I'm the manager, ma'am," Demetrius says. "Owner, actually."

"Is that so?"

She looks Demetrius over and frowns.

"What can I help you with?"

"Where are your shower curtains?"

Demetrius directs her toward the rear of the store. I open a lawn chair and take a seat. Cora crawls onto my lap and shows me her favorite colors of crayons. She's partial to shades of blue. Demetrius helps a thickset bald guy choose a fishing rod and reel.

"You're a talented artist, Cora," I say. I set her on her feet and stand. "You kids have fun on your camping trip."

"We will," Demetrius says. He walks me to the door. "I'll miss you."

"Call me when you get home."

It's sprinkling rain outside. I dash to the squad car. The wiper blades squeak as they scrape across the windshield. I switch them off and creep through town, peering through the drizzle.

A beanpole of a guy with shaggy hair, wearing a Metallica tee shirt and sporting dark shades, loiters on the corner, smoking a cigarette. He peers up and down the sidewalk; he may be dealing drugs. I pull over and idle at the curb. He ducks around the corner. I cruise along behind him. He climbs inside an older model Ford and drives away. I stay on his tail for a few blocks. He maintains the speed limit and uses his turn signals. Once he departs the town limits, I turn back.

A few blocks later, I come across a gang of teenagers harassing two younger boys. I flash my lights and pull over. "Is there a problem here?" The teenagers take off running. I help the younger boys onto their feet, dust off their clothes, and ask if they're okay.

The bright blue eyes of the pudgy kid with the freckles widen. "You're the cop who rescued Evan."

I nod.

"Cool!" the slighter kid with the blond cowlick exclaims.

Evan may have survived his ordeal, but he lost his innocence at far too young an age, which breaks my heart.

"You kids get home safely."

The boys thank me and dash away. I follow at a distance until they're inside their respective houses and make a U-turn.

Two blocks later, Jude Hewes flags me down. What is his problem? I pull over and hop out. Hewes reeks of cigarette smoke and beer.

"What's going on, Jude?"

"Those young hoodlums stole my trash can."

"What hoodlums would those be?"

"Same ones who broke into my garage the last time."

"I need names, Jude."

"Hell if I know the hoodlums's names."

"What did they look like?"

"I didn't see their faces."

"Were they white? Black? Hispanic?"

"Like I told you. I didn't get a good look."

"Did you actually see these hoodlums, Jude?"

"Well, um . . . I may not have set eyes on the lot. But I know they're behind this mischief."

To appease the old coot, I follow him around behind his garage.

"Yesterday I had two garbage cans here. Today, I only got one."

The ground nearby has been disturbed. I follow the crushed underbrush through the trees for a few yards and stumble upon a mangled pile of plastic debris.

"Jude, I believe you have a bear problem."

"I haven't seen any bears on my property."

"You haven't seen any hoodlums either, have you, Jude? Have a nice day."

Next stop, Mama Libby's house. I find her in the backyard, weeding her garden.

"What brings you by, son?"

I never tire of hearing Mama Libby call me son.

"I'm on patrol and found myself over this way."

Truth be told, after sorting through the evidence from my mother's case this morning, I need to be around someone who understands how much opening that old wound pains me.

"Have you had lunch?" Mama Libby asks.

"I'll grab a sandwich from the Gas & Go when I get back to town."

"Don't be silly. I've got a smoked turkey breast. If you're in a rush, you can take your sandwich and go."

That sounds a thousand times better than a day-old sub from the gas station. I help Mama Libby onto her feet and follow her inside the house.

"There's a pitcher of fresh-squeezed lemonade in the fridge," Mama Libby says. "Help yourself."

"Would you like a glass?"

"I haven't finished my coffee yet," Mama Libby says. "It's gotten cold, though." She heats up her coffee in the microwave while she fixes me a sandwich.

"I checked out my mother's cold case files from the evidence locker."

"Did you now?"

"I'm asking the crime lab to retest some of the evidence."

"Are you now?"

"Crime scene technology has advanced a lot over the past twenty years."

"Has it now?"

"Maybe I'll catch a new lead."

"What if they don't find anything?"

"At least I'll know."

"I know you don't want to hear this, Cal. But the odds of finding your mother's killer after all these years are slim to nil."

"I made her a promise, and I intend to keep my word."

"For how long?"

"However long it takes."

"Don't waste your life chasing ghosts, son. Life is for the living."

"I should hit the road before the chief catches me loitering on the job."

Mama Libby wraps my sandwich in paper towels and sends me on my way, more determined than ever to catch my mother's killer.

———

BACK AT THE STATION, Officer Washington needs the keys to the squad car so she can respond to a report of a shoplifter at the Gas & Go. I offer to ride along, but she'd rather handle the call alone. Settling at my desk, I catch up on paperwork. We must log every incident, no matter how banal, which seems a waste of time. Until I'm facing a defendant in court, and then my reports come in handy.

Across the room, Officer Lecoq is seated behind his desk, tying up loose ends before he takes off for the county fair this weekend. I wish him luck.

Dr. Webb calls. "The final reports from the lab came in. They found cyanogenic glycosides in the dead chickens, which metabolize into cyanide. But they also discovered trace amounts of a sugary substance."

"Why would anyone sweeten the berries?"

"Elderberries are quite bitter. The sweetness would make them more palatable to the flock."

As suspected, someone deliberately poisoned Rose and Trixie's flock. The Sinclairs strike me as the most likely suspects. But I need evidence. I call Rose and share what I've learned.

"I knew it," Rose says. "I'm at my wit's end with that couple."

"You need proof."

"Trixie keeps pressuring me to install security cameras, but that would set us back several thousand dollars that we don't have."

"I wish there was more I could do."

After I hang up, I leave my reports on the chief's desk, wish Lecoq luck again, and take off.

On my way home, I pick up Flower from Demetrius's cabin. Annie promised we'd dog-sit this weekend. The slobbery mutt hops inside the pickup. I climb behind the wheel. He crawls into my lap. I shove him onto the passenger seat and tell him to stay put, which he does for a few seconds before wiggling in my direction again. I scratch his chin and ask who he thinks poisoned those chickens. He yawns, apparently not interested in finding the culprit.

CHAPTER TWENTY

SATURDAY AFTERNOON, I patrol Main Street, giving downstaters directions and ticketing their double-parked vehicles. Officer Washington relieves me at five o'clock. I rush home, shower, and take Flower for a walk before driving out to the Roadhouse, where I'm charged with keeping the peace during tonight's PRIDE celebration. Vehicles crowd the parking lot. I find a spot on the shoulder, across the road from the bar.

Inside the Roadhouse, a bare-chested Trevor Speedman whips his sweaty shirt overhead like a lasso and prances around the dance floor. His sun-bronzed torso glistens with sweat under the prisms of the disco ball the club installed for the night. Rainbow-colored streamers drape from the ceiling. Trevor rips one down and wraps it around his neck like a scarf. He seems much happier since his divorce. As does Brandy.

Watching the celebration makes me miss Demetrius. I have two left feet, but he's dragged me onto the dance floor a few times, and I've done my best to keep up with his moves. He won't have cellular service in a tent in the woods, so I can't call him.

A commotion arises around the pool table. Lucy cracks a cue across Dolores's back. Dolores donkey kicks Lucy. Lucy doubles over. The on-and-off-again girlfriends become mean drunks after they've had a few too many. Dolores sweeps Lucy's legs. Lucy collapses to her knees and groans. Dolores lifts a chair overhead. I seize her arm and wrest the chair from her grasp.

"Not tonight, ladies," I say. I help Lucy onto her feet and escort the couple out the front door.

"Give me your car keys."

"You don't have any right to take our keys," Dolores says.

"I can arrest you for being drunk and disorderly if you'd rather. Let you dry out in a jail cell tonight."

"Fine."

Lucy tosses me her keys.

"Do you have someone you can call who can pick you up?"

"We'll sit here and sober up," Dolores says.

"That's not how this is going to work."

"What do you expect us to do?" Lucy asks.

"I'll call you a cab."

"You think we're made of money?"

"Here."

I offer Lucy a twenty-dollar bill.

"We don't need your charity."

"Speak for yourself, Dolores."

Lucy snatches the cash. I step inside. Gunner and Tanner rush around behind the bar, mixing drinks and drawing beers. I shout over the music for Gunner to call the cab company. "Can't you see I'm busy?" he calls back, and he tosses me the bar phone. "Call yourself."

Gunner sets a beer before a cute twink with a sweet smile. The husky fifty-something guy seated beside the twink pays. Middle-aged gays chase their lost youths the same way their straight counterparts do.

After ordering a cab, I make sure Dolores and Lucy don't wander off. A full moon illuminates the night sky. A warm breeze rustles the leaves in the trees.

A Chevy Baja pickup tricked out with a roll bar, off-road lights, and full skid plating from front to rear drives past the Roadhouse. I recognize Wayne Gerber behind the wheel. He and his buddies can't seem to keep their noses clean. A few minutes later, the fools speed past the bar again. I finger the straps of my holster, hoping I don't need to draw.

By the time their ride arrives, Dolores and Lucy have calmed down. They apologize profusely for their behavior, as they do every time that they cause a scene. I load the sheepish couple into the cab and send them home.

Wayne Gerber and his buddies cruise past the bar a third time. I radio Washington and apprise her of the situation. Things are quiet in town, so she'll head over our way. Perhaps if Wayne and his buddies see a squad car, they'll think twice about stirring up trouble tonight.

A rowdy gang of college boys pulls into the parking lot and piles out. On their way inside the bar, they jostle one another like overgrown puppies.

A late-model Mercedes coupe parks across the road. Luke and Jordan step out. The preppy couple in their matching navy-blue blazers and striped board shorts rent a cabin on the lake north of town every summer. They toss me sardonic salutes as they swagger past.

Wayne Gerber and his buddies cruise through the parking lot, whooping and hollering homophobic slurs, before they speed away. I step inside the bar and signal for Gunner. He rings up the drinks he just served, sets the guy's change on the bar, and rushes over. I let him know trouble may be brewing outside. He shares the news with Tanner. I promise to keep the pair posted.

Officer Washington pulls up in the squad car and idles on the shoulder of the road. She alerts the chief, who tells us to keep her posted.

Rose and Trixie pull into the parking lot in their moss green Jeep Wrangler with its rainbow-striped PRIDE bumper sticker.

Dressed in tie-dyed tee shirts and rainbow-striped balloon pants, the couple greets us with warm hellos. I ask if they've experienced any more troubling incidents on their farm. They haven't. I share that Wayne Gerber and his buddies have cruised past the bar several times tonight.

"If you need backup," Rose says. "I've got my Winchester in the Jeep."

"Officer Washington and I can handle Gerber."

"All right, then. Well, you know where I'll be if you change your mind."

An exuberant group of middle-aged downstaters who I gave directions to this afternoon spills out the door of the bar and piles into their rental car. As they pull out of the parking lot, Wayne Gerber and his buddies race past. The downstaters brake to a stop mere inches from the speeding pickup.

"Let's go!" Officer Washington shouts. I climb inside the squad car. Lights flashing and sirens blaring, we burn rubber out of the parking lot. The taillights of Warner Gerber's pickup flicker through the trees ahead. An SUV pulls over onto the shoulder so we can pass. Gerber merges onto the highway. Washington makes a sharp turn and floors the accelerator. The squad car fishtails and shoots up the ramp.

"We should alert the state troopers," I say. "Let them take things from here."

"I've got this."

Hunched forward over the steering wheel, Officer Washington veers into the left lane, speeds past a semi-truck and two passenger cars, and closes the distance on Gerber's pickup. Gerber brake checks us. Washington veers onto the shoulder to avoid a collision. Gerber speeds up. Washington stays on his tail.

"Let it go, Washington."

"You can't be serious?"

"Our job is to protect the Roadhouse tonight," I say. "Not pursue reckless drivers down the highway. That's the state's job."

"I hate it when you're right."

Officer Washington turns around at the first opportunity while I radio the state troopers and alert them to be on the lookout for Gerber and his buddies. Washington drops me off at the Roadhouse and returns to town. "It's Raining Men" blasts from the jukebox when I go inside. Scantily clad revelers crowd the dance floor. Several guys invite me to join in the revelry, but I politely decline.

Behind the bar, Gunner and Tanner look exhausted and more than a little buzzed.

"It's Raining Men" fades out, and "I Will Survive" plays. The dance floor erupts in song. I check my watch. The bar closes in thirty minutes. I take a walk around the parking lot and catch a pair of half-dressed college guys making out in the backseat of their car. When I suggest they get a room, they take off.

Back inside, Gunner and Tanner give the last call. Patrons settle their tabs and spill out into the chilly night. I make sure no one gets behind the wheel if they've had too much to drink.

Luke and Jordon invite me back to their cabin for a drink. I can't think of anything I'd rather do less right now. I politely decline. The indignant couple call me rude and stomp off.

After everyone leaves, Gunner offers me a shot of whiskey for the road, which I knock back before climbing into my pickup and driving home. The porch light shines, but the rest of the house is dark. I shuck off my boots, brush my teeth, and fall into bed without even taking off my uniform. It's been a long-ass day, and I'm looking at another twelve-hour shift tomorrow.

CHAPTER TWENTY-ONE

WHILE ON PATROL SUNDAY AFTERNOON, dispatch radios that the Sinclairs have reported seeing a prowler on their property. I respond to the call. As I drive past Rose and Trixie's farmhouse, Rose waves from her garden. I continue up the mountain and reach the Sinclairs's mansion. A scowling Bill Sinclair charges out the front door, his fists clenched, and scoffs.

"Of course, they would send you."

"Nice to see you again, Mr. Sinclair. I owe you and your lovely wife an apology. My behavior at the restaurant the other night was inexcusable."

"Too little, too late."

"You spotted a prowler on your property?"

"Like you give a shit," Bill says. "But yes, I chased the trespasser into the woods."

"Did you see his face?"

"Her face. It was that lesbian who lives down the mountain. Not the fat one, the tall one. Those vile women have harassed my wife and me ever since we moved here."

"How so?"

"They've made false accusations. Sued us. The tall one hikes across our property all the time."

"I see."

"I want to press charges."

"Did anyone besides you see the woman on your property?"

"I only saw the back of her head, but my wife caught a good look at her."

"That's right, Cal."

Daphne Sinclair stands in the doorway wearing a bathrobe. Her dark sunglasses and heavy makeup fail to conceal the bruises around her blackened eye. I wish I could say I was surprised, but I'm not.

"I spotted Trixie through the kitchen window, creeping around our yard, and hollered for Bill. He ran outside and chased the woman away."

"You're sure it was Trixie you saw?"

"I'd recognize that bony-ass witch anywhere."

"Were you aware that someone fed Trixie and Rose's chickens elderberries and they died?"

Bill and Daphne Sinclair eye one another and shake their heads.

"I grow elderberries in my garden," Daphne says. "And make syrup from them."

"May I take a look at your garden?"

"Why?"

"To satisfy my curiosity."

Daphne eyes Bill. He shrugs.

"Sure, follow me."

Daphne leads me around behind the house. If anything, her garden looks even lusher now than it did when Vona showed me around. I notice one of the elderberry shrubs is covered in bright green berries, while the other has been picked clean in patches.

"Why did you harvest the berries before they'd ripened?"

"I didn't," Daphne says. "A deer must've gotten into my garden again."

Did a deer eat the berries? Or did the Sinclairs poison Rose and Trixie's chickens?

"You drink gin, isn't that right, Mr. Sinclair?"

"Why?"

"We found an empty gin bottle in your wife's dressing room that bore your initials."

"When my husband visits me at the theater," Daphne says, "he likes to have a martini. Is that a crime?"

"Did you share your bottle with anyone that night?"

"No," Bill says. "But it wasn't locked up."

"Thank you for your time."

"What about that woman?"

"I'll pay Trixie a visit and get her side of the story."

"She'll lie."

"We'll see."

"If this harassment doesn't stop, I'm going to—." Bill Sinclair punches his palm with his fist. "My wife and I deserve to live in peace."

"Let me conduct my investigation, sir."

I climb behind the wheel of the squad car and cruise down the mountainside. Bill Sinclair is right. This feud must stop before someone gets seriously hurt.

A battered Ford Escort with a cracked windshield chugs in my direction. I recognize Vona behind the wheel and flag her down. As soon as I mention the Sinclairs, the evasive housekeeper clams up. I pass her my card and ask her to call me if she thinks of anything I should know.

"To what do we owe the pleasure?" Rose asks when I pull up and step out.

"I'm here on official business, I'm afraid."

"Oh, dear."

"Is Trixie home?"

"She's in the shower. She went for a hike earlier. Come inside." Rose stomps her feet on the mat. I follow her through the door. She hollers, "Trixie! Cal is here. He needs to speak with us."

"Be right down!" Trixie shouts from upstairs.

"Have a seat," Rose says. "Would you care for a cold drink?"

"A glass of water, if you don't mind."

"I offered, didn't I?"

Rose disappears down the hallway. I take a seat on the overstuffed couch with its crocheted afghan and scan the article on the cover of the *Nyes Landing Gazette* that's lying on the coffee table. Ernest Drucker's forthcoming trial is the biggest story this town has seen since I rescued little Evan Langford last year. Drucker will probably get convicted for making everyone sick, but the medical examiner didn't find any traces of tetrahydrozoline in Crispin.

"What brings you by, Cal?"

Dressed in a sweatsuit, with her short, spiky gray hair still damp, Trixie sits on the couch and puts on her socks.

"I'll cut to the chase. The Sinclairs claim you've been trespassing on their property."

"I went for a hike."

"They want to press charges."

"Let them," Rose says. "We've beaten their asses in court before, and we'll do it again if we must."

"This feud needs to end before someone gets seriously hurt."

Rose hands me a glass of cool water.

"We didn't start this."

"But you can finish it," I say. "Somebody needs to be the adult on the mountain." I stand. "I'm sure you have more important things to do. Think about what I've said."

I hope Trixie and Rose take my advice and watch their backs. My spidey sense tells me Bill Sinclair may be the sort of guy who could get away with murder if he wished.

———

AT THE END of my second twelve-hour shift in a row, I file my reports for the day, including the one on the Sinclair incident, and toss Sergeant Reeves the keys to the squad car. He and Washington are on night patrol. I clock out and drive home.

Annie feels nauseous and has a slight fever. She may have caught something from one of her students. She brews herself a pot of hot tea with honey and goes upstairs. I pour a hearty glug of whiskey into a highball glass and knock back every drop. The warm burn refreshes me.

Flower bounds around my feet. I pour another whiskey, plop down on the couch, and turn on the television. Flower leaps onto the couch and curls up beside me. He's not supposed to be on the furniture, but I won't tell. I lower the volume so I don't disturb Annie. I'm on my own for dinner. I wish I'd picked up pizza on my way home.

In ten minutes, *The Adventures of Priscilla, Queen of the Desert* comes on. I've never seen the campy road trip flick, but the year it came out, dozens of gay boys dressed as the drag queens from the movie marched in the PRIDE parade in the city, which I patrolled.

Before the movie starts, I find a pot of leftover roasted chicken and new potatoes in the refrigerator. Thanks to Annie, I'm eating healthier than I did in the city. I fix myself a plate, which I heat in the microwave, and return to the living room. Flower joins me.

Who would've thought a movie about drag queens in the Australian outback could make me laugh so much or cry so hard? I thought being a gay cop was tough.

It's nine o'clock. Demetrius should be home by now. I hope he's not stranded on the side of the road somewhere. Perhaps I should go look for him. Or would that be an overreaction? Before

I do anything, I take Flower for a jog around the block. When we return, I don't know which of us is more excited to see Demetrius's pickup parked in the driveway.

CHAPTER TWENTY-TWO

Monday morning, I rise at the first light of dawn and brew a pot of coffee. Ernest Drucker tainted the meatballs with eye drops at the opening night party, but the medical examiner didn't find any traces of tetrahydrozoline in Oliver Crispin. Am I crazy for doubting his findings?

When I reach the station, Suki sits behind the front desk, knitting a sweater for Daisuke. We exchange greetings, and I head back to the evidence room. Grabbing the bag with the red plastic cup that Crispin drank from and the bottles of gin and elderberry syrup from Daphne's dressing room, I rush back out of the station and drive an hour to the Forensic Investigation Center in Albany. The woman seated behind the reception desk arguing with someone over the phone ignores me. From her side of the conversation, I gather she and her husband can't agree on where to go for dinner tonight. I wait a moment for her to finish, and when she doesn't, I reach over the counter and hang up her call.

"Excuse me. You can't just—"

I flash my badge and explain what I need.

"Third floor. Elevators are down the hall on the right."

A baby-faced blond lab technician asks how he can help. I

explain the situation. From the way he's checking me out, I gather we may bat for the same team. I'm not above using that to my advantage.

"Listen, we may be dealing with a homicide here," I say. I lean over the counter and wink. "Anything you can do to help me expedite the results would be appreciated."

"I'll see what I can do," the lab technician says. He processes my information and passes me a claim receipt. His finger brushes against mine. I thank him for his time and dash out the door.

————

BACK IN NYES Landing by ten o'clock. I stop by the Sacred Root Apothecary. Padma Patel flips the closed sign on the door around so that it reads open and unlocks the front door. It's ten o'clock. I step inside. Cloying incense overwhelms my senses. Faint sitar music plays through speakers on the walls.

"Welcome to my little corner of the world, officer."

"I understand you're an expert on the healing properties of plants."

"The more I learn, the less I know."

"What's your experience with poisonous plants?"

"Why do you ask?"

I explain what happened to Rose and Trixie's chickens.

"They lost their entire flock?"

"I'm afraid so."

"How awful."

"Rose mentioned that you host a nature group?"

"We gather on Wednesday evenings and talk about what's going on in our lives. If anyone feels under the weather, I offer suggestions for natural remedies they might try."

"Are elderberries poisonous?"

"All parts of Sambucus, which is a member of the honeysuckle family, contain cyanogenic glycosides."

"What about elderberry syrup?"

"When cooked, elderberries lose their toxicity and can ease flu and nausea symptoms. French monks ferment a liqueur from the flowers of the plant that is quite delicious."

I thank Padma Patel for her time.

———

WHEN I REACH THE STATION, Chief Jimenez shouts, "Nowak, my office. Pronto!"

I rush down the hallway. The chief sits behind her desk with her arms crossed and that look of exasperation and anger on her face that I know all too well. "What the hell did you do?"

I shrug.

"I received an angry phone call from Bill Sinclair."

I explain the Sinclairs's trespassing complaint and Trixie's response.

"You're right. Without evidence," Chief Jimenez says, "there's not much we can do."

"I was thinking—"

"Whatever you're going to say—don't. I want you to stay as far away from the Sinclairs as possible."

"It's a small town."

"I mean it, Nowak. If I receive another call from the mayor, I am not going to be a happy camper."

And with that, the chief dismisses me. To distract myself from obsessing over the manner of Crispin's death, I take my mother's evidence box into a quiet room and read over the reports for the umpteenth time. It's obvious that the responding officers considered her a sex worker and felt that one of her johns had ended her life. My mother may have taken gifts from men from time to time, but she was not a prostitute.

When I receive the results back on the evidence we collected from the theater, perhaps I can convince my new friend there to retest the hair samples and fingerprints from my mother's case. I need to find out what the investigators in 1983 missed or, more likely, didn't bother looking into in the first place.

Officer Lecoq arrives at the station clutching a large trophy in his fist, which he sets on his desk. "My cockerel won Best in Show," he says, beaming with pride.

"Congrats, Lecoq," I say, although I have no clue what a cockerel is. I put away the evidence box, grab the keys to the squad car, and head out on patrol.

The weekend downstaters have gone home, so the streets are quiet. I spot Helena Potter strolling down the sidewalk arm in arm with Padma Patel and pull over to say hello.

"Officer Nowak dropped by the apothecary earlier today," Padma tells Helena. "He had some questions about elderberries."

"Someone fed Rose and Trixie's chickens elderberries," I say, "and they died."

"People can be so cruel," Helena says.

"I must get back to the shop," Padma says. "I will call you later, Helena. It was nice seeing you again, officer." She walks to the end of the block and crosses the street when the light changes.

"My heart breaks for Padma," Helena says.

"Why?"

"Her mother died when she was born. Her great aunt raised her."

"What about her father?"

"She never talks about him."

"How long have you been attending her support group?"

"We started meeting shortly after she opened her apothecary last year."

"Do Rose and Trixie attend these meetings?"

"They do," Helena says. "And Daphne Sinclair usually comes. Brandy Speedman pops by whenever she can. Annie even came a time or two."

"Padma isn't from around here."

"She grew up in India, but she attended college in the states."

"Is that so?"

"Why do you ask?"

"Just curious." I pull the spider-shaped silver brooch out of my pocket. "I believe this belongs to you."

"Where did you—?"

"Under Crispin's bed."

"Ollie was a troubled soul," Helena says. "But whenever we were alone, he made me feel like I was the only woman on earth. Like all the other frogs I've kissed, he didn't turn out to be my Prince Charming." Her eyes tear. She smiles. "But I miss him, warts and all."

Crispin had a way with women. And men, I suppose, too, when it suited his purpose. Like a chameleon, he adapted to his surroundings, and his manic energy both attracted and repelled me.

"He had a rough childhood," Helena says. "But who didn't, right? Look who I'm talking to."

It's none of my business, so I don't pry. No one really knows what makes another person tick.

As Helena walks away, I can't help but wonder what brought Padma Patel to Nyes Landing. This town is not exactly a cultural melting pot, and as far as I can tell, she doesn't have any ties to the community.

CHAPTER TWENTY-THREE

AFTER TURNING in my paperwork for the day, I rush home, take a shower, and put on the cleanest tee shirt I can find from the pile of clothes atop the chair in my room with a pair of blue jeans I've only worn a few times. As a final touch, I splash on a few drops of Calvin Klein's Obsession aftershave from the bottle Annie gave me for Christmas.

Streaks of dust and dried mud from the recent rain coat my pickup. Gas & Go shopping bags clutter the floor on the passenger side. I pull into the car wash. By the time I finish, the inside of the cab looks spotless, and the truck's chili-pepper red finish shines.

While I have cellular service, I call Demetrius and ask if he wants to have dinner.

"Why don't we stay in tonight? I'll make spaghetti and meatballs."

"If you're cooking, I'm coming."

"We'll see about that when you get here."

It takes me a second to catch his drift.

"I'm on my way."

"Pick up a loaf of Italian bread from the grocery store, would you? And a bottle of red wine vinegar."

I bump into Trevor Speedman at the grocery store. He wears a headband with a mesh tee shirt over his bronze torso. The dude epitomizes California pretentiousness. It's hard to believe that a year ago he was on the verge of an emotional breakdown over his marriage going south.

Trevor gives me a bro hug and smacks my ass. I pull away.

"How much longer are you in town?" I ask.

"Why? Are you ready for me to leave?"

"Just making conversation."

"Talk is overrated," Trevor says. "I rented this quaint creekside bungalow. There's a liquor store next door. Why don't we grab a bottle of whatever you drink and go back to my place?"

"That's not happening," I say. "I'm just here to grab a few items. Demetrius is cooking tonight."

"What are we having?"

"We're not having anything."

"You're no fun."

The bakery offers several types of Italian bread. I choose a small, round loaf and find the condiments aisle. One brand of vinegar looks the same as another. I buy the least expensive bottle. As I pass through the frozen food section, I decide we need ice cream. I prefer chocolate, but Demetrius is a plain vanilla man, so I choose Neapolitan. Maybe he'll try the strawberry. If not, I'll eat that, too. I grab a can of whipped cream, pay, and go.

Aromas of oregano and basil fill the cabin when I step through the door.

"I'm in the kitchen, babe!"

Demetrius leans over the stove, stirring a pot of simmering marinara sauce. I set the shopping bag on the counter. He pulls out the carton of ice cream and shoots me a side-eyed glance.

"I brought dessert."

Demetrius slices the loaf of bread and sets it on the table alongside a bowl of fresh green salad. He whips up a dressing using the red wine vinegar, some olive oil, and dried herbs, like the chefs on those cooking shows he and Annie watch do.

"Would you like a beer?" I ask.

I put the ice cream in the freezer and set the whipped cream in the fridge.

"Sure."

I grab two bottles and dig the bottle opener out of the utensil drawer.

Demetrius stirs the cooked meatballs into the marinara sauce and lowers the flame under the pan. "Dinner will be ready soon." He slips his arms around my waist and kisses me. "Did you miss me this weekend?"

"I didn't have anyone to dance with at the PRIDE celebration."

"I'm sure that broke your heart."

"Dancing's okay when you have the right partner."

"Am I the right partner?"

"What do you think?"

I kiss Demetrius. My hands slip under his tee shirt and rove over his smooth torso. He gropes my crotch through my jeans. We have our issues, but sex is not one of them.

Demetrius pulls away. "I need to stir the sauce before it burns."

"Screw the sauce," I say, and I turn off the burner. Our lips lock in a passionate kiss. We come up for air. I yank off his tee shirt and loosen his fly. He shoves my tee shirt up over my head. I yank the darn thing off and toss it onto the floor.

"Hold on," Demetrius says. He grabs the whipped cream from the refrigerator and shakes the can. "I've always wanted to try this." He squirts a blast into my mouth. Snatching the can, I swirl whipped cream over his stiff nipples and lap up every drop with my tongue. I tug down his briefs and squeeze whipped cream over his crotch.

Flower bounds around our feet. I shove the dog aside. Taking that as an invitation to play, he leaps on me and knocks the can out of my hand. Whipped cream spurts across the kitchen. Flower licks up every drop he can reach.

"Let's wash up," Demetrius says. "We can fool around after the hellhound goes to bed."

Demetrius finishes cooking dinner while I take Flower outside. His glow-in-the-dark collar makes it easy to spot him in the dark.

A warm breeze rustles through the leaves in the trees. It's unusually warm this summer. The high today reached eighty-three degrees, and the night isn't much cooler. I'll bet it's miserable in the city with all that concrete.

I hear voices but Demetrius is inside the cabin, and Flower can't talk. I hear the voices again and realize it's my radio, which I left in the pickup. I answer the call.

"There's an incident at the Roadhouse," Suki says. "Washington and Lecoq are dealing with a three-car collision on Main Street, and Reeves is on a date in New Paltz. Or was, rather. He's driving back now, but he's still an hour away, and I hate to bother the chief."

"I'll handle the call at the Roadhouse. Give me the particulars."

Grabbing a pen, I scribble down the details she shares. Our transmission ends.

A dog barks in the distance. Flower must've wandered out of the yard while I was distracted. I call his name. He doesn't respond. My heart races. If I've lost Demetrius's dog, I'll never forgive myself. I race around behind the cabin and scan the backyard. A faint glint of light through the trees catches my eye. I venture into the dark woods, something I couldn't have done a year ago. Knowing Demetrius is a shout away bolsters my nerve.

Flower bounds my way, wagging his tail. He clutches a dirty tennis ball in his mouth, which I confiscate after a brief but intense tug-of-war. I scold the dog for running away. He licks my face. We go inside, and I break the news to Demetrius that duty calls.

"It's a good thing that marinara sauce freezes well," Demetrius says.

"I wish I didn't have to go."

"I fell in love with a cop," Demetrius says. "I have no one to blame but myself." I hug him from behind and nibble on his neck. He giggles.

"I'll be back as soon as I deal with this issue."

————

OUTSIDE THE ROADHOUSE, Trevor Speedman sits on the ground, his tan face a bruised and bloodied mess. My mother's friend, Charlie, bandages Trevor's wounds.

"That dickhead, Wayne Gerber, and his posse of pricks jumped Trevor in the parking lot and beat the crap out of him," Charlie says. "Then the cowards sped away."

I examine Trevor's wounds. He may require stitches.

"Stand up, Trevor. I'll drive you to the emergency room."

Charlie and I help Trevor onto his feet. Trevor winces and says, "I'm okay." His busted lip slurs his speech.

"You are not okay," I say. "You're bleeding. Here." I pass Trevor a tissue. "Wipe your mouth."

Once I situate Trevor inside my pickup, I radio Suki and ask her to alert Washington and Lecoq that Gerber and his thugs are on the rampage tonight.

Following an hour-long drive through the mountains, during which Trevor manages not to bleed all over my pickup, we reach the hospital. A car accident on the interstate has the emergency room personnel rushing around, caring for the injured victims. I need to call Demetrius, but I left my cellular phone in my pickup, and I don't see a pay phone nearby.

By the time a weary young triage nurse with a reassuring smile squeezes Trevor in, it's two o'clock in the morning. After examining his wounds, she concludes he's suffered scrapes and contusions but hasn't broken any bones. "If your headaches don't subside over the next twenty-four hours," she says, "we'll need to do an MRI." A young Chinese doctor whose name I can't pronounce prescribes painkillers. Trevor signs his paperwork and pays his bill. We drive back to town. I drop Trevor off at his bungalow and buy a microwave burrito at the Gas & Go, which I eat in the pickup. I let myself into Demetrius's cabin and brush my teeth before crawling into bed. I snuggle against his back and whisper in his ear, "Sorry."

"I'm just glad you're alive," Demetrius says. He scoots over to the edge of his side of the bed and hugs his pillow against his chest. I take the hint and leave him be.

CHAPTER TWENTY-FOUR

It's a beautiful Tuesday morning. I let Flower out to do his business and give him his breakfast. To make amends for running out on Demetrius last night, I fry a half dozen sausage links and scramble as many eggs. While I'm cooking, I burn the toast and start over with two new slices of bread. I pour myself a second cup of coffee and take a long gulp. I'm running on fumes.

Demetrius shuffles into the kitchen. "I need caffeine." His hands shake. He sloshes coffee over the rim of his cup. "Shit!"

"It's just a little spill."

I grab a wad of paper towels and wipe up the mess.

Demetrius's eyes well with tears. "I tossed and turned last night," he says, his voice quavering, "terrified you'd been in an accident or, worse, shot dead. I called you a dozen times and never heard back."

I explain what went down last night.

"When you rush out of the house on an emergency call and I don't hear from you, I fear the worst."

"You're right. I'm a lousy boyfriend."

"Don't do that."

"Do what?"

"Play the 'I'm damaged goods' card."

"What do you want me to say?"

"I don't know what I would do if something happened to you."

I enfold Demetrius in my arms.

"Nothing's going to happen to me."

"You don't know that."

"I won't leave you in the dark like that again."

I scoop a mound of scrambled eggs onto a plate, add three sausages, lay a slice of toast on top, and pass Demetrius his breakfast.

"Eat up before your food gets cold."

"I'm not hungry."

Demetrius sets his plate on the counter and nibbles on a slice of toast. I slap scrambled eggs and sausage links between two slices of toast and wrap a paper towel around the sandwich. He takes a bite of scrambled eggs and says, "The eggs are a little dry."

"I'm off." I kiss his cheek and whisper, "I really am sorry."

Demetrius is right. I should've called, and I didn't, and that's on me.

———

Following an uneventful morning, I grab lunch and afterward attend Oliver Crispin's memorial service at the theater. Crispin's estranged sister shipped his body home to Ohio for burial, and none of his friends from the theater were invited to the funeral, so this is their chance to say goodbye.

A blowup of Crispin's headshot rests on an easel, which stands beside a podium center stage surrounded by several lush floral sprays of lilies and carnations. Their strong scents fill the auditorium. I stand at attention to the right of the entrance. Washington mirrors me on the left side. The chief and sergeant sit on either side of the aisle far enough back that they can monitor the crowd. Lecoq is patrolling the streets, prepared to respond to any calls that come in while the rest of us are here.

Seated up front, wearing a black dress and hat with a veil that covers her face, Daphne sobs. Bill passes her a handkerchief and whispers in her ear. She sobs louder.

Helena Potter and Bo Satterlee slide into the back row. Ernestine Middleton takes a seat on the aisle and whispers into a digital voice recorder.

Mayor Lucille Miller strides through the door wearing a navy-blue suit, every hair on her auburn head in place. She catches my eye. I smile. She scowls. I am definitely on the woman's shit list.

Nadine arrives arm in arm with Stanley. They smile and nod my way and take seats in the middle of the auditorium. Howie follows the couple into the row. Annie stayed home with the flu.

Ernest and Terrell shuffle through the door. Ernest peers around. Sweat beads dot his forehead. Terrell dabs a tear from his eye. He seems genuinely sad.

Daphne gives the performance of her career, weeping and wailing like some tragic Shakespearean actress. I'm surprised she doesn't rend her hair and gnash her teeth. Bill gives the whispering onlookers a sheepish smile.

It occurs to me that one doesn't have to become an actor to play a role. We adjust our behaviors throughout the day, depending upon who we're interacting with. For instance, I'm a different person around the chief than I am around my boyfriend.

Rose and Trixie slink through the door and sidle up against the wall beside me. "We weren't going to come," Rose whispers. "But Trixie convinced me we should put in an appearance."

Padma Patel strolls through the door looking regal in a ruby red and black jacket and matching slacks. She wears her shiny black hair twisted into an elaborate crown of braids atop her head. Her golden bracelets jingle when she walks. She glides into a seat beside Helena.

"That woman is so beautiful," Trixie exclaims.

Padma's enigmatic smile reminds me of that Mona Lisa painting.

Several more locals and a few of Daphne's friends from the city gradually fill the auditorium. I'd estimate fifty to sixty people came, which is frankly more than I expected. Crispin didn't live here for long and, aside from the women he slept with, no one knew the guy well.

Bill steps on stage and gives a speech that mentions the contributions he and his wife have made to this town more than the guy we're here to memorialize and introduces his wife. Suddenly able to contain her grief, Daphne rushes up the steps onto the stage like she's accepting an award.

"Oliver—Ollie to his friends—was the most talented actor I've ever worked with. Acting with him was a privilege I'll treasure forever."

Ernest Drucker scoffs so loudly that people turn around and stare in his direction. He slides down in his seat.

"Ollie would have become a big star one day." She dabs her eyes with her handkerchief. "But he had his demons, and they—" She covers her face with her hands and rushes offstage. For all her drama, her grief appears genuine.

Although Daphne and I ran in different circles in high school, our class was small, and she was one of the few people who stood by me when I came out as gay. I can't help but feel bad for her. She poured her heart and soul into this theater, and now it may have to close.

Bill Sinclair steps up to the podium. "Please excuse Daphne. She's understandably upset. We all miss Oliver." A screen lowers from the ceiling. "My wife put together this slideshow celebrating his life."

An image of Daphne and Crispin laughing fills the screen. That sad Enya song "Only Time" underscores the slides. Several women weep. Padma Patel catches Bill Sinclair's eye. A faint smile flashes across her face and leaves so fast I wonder if I imagined seeing it in the first place. Bill remains stoic, but I'm sure he doesn't enjoy seeing images of his wife with her dead lover. I wouldn't be surprised if he served Crispin tainted gin to get the guy out of the picture. I'll know more when I receive the report back from the crime lab. If it's clean, I'll drop my investigation and admit I'm wrong, something I probably couldn't have done a year ago.

A final image of a smiling Crispin looking up at the sky with the words "Oliver Tyler Crispin, November 8, 1967–June 16, 2003" freezes on the screen.

Terrell takes the stage and sings a song about walking through a storm and holding your head up high. His deep bass voice resounds off the walls. The mourners file out of the theater. Their mood remains sober until they reach the sidewalk, and then it's back to business as usual. I hardly knew Crispin, but I feel bad for the guy. I hope when my time comes, I'm not so easily dismissed.

"Maya?" A woman says. "Maya Kumar?

Padma Patel turns around. A look of alarm flashes across her face. She regains her composure and says, "You must have me confused with someone else."

"I'm sorry . . . you look like this girl I went to college with."

"You attended college in Mumbai?"

"No, NYU."

"Then I do not see how we could have met at school."

On her way out of the theater, Mayor Miller calls me aside. "I hope you're satisfied now, officer, and will let the Sinclairs grieve in peace." Her mouth smiles, but her eyes do not. "I would hate for you to tarnish that reputation you've worked so hard to rebuild."

The mayor wants to keep the Sinclairs, and Bill in particular, happy. That must be why she's pushing so hard for me to drop this investigation. Given she's up for re-election next year, I'd think she'd do everything in her power to prove she's tough on crime.

CHAPTER TWENTY-FIVE

WHEN I REACH the station Tuesday morning, Suki grins and whispers, "You have a visitor." She nods toward the reception area. I recognize my young friend from the Forensic Investigation Center in Albany. He doesn't notice me, which gives me time to duck into the men's room and relieve my coffee-logged bladder. I wash my hands, comb my fingers through my hair, and check my smile in the mirror. I'm glad I did, too, because I have bits of egg caught between my teeth.

My young friend stands when I approach. "Officer Nowak," he says. "I'm glad I caught you. We need to talk."

"Follow me."

"Not here."

My young friend peers around.

"What's going on?" I ask.

"I'm not sure, and somebody above my pay grade doesn't want us to find out."

"What is your name, young man?"

"I'm not that young. I turn twenty-four next month."

"Happy early birthday, um——?"

"Kaden."

"Let's take a walk."

I lead Kaden away from Main Street and turn right onto Mt. Pleasant Way. We stroll down the deserted sidewalk.

"You're not wearing a wedding ring, Officer Nowak."

"That's very observant of you. Now, what did you find out?"

"First of all, my supervisor put the kibosh on your request. She claims the case is closed."

"Technically, that's true."

"But you think our lab missed something."

"Not on purpose."

"It's not like my supervisor to be so adamant about letting go of a questionable case. So I took the liberty of running my own tests after hours."

"And?"

"I found trace amounts of atropine and scopolamine on the red plastic cup, but the results were inconclusive."

"What else?"

"Tests of the gin bottle came back clean, but the syrup tested positive for high levels of both toxins."

"I thought elderberries were safe to consume."

"Raw elderberries can be toxic, but you'd need to consume more of the cooked berries than you can eat before you'd get sick."

"So, what happened?"

"Best guess. Those weren't elderberries in the syrup."

"What were they then?"

"I'm not a botanist."

"Could a person die from drinking the substances you found?"

"There's a good chance, yes. Especially if they'd also consumed alcohol and illegal drugs, as I understand your victim did."

"Good job, kid."

"I stuck my neck out for you."

"I owe you one."

————

I still owe the Sinclairs a formal apology. Vona answers when I arrive at their door.

"Mrs. Sinclair is not home."

"Is Mr. Sinclair here?"

"He's laid up in bed with the flu."

"Perhaps you can help me."

Vona crosses her arms over her chest and sighs. "I'm not supposed to talk to the police."

"Why not?"

"Vona?" Bill Sinclair shouts from upstairs. "Who's that at the door?"

"Please leave."

Vona tries to shut the door. I block her attempt with my boot.

"Who brewed the elderberry syrup you brought to the theater?"

"If the police come around asking questions, Mr. Sinclair said I should give you his attorney's card."

Vona passes me a third business card to go with the two I already have.

"Do you have an attorney, Vona?"

"Why would I—?

"Good day."

I withdraw my boot. She slams the door in my face.

————

As I drive down the mountain, I spot Trixie hiking through the trees. I pull over and step out. She waves. I stumble through the underbrush and catch up with her.

"I'm taking my morning constitutional," Trixie says. "That's what my grandmother called the walks she always took after breakfast."

"I hope you're staying away from the Sinclairs's house?"

"Have you told them to stay away from our farm?"

"If you catch them trespassing, we will."

"I'm sorry, Cal. I shouldn't take out my frustration with those awful people on you. I'll steer clear of their property."

WHEN I GET BACK to town, I stop by the hardware store. Demetrius is helping a stocky guy with a bushy beard choose a hunting rifle. I pick up the book on poisonous plants in the Catskills that I noticed the other day and thumb through the pages. There's a section on elderberries. I study the pictures of the woody shrubs with their clusters of white flowers and dark-purple berries. The article concludes with a brief paragraph that mentions the nightshade family, which includes belladonna, a plant so toxic that if an open wound brushes against the leaves, roots, or fruits, the reaction can be fatal.

"The Winchester XRT is a great little rifle, but so is the Remington 700," Demetrius says. "You can't go wrong with either."

"Let me think it over," the stocky guy with the bushy beard says. He thanks Demetrius for his time.

"What are you reading?" Demetrius asks me.

I hold up the book's cover and share what I learned from Kaden.

"You're convinced someone poisoned Oliver Crispin?"

"The elderberry syrup we confiscated from Daphne's dressing room contained lethal amounts of toxins not found in elderberries."

"Bill Sinclair puts elderberry syrup in his martinis."

"True."

"Why didn't he get sick?"

"He has the flu."

"It's going around."

"That's true. Annie stayed home from school again today."

"I thought you'd closed the Crispin case."

"If I can prove he was poisoned, the chief must reopen the investigation."

"That won't bring him back."

"But it will bring his killer to justice."

After I leave the hardware store, I stop by the bank. Daphne Sinclair is waiting in line for a teller. We exchange pleasantries. She confirms Bill is in bed with the flu.

"My husband never sleeps this much," Daphne says. "I'm worried."

"May I ask you a question?"

Daphne narrows her eyes. "That depends."

"You brew your own elderberry syrup, right?"

"Bill takes a splash in his martinis."

"Did Crispin drink the syrup in his cocktails?"

"Ollie only drank cocktails when chugging straight from the bottle wasn't an option."

"We found a bottle of elderberry syrup in your dressing room."

"Vona brought me a bottle from the batch she'd made that day."

"Vona brewed the elderberry syrup we found in your dressing room?"

"I would've brewed it myself, but I had too much to do at the theater that day."

"Next!" a teller shouts.

Daphne excuses herself and steps up to the window. Vona told me she'd stained her fingers brewing elderberry syrup, but I failed to connect the dots.

While on patrol later that night, I spot Vona coming out of Maestro's Pizzeria, juggling a large pizza box in one hand and cradling a squirming baby in her other arm. A young girl follows her mother, clutching a shopping bag bearing the restaurant's logo. An even younger boy toddles behind his sister, sucking his thumb. I pull over to the curb and step out.

Vona spots me and rushes across the parking lot toward her car. Her children run after their mom. I catch up with the woman and her children before she drives away.

"This is harassment, officer."

"Did you know Oliver Crispin?"

"I met the guy a few times," Vona says. "When he'd stop and visit with Mrs. Sinclair."

Her inflection on the word visit implies they did more than catch up on the latest gossip.

"Were they having an affair?"

"What the Sinclairs do behind closed doors is none of my business."

She knows more than she's saying, but I can't force her to talk.

"Did you ever date Oliver Crispin?"

"When do I have the time to go on a date? I have three kids, two jobs, and an ex-husband with a mean streak."

"Were you working for the Sinclairs when they were sued by Rose and Trixie?"

"I don't get involved in disputes between the Sinclairs and their neighbors."

"Are you sure those were elderberries in that syrup you brewed?"

"Why do you ask?"

"When the crime lab tested the syrup you made, they uncovered lethal substances not found in elderberries."

"I used the berries Mrs. Sinclair said I should."

"Good luck convincing a jury of that."

"What are you talking about?"

"The syrup you brewed may have killed someone."

"I have to go."

Vona rolls up her window and speeds away.

———

As I cruise through the quiet streets of town, I remind myself that the obvious answer is often the truth. But I cannot accept that Crispin died of a mere overdose. If I can connect him to the tainted elderberry syrup, then I'll have evidence I can build a case around. Perhaps if I share what I've learned with the medical examiner, he'll agree to retest the samples he collected from the actor's autopsy.

Vona brewed the syrup in question and has made it clear she does not want to talk to me. But what reason could she have for wanting Crispin dead? Bill Sinclair certainly had good reason to want Crispin out of his life and likely the means to cover his tracks. Several women, including Daphne, Helena, and Brandy, had affairs with the guy. They were all at the theater that night. Could one of them have poisoned Crispin out of jealousy?

A lavender glow over the mountaintops signals the arrival of dawn. I return to the station and file my paperwork, which doesn't take long because nothing much went down tonight.

Sergeant Reeves swaggers through the door, grinning like a fool. "I'm telling you, man. That Roxie is a tigress between the sheets—"

"Too much information, Reeves," I say, and I toss him the keys to the squad car. "I'm out of here."

As I drive past The Golden Swirl, the aroma of freshly baked cinnamon rolls makes my mouth water. I turn around and pull into the parking lot. Even this early in the morning, there's already a line at the counter. I await my turn. The rail-thin woman who takes my order must never eat the pastries she serves. She drizzles caramel syrup over two cinnamon rolls and sprinkles chopped black walnuts on top. I pay her and go.

When I reach Demetrius's cabin, I let myself inside.

"Demi! It's me!"

"In here!" Demetrius hollers back. He's seated in the kitchen in his boxer shorts, sharing a waffle with a bandaged-up Trevor, who's wearing Demetrius's bathrobe.

"I'm sorry . . . ." I stammer, unable to believe my eyes. "I didn't mean to interrupt—"

"You're not—"

"I know how much you like the cinnamon rolls from The Golden Swirl. But . . . I see you're . . . already eating. I should go."

Setting the bag from the bakery on the table, I rush out the door. Did Trevor get drunk and stay over again? This is becoming a habit. Why didn't Demetrius tell me Trevor was spending the night? Did they—?

"Cal, wait!"

Before I make an even bigger fool of myself, I hop behind the wheel and speed away. I don't get far before I pull over and beat my fists against the steering wheel. Trevor may be a mess, but he's hot, and he says and does whatever he pleases. That sort of unapologetic confidence can be intoxicating.

Still hungry, I pay the bakery another visit.

"You already finished two cinnamon rolls?" the rail-thin woman behind the counter asks.

"Those were for a friend," I say. "But they smelled so good that I had to have one for myself."

"Here you go. I threw in a few niblets, too."

I drop my coin change into her tip jar and thank her for the treats.

As soon as I get home, Annie passes me the phone and says, "Call Demetrius."

"What?"

"How could you think he was sleeping with Trevor Speedman? Or anyone else? He loves you. Why can't you see that?"

"I do see that. I just . . . they looked so chummy, sharing their breakfast." I sigh and say, "I'll make this right." I hold up the bag from the bakery. "But first, I'm eating my cinnamon roll." I pinch off a big bite and stuff the gooey goodness in my mouth.

"I have to go," Annie says on her way out the door. "I'm meeting with a parent before class."

The longer I wait, the harder facing the music will be. I call Demetrius. He picks up on the first ring.

"Cal, I'm sorry . . . nothing—"

"I'm an idiot, okay? I don't know what came over me."

"You don't trust me?"

"It's not that. I'm a mess."

"I wish you'd stop saying that."

"How come you're so perfect?"

"That's ridiculous. Nobody is perfect. Least of all me."

"You always know the right thing to say and the right thing to do. I feel like I'll never deserve you."

"You're tired, and you're rambling. Get some rest. We'll talk later."

CHAPTER TWENTY-SIX

A KEY RATTLES in the front door. Annie must be home from school. I sit up in bed, yawn wide, and stretch my shoulders and arms. Shifting back and forth between day and night shifts has thrown my internal clock out of whack. I climb out of bed, splash some water on my face, and step out into the living room.

"I hope I didn't wake you," Annie says.

"I didn't mean to sleep this long."

"I suppose you've heard?"

"Heard what?"

"They hospitalized Bill Sinclair today."

"I knew he had the flu," I say. "But I didn't realize it had gotten that bad."

"Are you hungry?"

"I have work to do."

I put on my boots and take off.

Vona answers the Sinclairs's door.

"What do you want, officer?"

"I heard Bill Sinclair's in the hospital. What happened?"

Vona glances around and whispers, "Mr. Sinclair has been ill for the past few days. Everyone thought he had the flu. But this morning, he threw up so many times that Mrs. Sinclair told me to call nine-one-one. When the paramedics arrived, they rushed him to the hospital."

"Any idea what might have made him sick?"

"Vona?" A woman's voice that I don't recognize says. "Who's that at the door?"

"You should speak to the Sinclairs's attorney."

Vona shuts the door in my face.

As I drive through the mountains, my mind races. Bill Sinclair adds elderberry syrup to his martinis. Crispin drank Sinclair's gin at the theater that night. Did he try the syrup, too? Vona brewed the batch in question. Did she poison her employer? All I have are questions. I need answers.

When I reach the hospital, the nurse behind the information desk directs me to the fourth floor, where I find Daphne pacing the waiting room.

"They're drawing Bill's blood," Daphne says. "I can't watch."

"What do his doctors think might be wrong?"

"They're not sure. It's not a virus, though, so they've ruled out the flu."

"Vona brew the elderberry syrup we found in your dressing room, right?"

Daphne nods.

"Was that the only bottle she brewed?"

"It's not worth the effort to brew one bottle at a time."

"What happened to the other bottles?"

"They're in my kitchen pantry," Daphne says. "And we keep a bottle on the bar."

"I need to speak with your husband."

"Why?"

"A hunch."

I follow Daphne down the hallway and around the corner into

Bill's private hospital room. Bill lies propped up on his bed, his face ashen, sipping water from a bottle through a straw.

"How do you feel?" I ask.

"I've drunk gallons of water the past few days, yet I'm still thirsty," Bill says. "And my stomach is on fire."

"My poor baby," Daphne says. She fluffs Bill's pillows.

"May I have a moment alone with your husband?"

"Whatever you have to say to Bill, you can say in front of me."

"Give us a minute, Daphne," Bill says.

"I'll be right outside the door if you need anything, honeybun."

Daphne steps out into the hallway and closes the door.

"All right, officer. You have my attention. What's this about?"

"Someone may be trying to kill you."

Bill's eyes narrow. After a moment, he smiles.

"I would laugh in your face, officer. But you look so serious."

"Hear me out."

I explain the toxicology lab's findings.

"You believe someone poisoned me?"

"How else do you explain the tainted syrup?"

"I can't."

"Did your wife sign a prenuptial agreement?"

"I saw no need, officer," Bill Sinclair says. "I'm an old man. I have no children. And my siblings have everything they need and more."

"Ask your doctors to test for the toxins atropine and scopolamine. If I'm wrong, I'll have wasted their time. But if I'm right, we might save your life."

Bill Sinclair summons his doctor. I explain what the toxicology laboratory discovered.

"I believe we can test for that," the doctor says. He looks at Bill Sinclair. "If you wish."

"Run the damn test."

———

ON THE DRIVE back to Nyes Landing, I'm feeling rather pleased with myself. I suspected all along that Crispin didn't overdose on booze and drugs alone. But no one listened, and now Bill Sinclair is hospitalized. If he's abusing Daphne, she might want him dead. But why would she kill Crispin? Perhaps Bill was the intended victim, not Crispin, like in that play script I found in Daphne's dressing room.

When I reach town, I stop by the Gas & Go, fill up the tank of my pickup, and grab a cup of black coffee. I take a gulp on my way out the door. I only slept for a few hours last night, and I tossed and turned through those.

Back on the road, I get the caffeine jitters. I stop by the local florist and buy a bouquet of daisies. While the clerk wraps my bouquet, she tells me daisies are her daughter's favorite flower. Her daughter is going through a divorce, and she is worried about how her grandkids are going to take the news. I wonder if Cora is going to have issues when she gets older because her parents are divorced and her dad is bisexual.

Demetrius's face lights up when I hand him his bouquet. I should bring him flowers more often. He gives me a kiss. I hug him and whisper, "I'm a fool. Forgive me."

"For what? Bringing me breakfast and flowers?"

A young couple asks where they can find the paint supplies. Demetrius points them toward the right aisle. As soon as they are out of earshot, he whispers, "How could you think I'd sleep with Trevor Speedman?"

"He's hot."

"You think Trevor is hot?"

"You don't?"

"He's too...blond for me."

"You two have a lot in common."

"Because we're bisexual and divorced?"

"Well, yes."

"That's not how love works, Cal."

"It was silly of me."

"You wouldn't get jealous if you didn't care."

"Of course, I care."

"I should put my flowers in water," Demetrius says. He repurposes an empty paint can as a vase and arranges the bouquet, which he sets on the counter by the cash register.

The young couple dumps several paintbrushes, a bag of drop cloths, and various other supplies on the counter. While Demetrius rings up their purchases, they ask where they can get a decent cheeseburger in this town. He recommends our favorite burger joint, the Jukebox Junction.

"I should get going. I need to get dressed for work. I'm on patrol in a few minutes."

Demetrius kisses me and says, "I love you."

If what I'm feeling right now isn't love, I don't know what is. So why don't I say the words back? Instead, I say, "I'll call you later," and I duck out the door.

———

THAT AFTERNOON AT THE STATION, I review the evidence from my mother's case, hoping I can find a clue I've missed. Every time I look at these horrible reminders of her brutal end, my desire for revenge, or justice, rather, deepens. The investigators didn't cover much ground. I call the Forensics Investigation Center. The operator transfers me. The phone rings several times.

"Kaden, here."

He sounds out of breath.

"This is Officer Nowak."

"Nyes Landing's hottest cop."

Considering the competition, I'm not sure that's much of a compliment.

"I'm looking into a cold case from 1983. I need some fingerprints and hair samples retested."

"I'm about to leave for the day."

"I'm already on the road now. I can be there in under an hour."

I'm lying, but I need his help.

"One hour, and then I'm out of here," Kaden says. "And you have to buy me dinner."

"Fine."

"Somewhere nice."

Grabbing the box, I rush out the door.

Ninety minutes later, I step off the elevator at the Forensics Investigation Center. Kaden stands leaning against the wall with his arms crossed over his chest. "You're late." He sounds upset, but there's an impish glint in his eyes.

"A car wreck on the highway slowed me down."

"Show me what you have."

I follow Kaden inside a conference room and set the box of evidence from my mother's case on the end of a long table. He slips on a pair of gloves, lifts the lid, and glances over the police report.

"Dede Nowak, huh? A professor of mine referenced this case when I was in college. The brutality of the assault left a lasting impression on me. Any relation?"

If Kaden is going to help me solve my mother's case, he needs to know the truth. I take a deep breath and recount the facts as best I can. When I finish, my eyes are dry, but Kaden has tears streaming down his cute mug. I pass him a tissue and tell him I'm fine when he asks, which is far from the truth.

"No promises," Kaden says, "but I'll see what I can do."

Kaden records the samples and locks the bags inside an evidence cabinet.

"Where do you want to go for dinner?" I ask.

"I was kidding about that."

"It's the least I can do."

"You have a boyfriend."

"We have to eat, don't we?"

"I know just the place."

The quaint mom-and-pop bistro that Kaden recommends is closed, as is the pizzeria next door. We end up seated on stools in front of a street cart, having some of the best tacos I've ever eaten.

Kaden asks about my boyfriend. I launch into the story of how Demetrius and I met, and before I know it, I'm singing his praises.

"Sounds like a great guy," Kaden says.

"He is," I say. "What about you?"

"I had a boyfriend in college, but we broke up after graduation. He took a job in Texas, I think, or maybe it was Tennessee. We kept in touch for a while. But then he met some guy, and we drifted apart."

"That's a bummer."

"Did you always know you were gay?"

"I always knew I was different," I say. "But when I started playing sports, I realized I was gay. What about you?"

"My first crush was on Fred in the *Scooby-Doo* cartoons. I was four."

"Were your parents supportive?"

"My mother tried to pray the gay away," Kaden says, "and when that didn't work, my stepfather figured he'd beat the queer out of me."

"That's terrible."

"That's life."

"By the time I came out, my mom had died," I say. "And my dad had taken off long before that. For all I know, he may have passed away, too."

"At least I know where I stand with my parents."

A young couple buys tacos and sits on the curb to eat. We have finished eating, so we offer them our stools.

"Would you like to grab a drink?" Kaden asks.

"I should hit the road," I say, before I do anything I'll regret.

CHAPTER TWENTY-SEVEN

After working thirteen shifts in a row, I finally have a day off tomorrow, and I plan to unwind and have a good time at Brandy Speedman's birthday party tonight if it kills me. When I reach Demetrius's cabin, I let myself in. He looks festive in a pink shirt and maroon pants. I should incorporate more color into my wardrobe. I'm not living in the city anymore, where I wore black and darker colors everywhere.

Flower leaps on me. I scratch his head. He slobbers on my jeans. I grab a paper towel.

"Flower, leave Cal alone." Demetrius tosses me a bottle of water and opens another for himself. "We should hydrate before we go drinking."

Demetrius shuts Flower in the spare room with his food and water bowls and his many toys. I toss Demetrius his jacket. He offers to drive. We take the highway through the one-stoplight hamlet of Capachick, continue down the mountain into the valley, and pull into the crowded parking lot of Brandy Speedman's winery. Several vehicles display out-of-state license plates.

Inside the renovated colonial-era barn, a vivacious young

woman with spiked blue hair spins tunes atop a small stage on the far side of the cavernous room. Servers dressed in starched white shirts and neatly pressed black slacks rush around the spacious room serving cocktails and fancy appetizers. The bougie catering company from the city must have cost Brandy a fortune. They're not serving Irish whiskey at the bar, but they have a Woodford Reserve double-oaked bourbon that will do the trick.

Demetrius sets his present for Brandy on a table near the entrance, which is piled high with elegantly wrapped packages. I slip my card between two of the gifts.

The DJ plays "Everybody Dance Now." Sergeant Reeves spins his date, Roxie, around the floor. Who knew the guy had moves like that? Marta swirls around Chief Jimenez, swishing her skirt. Several other couples join in the raucous celebration. I take Demetrius by the hand.

"Would you like to dance?"

"Are you sure?"

"It's your toes I'll be stepping on."

Demetrius shimmies around the floor, seducing me with his eyes. I may not be much of a dancer, but I've drunk enough whiskey to let go and make a fool of myself.

In an abrupt shift of mood, that Shania Twain song "From This Moment On" plays. Demetrius draws me close. My heart races. I can't escape without looking like an ass, so I attempt to follow his lead around the floor, which proves impossible. He gives up and follows my lead. We finish with a lingering kiss, and he tells me he loves me. This time, I muster the courage to say the words back.

"You mean that?"

Despite my fear that this feeling can't last, I say the words again.

Brandy Speedman makes a grand entrance on the arm of local attorney Daniel Fields, who represented Annie when she was charged with Kit's murder last year, and sweeps through the crowd in a magenta gown, kissing cheeks and thanking her guests for coming.

"My favorite gays," Brandy says. "Don't you look festive, Demetrius." She kisses his cheek.

"You look like a million bucks, Brandy," Demetrius says. "Happy birthday!"

Brandy looks me over and straightens my collar. "Cal, you should let Demetrius dress you."

A rowdy Trevor Speedman collides with a young server. The young server loses his balance. A large tray of dirty glasses crashes across the floor, bringing the party to a standstill.

"I thought after the divorce, I wouldn't have to deal with his crap anymore," Brandy says. She apologizes to her guests and drags her inebriated ex-husband aside.

Daniel Fields brings Brandy a drink. Helena and Bo duck out the door, probably intending to smoke something illegal in the parking lot. I'm off duty, so I turn a blind eye. Demetrius goes to the men's room. I grab another drink from the bar.

Chief Jimenez sidles up beside me and orders a rum and diet soda. "I suppose you heard," she says.

"What now?"

"Bill Sinclair slipped into a coma."

"Same as Crispin did."

"The Crispin case is closed."

"Maybe we should reopen it?"

"Don't test me, Nowak."

That Ricky Martin song about shaking your bonbons plays. Marta coaxes the chief onto the dance floor.

Demetrius returns with Annie. "Look who I found."

"Hey, roomie," Annie says.

"When did you get here?"

"Howie tuned up my car today, so I took him to dinner at the diner. We just arrived."

Howie shuffles up. He's combed his hair and trimmed his beard. His shirt is pressed and his shoes polished. "What's up, Cal?"

"Not much. How are you doing?"

Howie shrugs. "Could be better, could be worse." He turns to Annie. "What would you like to drink?"

"A glass of white wine."

Demetrius leans in and whispers, "Are they—?"

"I don't think so," I whisper back.

"What are you two smiling about?" Annie asks.

"I need another drink," I say. "How about you?"

"I'm fine," Demetrius says.

Helena and Bo catch up with me at the bar. Their eyes look bloodshot, and they reek of patchouli.

"Can I ask you two a question?"

"What about?" Helena asks.

"That night at the theater."

"Fire away," Bo says. He nibbles on a cheese straw from the basket on the bar.

"Did either of you see Oliver Crispin drink gin that night?"

"Not me," Bo says. "But I was pretty wasted."

"Ollie was a wild man that night," Helena says. "He imbibed anything and everything within reach. He even chugged a glug of that nasty elderberry syrup Bill Sinclair likes."

"Crispin drank elderberry syrup that night?"

"Bill doesn't like people touching his stuff," Bo says. "Ollie didn't give a damn."

That explains the hallucinations. And now, Bill Sinclair is in a coma.

Chief Jimenez and Marta slip off the dance floor and return to the bar.

Sergeant Reeves and Roxie lead the crowd in the Macarena. Helena and Bo join in the raucous line dance. Demetrius keeps the beat from the sidelines.

"Demi, I need to speak with the chief."

"Care to dance, Marta?"

Demetrius leads Marta onto the dance floor, and they join in the Macarena.

"What's on your mind?" Chief Jimenez asks.

"There's been an interesting development in the Crispin case."

"That case is closed, Nowak. How can I get that through your thick skull?"

"Crispin was poisoned. That's a fact. And I believe Bill Sinclair may have been the intended target."

Chief Jimenez takes me by the arm and leads me over to a quiet corner. "Nowak, I've had about all of your insubordination I can take."

I share what I learned from Kaden.

"You think Daphne Sinclair is trying to kill her husband?"

"She had the means, motive, and opportunity. But she didn't count on Crispin drinking the tainted syrup straight out of the bottle."

"Even if you could prove that—which you can't—it won't bring Crispin back?"

"So we let a killer go free?"

"Let's see if Bill Sinclair's doctors find anything," Chief Jimenez says. "In the meantime, stay out of trouble."

Trevor Speedman taps a fork against his wine glass and asks for everyone's attention. The DJ fades out the music, and the crowd hushes.

"Tonight, we're here to celebrate the birthday of my best friend, Brandy," Trevor says. "We spent five mostly fun-filled years as husband and wife. Though that chapter in our lives has closed, my love and admiration for her endure." His words slur. "Brandy, you are one of a kind." He stumbles and catches his balance. "Happy birthday to the best ex-wife a man could ask for!"

We all raise a glass to Brandy.

"Help me out here, boys," Brandy whispers. She takes the

microphone. Demetrius and I lead Trevor aside and convince him to drink a bottle of water.

Brandy thanks everyone for coming. "We have plenty of good food and wine and great music," she concludes. "Enjoy yourselves!"

Daniel Fields embraces Brandy. She leans her head against his chest.

"I have to relieve Lecoq at the crack of dawn," Sergeant Reeves says. "So we're going to bounce." He grabs Roxie's ass on their way out the door.

"We're off, too," Chief Jimenez says. "Watch your step, Nowak."

"Roger that, boss."

The DJ cranks up the volume. Raucous guests crowd the dance floor, while their milder-mannered counterparts stuff their faces with sliders, flatbread pizzas, and a dozen different flavors of gourmet cupcakes. The booze flows freely. I've drunk enough bourbon to let loose and make a fool of myself with Demetrius on the dance floor.

Around midnight, the party reaches its zenith, and by one o'clock the festivities have wound down.

"That was fun," I say. I stagger against the bar.

Demetrius takes my arm and steadies me. "You're drunk."

"I'm having a good time."

"I'm glad."

We kiss.

Annie and Howie say their goodbyes and take off.

"Are you about ready to call it a night?" Demetrius asks me.

"Lead the way."

Demetrius wraps his arms around my waist and leads me outside. I lean on him for support and try not to trip over my own feet. My hands rove over and under his shirt. He helps me crawl inside his pickup and drives us home. We rush inside. He takes Flower for a walk while I nibble on a piece of dried cinnamon roll from the bag on the kitchen counter. I never got around to eating anything tonight.

Flower bounds inside the cabin. Demetrius locks the door. He takes my hand and leads me down the hallway into his bedroom. We strip off our clothes and tumble into bed in a passionate embrace.

CHAPTER TWENTY-EIGHT

SUNDAY MORNING, I'm lying in bed curled up next to Demetrius, looking forward to sleeping in, when his phone rings. He answers, listens for a second, and passes me the receiver. "It's for you."

Sitting up in bed, I rub my throbbing temples and take the receiver. "Hello?"

"I'm sorry to bother you," Annie says, "but Bill Sinclair's doctor needs to speak with you."

I gesture for Demetrius to pass me the pen and notepad on his nightstand, which he does, and I scrawl down the phone number.

"Did you and Demetrius have a good time last night?"

From the lilt in her voice, I figure Demetrius told her I said the L-word, and she wants details. I thank her for calling and hang up.

"Don't tell me," Demetrius says. "You have to work." He snuggles against me. "I asked Lamonte to cover the store so we could spend the day together."

"I need to make a quick call."

"I'll brew a pot of coffee."

Demetrius climbs out of bed. I admire the view. He slips on a pair of sweatpants and pads out the door. My boxer shorts lie on the floor near the door. I put them on. The phone rings three times before the doctor answers.

"Thank you for returning my call, Officer Nowak. We found atropine in Mr. Sinclair's urine. I'm still waiting on the final toxicology report, but it appears your theory about someone poisoning Mr. Sinclair may prove true."

"Will he be okay?"

"Hard to say."

The doctor promises he'll keep me in the loop.

Demetrius brings me coffee in bed and joins me with his cup. I share what the doctor told me.

"You really think Daphne is trying to kill her husband?"

"She didn't sign a prenup, so she stands to inherit a fortune."

"What about Vona? I thought she brewed the poisonous syrup."

"I can't imagine what she'd have to gain, but I haven't ruled out anyone."

"What do you want to do today?"

"Whatever you do."

Demetrius leaps out of bed.

"Okay, a long hike through the woods it is."

"Wait a minute—"

"I'm kidding. I'm going to fix breakfast."

While Demetrius is busy in the kitchen, I call the chief and share what I learned from Sinclair's doctor.

"That's still circumstantial, Nowak," Chief Jimenez says. "Bring me hard evidence, and I'll reopen the case."

"I'll keep digging."

"Nowak—be careful who you piss off, yeah?"

I take a quick shower, throw on my clothes, and find Demetrius in the kitchen, scrambling eggs and frying bacon.

"Grab the bottle of champagne and the orange juice from the fridge," Demetrius says.

"What are we celebrating?"

"A day off together."

This must be what happiness feels like.

Demetrius scoops scrambled eggs onto our plates, adds two slices of bacon and a slice of whole wheat toast while I pour the mimosas, and we sit down and eat our breakfast.

"I was thinking that we could drive into Kingston," Demetrius says. "Maybe have lunch at the farmers market and see a movie afterward. The new *Matrix* is playing at the Hudson Valley Cineplex."

"That's in the mall, right? I need to buy new sneakers."

"Annie said she'd stop by this afternoon and take Flower for a walk."

"What did you put in these eggs?"

"You like them?"

"Heck, yeah."

"I added a few spoonfuls of that salsa I made."

After we finish eating, I clean up our mess while Demetrius showers and gets dressed. We take his pickup because its cab is roomier. When we reach the highway where I have cellular service, I receive an alert that I have three new voicemails. I play the first one, which is from Mama Libby.

Cal, I'm sorry to bother you. But I need your help. I think I have squirrels in my attic again.

I tell Demetrius.

"Should we check on her?"

"I'll drop by tomorrow and have a look around."

I play the second voicemail. A garbled woman's voice whispers, "*Those women are lying.*" At least, I think that's what she said.

Which women are lying? About what?

The third voicemail plays.

Officer Nowak, this is Padma Patel from the Sacred Root Apothecary. It is urgent I speak with you.

I call Padma back, but our connection is weak. She sounds distressed. I miss every other word she says. I tell her I'll meet her at her shop and end the call.

Demetrius and I are halfway to Kingston. He is not going to like this. I break the news that we must turn around. He gives me the silent treatment all the way back to town and brakes to a tire-screeching halt before the Sacred Root Apothecary.

"I'm really sorry," I say.

Demetrius stares straight ahead. I climb out. His pickup speeds away.

Padma Patel greets me at the door.

"What seems to be the trouble?" I ask.

"Last autumn, I froze several bags of belladonna berries that I harvested from my plant," Padma says. "This morning, I opened my freezer to get some ice and noticed a bag was missing."

"That's your emergency?"

"I have been robbed, officer."

I am not happy that my day off was cut short for this, but since I'm here, I might as well have a look around. "Where is your freezer?"

Padma leads me through a beaded curtain into the stockroom. A refrigerator with a top freezer stands in the corner.

"Are you sure you didn't consume the bag and forget?"

"I keep impeccable records, officer." Padma takes out a ledger and shows me how she logs everything she harvests from her garden and all the wild herbs and flowers she gathers from the woods and fields around town. Her handwriting is very neat. "I should have four bags of belladonna berries." She opens the freezer door. "As you can see, I only have three."

"Who else has access to your shop?"

"I am the sole proprietor."

"Has anyone else come back here? A delivery person, perhaps?"

"I oversee all my deliveries."

"What about the women in your support group?"

"Of course, my friends come and go freely when we meet," Padma says. "But I cannot believe one of them would steal from me."

"Who attends these meetings?"

"I do not wish to cause trouble for anyone. But belladonna is highly toxic and must be handled with extreme care. In the wrong hands, it can be lethal."

Belladonna contains the same toxins that Kaden found in the syrup we confiscated from the theater.

"I need the names of your members."

"I am not sure I should—"

"If I must get a warrant, I will."

"I suppose it is no secret who attends," Padma says. She consults her ledger. "Daphne Sinclair, Rose Ryland, Patricia Sylvester, and Helena Potter attend most sessions. Brandy Speedman came a few times. Annie Nye joined us once."

I thank Padma for her time.

Once I'm outside, I call Demetrius. He doesn't answer his phone. He may not have gotten home yet, or he could be outside with Flower. I leave a message and start walking home. I'm in the middle of a murder investigation. Perhaps not officially. But he could be a little more understanding.

"I didn't expect you home today," Annie says with a sly grin when I walk through the door.

"Duty calls," I say.

I go into my room and shut the door.

"What did you do, Cal?" Annie asks.

"I don't want to talk about it."

"What is going on with you?"

I open my door.

"I had to work! I'm investigating a murder!"

"Don't yell at me."

"I don't know what everyone expects from me."

"Tell me what happened."

I do. She pours me a whiskey.

"Drink this and calm down."

"I'm fine."

"Finish your drink and call Demetrius."

"I'm not going to apologize for having to work."

"You two were looking forward to spending the day together."

"My pickup is at his place."

Annie grabs her keys. "Come on, let's go."

Once we're on the road, the chief calls and asks me if I have any updates. I'm not ready to divulge what I've learned from Padma yet.

"If your hunch is right," Chief Jimenez says, "we need evidence before anyone else gets hurt."

"What do you suggest I do?"

"You went to school with Mrs. Sinclair. Console her."

"I'll give it my best shot."

When Annie finds out I must go back to work, she drops me off at my pickup and drives away, clearly pissed off at me now, too.

———

DAPHNE INVITES me inside and asks if I'd like a cocktail. She stumbles and catches her balance. She must've already had a few drinks. I decline her offer. This may be my day off, but I'm here on official business. She suggests we take a seat. I follow her into a stylish living room that has a vaulted ceiling and panoramic floor-to-ceiling windows and join her on a couch that's so ugly it must be expensive.

"How is Bill doing?"

"He's still in a coma. His doctors sound hopeful, though."

"Have they diagnosed what's wrong?"

"They seem to think he may have been poisoned."

"How are you holding up?"

Daphne takes a sip of her drink and stammers, "I don't know what I'll do if—" She covers her mouth with her hand.

"How did you and Bill meet?"

"I was in the chorus of *42nd Street* on Broadway, but I understudied Celeste Fontaine, who played the lead. I should've had her role. I was a better tap dancer. But that's show business. Anyhow, she came down with laryngitis one night, so I went on." Daphne takes a drink and smiles wistfully. "After seeing my performance, Bill bribed his way backstage and invited me out for a late dinner at Le Bernardin. I'd never experienced such elegance. On our way out of the restaurant, he literally swept me off my feet when I stepped on a subway grate and broke off the heel of my shoe."

"Has Bill ever struck you?"

"What sort of question is that?"

"One that deserves an answer."

"I'd like you to leave now."

"I'm trying to save your husband's life."

"By interrogating me?"

"I need your help."

"How so?"

"Is brewing elderberry syrup difficult?"

"Not at all. It only requires four ingredients—frozen elderberries, honey, water, and a little lemon juice."

"Are you familiar with belladonna?"

"Padma taught us about the history and medicinal uses of deadly nightshade. All parts of the plant are extremely poisonous."

Daphne does not appear the least bit nervous, which makes me doubt she took the berries. She's not that good of an actress.

"Well, I won't take up any more of your time.

———

FLOWER BARKS, announcing my arrival before I even reach the door. I let myself in. The dog wags his tail when he sees me. I pet his head and scratch under his chin. Demetrius lies curled up under a blanket on the couch, reading a book. He doesn't glance up.

"I know you're disappointed. But I—"

"I should be used to this by now."

"I don't know what you want me to say."

"You cut our camping trip short, and then you leave me high and dry today. Just once, I'd like to come first."

"That's not fair."

"Maybe not. But that's how I feel."

"It's only six o'clock. I left my radio in the pickup. I turned off my cellular phone. I'm yours for the night." I flop down on top of Demetrius and take away his book. "You can read *Wildlife of the Adirondacks* later." I toss the book onto the coffee table and give him a kiss. "What do you want to do? Go out? Stay in?"

"So long as we're together, who cares?"

CHAPTER TWENTY-NINE

"WHERE HAVE YOU BEEN?" Suki asks when I arrive at the station on Monday morning. "The chief's trying to reach you."

"Oh, shit."

I left my radio in my pickup and forgot to turn my cellular phone back on this morning. I have seven voicemails.

"What's going on?" I ask Suki.

"There was an incident at the Roadhouse last night."

"What happened?"

"Someone attacked Gunner while he was locking up."

"Is he okay?"

"He's in stable condition at the hospital. Sergeant Reeves took his statement."

"Where's the rest of the team?"

"Washington took the bus to the city. It's her day off. Lecoq is responding to a trespassing complaint, and the chief is meeting with the mayor."

"What can I do?"

Suki holds up a Post-it note.

"Gladys Crabtree reported a prowler."

"Again?"

"She's an old woman who lives alone. She gets scared."

"Fine."

Gladys Crabtree lives next door to Annie and me. When I arrive, she leads me around behind her house. Trash litters her lawn. Someone—or more likely something—has rummaged through her garbage cans.

"Just look at this mess," she says. Her breath reeks of gin, and it's only ten o'clock in the morning.

"Did you see anyone in your yard?"

"Not exactly—"

"Have you spotted any raccoons recently?"

"A skunk chased Mr. Squiggles the other day."

Gladys Crabtree owns a Pomeranian named Mr. Squiggles. Given half the chance, she'll brag your ear off about his championship bloodline.

"I'd bet that's your culprit. All the same, I'll write up a report and alert my team to keep an eye out for prowlers."

"A fat lot of good that will do."

"If you see or hear anything suspicious, let us know."

I take off before she gives me any further grief and drop by Mama Libby's house. She's watching Dr. Phil help an angry couple sort out their marital issues on the television.

"Have you had breakfast?" Mama Libby asks.

"I'll grab a donut and coffee from the Gas & Go."

"Don't be silly. I baked blueberry muffins this morning."

Mama Libby picks and freezes wild blueberries every summer. Her muffins have crisp tops and moist, flaky centers. I glance out the window. The lawn needs mowing.

Sparky races around inside her kennel, barking at the squirrels playing on the lawn. She can be a handful. Smart dogs often are. Without her, though, I might never have found little Evan Langford last year. I step outside. Sparky leaps on the fence and whines. I slip through the gate, careful not to let her escape, and pet her for a few seconds before she dashes away and races around in circles. I wish I had her energy. I rinse out and fill her bowl with fresh water from the garden hose.

"Cal, what's the skinny?" Moses says. The old guy hustles down the stairs from his apartment over the garage and hobbles across the lawn.

"How's life treating you, Moses?"

"I had to put down Midnight. She got the leukemia."

Midnight was Moses's mean old cat that he treated better than some people treat their children.

"I'm sorry to hear that, man."

"I watched members of my platoon die in front of my eyes when I was in Nam. But I've never wept like I did for that darn cat."

I've never owned a pet, but grief is grief.

"I wish I could stay and chat," I say, "but I'm on patrol."

Moses follows me inside the house. Mama Libby shoves a bag into my hands.

"Here are enough muffins for you to share."

"I'll come over soon and mow your lawn."

"You don't need to do that. I know how busy you are."

"I always have time for you."

"You're too good to me, Callum Nowak."

"After all you and Papa Frank did for me, it's the least I can do."

"Frank would be proud of you."

"I took the hair and fingerprint samples from my mother's case to the crime lab in Albany."

"Are you sure that's wise?"

"She deserves justice."

"At what price?"

"I know you think I'm in over my head, but I can handle this."

"I hope so, son."

THAT AFTERNOON, I cruise through the town. The downstaters have gone home, leaving the locals free to enjoy a leisurely day. I stop by the hardware store. Vona is paying Demetrius for a new garden hose. When she sees me, she rushes out the door. I chase after her.

"Excuse me, Vona. I'd like to ask you a few questions."

"I've got nothing to say to you."

I catch up.

"How is Mr. Sinclair feeling today?"

"I haven't heard."

Vona refuses to look me in the eye.

"If he dies, Vona, you could be in a lot of trouble."

"I haven't done anything wrong."

"You might want to get yourself a good lawyer."

"I only did what I was told."

"Famous last words," I say.

Vona speeds out of the parking lot in her rundown Ford Escort. I wonder if she has a record. That would explain her reluctance to talk to the police. Perhaps I should run a background check. If she's committed minor crimes in the past, I don't care. It's in her best interest to come clean.

"Are you okay, babe?" Demetrius asks.

"Fine," I say. "I'll call you later."

Leaping behind the wheel, I chase Vona. I'm getting desperate for a break in this case. A school bus pulls in front of me. I can't pass without endangering its young occupants. By the time the bus turns down a side street, I've lost sight of the Escort. I turn around and return to the station.

Chief Jimenez calls me into her office and asks for an update.

"The Sinclairs's housekeeper is hiding something," I say, "and I intend to find out what."

"You've got nothing but circumstantial evidence and theories. You need to drop this."

"But—"

The chief's phone rings. She dismisses me with a wave of her hand. I take a seat at my desk and fill out my reports. If I don't convince Vona to talk soon, I'm going to have to drop this investigation, and I don't want to do that.

After I turn in my paperwork, I head over to the Nyes Landing Diner for lunch. Taking a seat on a stool at the counter, I look over the specials scrawled on the chalkboard mounted on the rear wall. The crispy trout tacos with jalapeño slaw sound good. I order those with a cup of black coffee.

Helena Potter climbs onto the stool beside me and asks how things are going.

"Did you know Padma Patel grows belladonna in her garden?" I ask.

"She showed us her plants when we discussed the nightshade family. She keeps bags of the berries in her freezer, which she dries and grinds into a powder that in microdoses relieves her migraines."

"How well do you know Padma?"

"I met her when she moved to town last summer, and we became friends. But I'm not sure anyone really knows her."

"Why do you say that?"

"Her aura is a murky gray."

A self-professed psychic, Helena believes people radiate auras that reflect our emotional and spiritual states.

"She carries deep sorrow in her heart."

"Losing one's mother will do that to a person."

"Of course you can relate."

"What brought Padma to Nyes Landing?"

"A change of pace, I suppose. She went to college in the city."

"She did?"

"Earned her master's degree in business administration from NYU."

Padma told a woman at Crispin's memorial service she'd gone to college in Mumbai. Perhaps that's where she earned her bachelor's degree. But if she attended NYU as well, why would she deny that?

"Did the Sinclairs's housekeeper ever attend one of Padma's meetings?"

"Vona? Not that I recall."

If Vona never attended one of Padma's meetings, it's unlikely she had an opportunity to steal the berries.

"Do you know where Vona lives?"

"You know those prefabricated houses out east of town?"

I nod.

"Around there somewhere."

Helena orders a milkshake to go. My tacos arrive. I ask for a refill of my coffee. Helena pays and leaves with her drink.

AFTER LUNCH, I pay the Sinclairs a visit. Daphne answers the door and invites me inside. I ask how her husband is doing.

"Bill is still in a coma."

"I'm sorry to hear that."

"I try to be strong, but . . ."

"Is your housekeeper working?"

"Vona took the afternoon off. One of her kids is sick or something. It's just as well. I'm not in the mood for company."

"How are you holding up?"

"I'm not." Daphne shuffles behind the bar. "Would you care for a cocktail?"

"I'm on duty." She pours herself a bourbon, neat. I notice a bottle of elderberry syrup on the counter. "Is this from the batch Vona brewed?" She nods. "Can I take it?"

"May I ask why?"

"It might be poisonous."

Daphne's jaw drops.

"Do you have Vona's address?"

"Of course." Daphne grabs her address book, a notepad, and a pen. "You don't think she—"

"I'm not sure about anything right now."

Daphne jots down Vona's address.

Officer Lecoq radios that he needs the squad car. I've been so busy that I lost track of time. My shift ended an hour ago. I return to the station and hand off the keys. Before I leave, I update the chief on my conversations with Daphne and Helena.

"Bring me evidence I can take to the prosecutor's office," Chief Jimenez says.

"I'm still digging."

"Dig faster."

I call Kaden. He agrees to test the elderberry syrup that Daphne gave me.

"It'll have to wait until tomorrow, though," Kaden says. "I'm on my way out the door."

"Hot date?"

"What's it to you?"

"I'll bring the sample by the lab first thing tomorrow."

After we hang up, I rush home, shower, and put on a tee shirt and blue jeans.

"Are you seeing Demetrius tonight?" Annie asks.

"I have to work," I say, and I rush out the door before I catch an earful for neglecting my boyfriend.

Once I reach the development where Vona lives, I drive around for several minutes before spotting her Escort parked in front of a small, gray modular house. I pull over and hop out. Before I even reach the porch, I hear kids laughing and shrieking. Hoping I look less intimidating out of uniform, I ring the bell.

"Quiet!" Vona shouts. She peeks through the curtain and, seeing me, cracks the door for an inch or so. "What do you want?"

"If you don't mind, I'd like to ask you a few questions."

"I do mind. I thought I'd made that clear."

"Someone poisoned Mr. Sinclair," I say.

"What's that got to do with me?"

"If the laboratory tests the elderberry syrup you brewed and finds the same toxins the doctors found in Mr. Sinclair's system, you're going to have some explaining to do."

"I didn't poison anyone. Now, please leave."

"If you did nothing wrong, talk to me, and I can help you."

Vona's baby cries.

"You're scaring my children, officer."

"If I were you, I wouldn't leave my fate in the hands of the Sinclairs and their lawyers."

Vona slams the door in my face. I'm getting nowhere with her.

When I reach the highway, my phone rings.

"Hey, babe. Are you okay? The way you ran off today . . . I was worried."

"I'm on a case."

"Why don't you come over and let me help you unwind?"

"I would, but—"

"Whatever."

Demetrius hangs up. I hope he doesn't call Annie and complain. I don't need the grief tonight.

CHAPTER THIRTY

TUESDAY MORNING, I'm out the door before Annie leaves for school. I must know if the elderberry syrup I confiscated from the Sinclairs's bar contains the same toxins found on the empty bottle from the theater. When I reach the Forensics Investigation Center, I ask for Kaden. He meets me at the front desk. "Step into my office, Officer Nowak." I follow him down a long hallway. Once we're behind closed doors, he says, "If anyone finds out I'm doing this for you, I could lose my job."

"If this bottle contains the same toxins as the one from the theater, we could be looking at a homicide."

As I'm driving back to town, Suki radios that Mama Libby has slipped and fallen. She doesn't have any further details. I speed south through town, cross over Esopus Creek, and pass through the woods. An ambulance sits in Mama Libby's driveway. I find her in the backyard, being examined by medics.

"My God, what happened?"

"Relax," Mama Libby says. "I'm fine."

"You're not fine, ma'am," the middle-aged woman medic says. "You've sprained your ankle."

"Is that all?" Mama Libby says.

"You need to stay off your feet for a few days," the younger guy medic says, "until the swelling goes down."

Mama Libby reaches for my hand. I help her up and lead her inside the house. The medics check her vitals and bandage her ankle.

"Shall we transport you to the hospital?" The woman medic asks.

"I am not setting foot in that deathtrap."

"In that case, ma'am, you'll need to sign our release form."

Mama Libby scrawls her signature where she's told to, and the medics leave. By this point, her ankle has swollen to the size of a softball.

"I'm moving back in until you're on your feet."

"No, you're not."

"You're going to need help."

"You work all the time."

Mama Libby is right. I'm hardly ever home.

"Okay, you win. But you're going to need crutches. Let me see if I can rustle up a pair."

"All this hoopla over a sprained ankle."

"Humor me, okay. I worry about you."

"Who's patrolling the town while you're fussing over me?"

"I can take a hint."

———

HOPING I can catch Vona before she leaves work for the day, I drive up to the Sinclairs's house and ring the bell. Hearing sobbing, I ring again. A woman who resembles an older version of Daphne answers the door.

"Yes, officer?"

"I was hoping I might speak with Vona."

"We sent the housekeeper away so my sister can grieve in peace."

"Has something happened?"

"Her husband passed away."

"Bill Sinclair died?"

"We just returned from the hospital."

"I'm sorry for your loss," I say, and I beat a hasty retreat.

On my way down the mountain, I radio the chief and share the news about Bill Sinclair. "I'm on my way to the hospital. I'll see what I can find out from his doctors."

"Tread carefully, Nowak."

Someone poisoned Bill Sinclair, of that I'm certain, and Vona brewed the questionable syrup. But who stole Padma's belladonna berries?

When I reach the hospital, I stop by Gunner's room. Purple bruises cover his face, and his blackened eyes are almost swollen shut.

"I look worse than I feel," Gunner says.

"Whoever did this should be—"

"Don't go off half-cocked, Nowak. I've gotten my ass kicked for being a faggot before, and I will again."

"That's not right."

"That's life."

"I'm going to catch whoever did this."

"Not if I catch him first."

"Don't do anything stupid."

"I won't if you won't."

Gunner's nurse needs to change his bandages. I promise I'll look in on him later and excuse myself.

The nurse at the reception desk tells me one of Bill Sinclair's doctors will speak with me in a moment. While I wait, I buy a cup of disgusting coffee from the vending machine, which I choke down for the caffeine rush.

"Officer Nowak," says a tall, silver-haired doctor with a warm smile. "I'm Dr. Norris, Mr. Sinclair's attending physician. Why don't we step into my office?"

I follow Dr. Norris inside a bright white office at the end of the hallway.

"I'm sad to report your instincts were correct, officer. Mr. Sinclair had lethal amounts of atropine, scopolamine, and hyoscyamine in his system at the time of his death. Our lab results will corroborate your evidence."

I don't have any evidence, but he doesn't need to know that.

"I appreciate your help, doctor. I'll be in touch."

WHEN I REACH HOME, Demetrius and Annie are seated on the couch, watching television. Annie has a stack of her students's papers piled on her lap that she's marking up with a red pen. Without glancing up, she says, "There's fried chicken and mashed potatoes in the kitchen."

"You read my mind."

Flower comes bounding into the room and leaps on me. I scratch his ears.

"Go change," Demetrius says. He gives me a kiss. "I'll fix you a plate."

I slip on a sweatshirt and pants, hang up my uniform, wash my face, and join Demetrius and Annie on the couch.

"I can't believe Bill Sinclair is dead," Annie says. "I must call Daphne tomorrow. Or better yet, pay her a visit and find out what she needs."

"When I stopped by earlier, her family was with her," I say.

"What happened?" Demetrius asks.

"His doctors found lethal toxins in his system."

"My God," Annie gasps. "From what?"

"We're not sure yet."

"You need to eat," Demetrius says, and he thrusts a fork into my hand.

"Mama Libby fell and sprained her ankle today," I say. I scoop up a bite of mashed potatoes and savor their buttery goodness.

"Oh, no," Annie says. "Is she all right?"

"She needs to stay off her feet for a few days. Like that's going to happen. I offered to stay over, but she declined my help."

"I'll stop by tomorrow after school and see how she's doing," Annie says.

"We'll take turns looking after her," Demetrius adds.

"What are you guys watching?" I ask. I bite into a chicken thigh that's crunchy on the outside but juicy on the inside.

"The Lifetime movie of the week," Demetrius says.

"The channel for women and gay men," Annie says.

"Not this gay man," I say.

"How can you not feel sorry for that poor little girl on the screen?" Demetrius asks. "She's dying of a rare childhood blood cancer."

"The movie is based on a true story," Annie says. "How sad is that?"

"You two are hopeless."

While I eat dinner, I review the next steps in my investigation. I need Kaden to rush those results. Then, I must convince Vona that if she's not guilty, she needs to come clean before she gets charged with murder.

Flower crouches at my feet and eyes my plate. He yawns and licks his chops.

"Leave Cal alone, Flower," Demetrius says. "You know you're not allowed people food."

"If that poor little girl dies," Annie sobs. "I'm never going to watch another one of these movies."

"She won't die," Demetrius says.

Life has taught me that in true stories, little girls and boys often die, but I keep that thought to myself. In the end, the poor kid does die, and from the tears streaming down Annie's and Demetrius's faces, you'd think they'd known her personally.

"I have an early meeting in the morning," Annie says, and she tosses Demetrius the remote. "Goodnight, boys."

Demetrius and I curl up on the couch. He switches channels, and we watch a nature program about ants. I doze off. He shakes me awake. "Go to bed." He shoves me toward my room. "I'll take Flower for a walk and join you."

CHAPTER THIRTY-ONE

BY THE TIME I crawl out of bed on Wednesday morning, Annie has left for school. I find a pot of coffee in the kitchen and pour myself a cup. Flower scampers around my feet. I open the back door. The dog rushes outside and races around the backyard. Unlike Sparky, though, I can trust him not to run away. He's braver at home in his own yard, but when he's over here he stops in his tracks every few seconds and looks back over his shoulder, as if he's making sure I'm still there.

When Flower finishes his business, I toss him a doggie biscuit from the jar Annie keeps on the counter for his visits and dump half of a can of food into his bowl. He gulps down the chunky brown stew.

"Morning, babe," Demetrius says, shuffling into the kitchen. He yawns and pours himself a cup of coffee.

"Are you hungry?" Demetrius asks.

My phone rings.

"Nowak here."

"It's Kaden from the crime lab."

"Did you find something?"

"Yes and no."

"What does that mean?"

"Not over the phone."

"Where are you?"

"At a diner in Woodstock."

"What are you doing there?"

"I had a meeting with a detective on another case."

I write down the location and tell him to give me an hour.

"You're kidding me," Demetrius says when I hang up.

"I'm sorry. It's just—"

"I'll let myself out."

"I don't deserve you."

———

KADEN WAVES from a booth in the rear of the crowded diner. His fingers tap the tabletop. He's had too much caffeine. I slide into the seat across from him. A woman who could be anywhere from forty to sixty approaches and asks if I'd like coffee. I nod and study the menu she hands me.

"Have you eaten breakfast?" Kaden asks.

"Nope."

"Me either," Kaden says.

The woman brings my coffee and asks if we're ready to order. I defer to Kaden.

"I'll have an egg white omelet with spinach and feta cheese."

"Home fries or sliced tomatoes."

"Sliced tomatoes."

"White, wheat, or rye toast?"

"No toast."

The woman looks at me.

"And for you?"

"The western omelet with home fries and wheat toast."

The woman collects our menus and goes into the kitchen.

"So? What did you find?"

"I didn't get any hits on the fingerprints from your mother's case, and the hair strands didn't turn up any matches."

"That doesn't leave much room for good news."

"I may have located your father."

I haven't thought about my old man in years.

"That asshole is still alive and kicking, huh?"

Kaden slides a snapshot across the table.

"Martin Nowak. Fifty-three years old. His last known address was in Troy, New York, but that was four years ago. He may have moved since then."

The woman brings our omelets and refills our coffee mugs. I've lost my appetite. Excusing myself, I dash off to the men's room and splash some cold water on my face. My father left my sister and me with our mom. After she died, he could've come back for us, but he didn't. He doesn't want anything to do with me. And I feel the same way about him. Good riddance.

When I return, Kaden hasn't touched his food.

"You didn't need to wait for me."

"Are you okay?"

"What about the elderberry syrup?"

I take a large bite of my omelet, swallow it down with a swig of coffee, and nibble on my toast.

"I hope to receive those results today."

"Call me the minute you do."

Kaden slips me a note. "Your father's address. In case you . . ."

I slip the note into my pocket.

We finish breakfast. I thank Kaden for his help, pay our check, and go.

———

BEFORE GOING ON PATROL, I check on Mama Libby. When she doesn't answer the door, I dash around behind the house, afraid she may have fallen again. I find her watering her garden while

Moses tells her about all the unusual vegetables he ate during his tour of duty in Nam.

"If you don't stay off your feet," I say, "your ankle won't ever heal."

"Shouldn't you be out protecting the town from jaywalkers?"

"I'm on my way to the station now. I thought I'd see if you needed anything."

"Sparky needs a bag of kibble."

"I'll stop by the feed store."

"Are you hungry?"

"I just ate breakfast," I say. "I'll bring that kibble by later."

When I reach the station, I lock the cold case files from my mother's case in the closet. I'm disappointed that the lab tests didn't turn up any new leads. At this rate, I may never find her killer, and that's not an option.

"Nowak, have you spoken to the Sinclairs's housekeeper yet?" Chief Jimenez asks.

"She won't talk to me. But I spoke with Bill Sinclair's doctor. They found lethal amounts of atropine, scopolamine, and hyoscyamine in his system. The toxins that are found in belladonna berries. Someone stole a package of belladonna berries from Padma Patel's freezer. Daphne attends Padma's support group meetings. She could've committed the theft. But so could any of the other women at those meetings."

"Slow down, Nowak. What meeting?"

I tell her about the group Padma hosts.

"You say they meet on Wednesday nights?"

"That's right."

"It's Wednesday."

"And you want me to—?"

"What are you waiting for?"

———

WALKING into the Sacred Roots Apothecary a few minutes before six o'clock, I inhale a myriad of scents—some spicy, some floral, some harder to describe. Rows of candles and boxes of incense line a set of wicker shelves. Bottles of essential oils fill a glass cabinet. Some promise they'll energize you, while others claim they'll put you to sleep. Hypnotic sitar music plays faintly in the background.

Padma steps out of the back room.

"Officer Nowak, what brings you by?"

"I thought I'd check out one of your meetings. Maybe I can learn a thing or two. If men are allowed, that is."

"I welcome any chance to share the benefits of honoring the natural world."

Padma welcomes Rose and Trixie into her shop. Trixie sets a plastic tub on the refreshments table and announces she made granola. Helena arrives moments later and shares her vegan brownies.

"I didn't realize we were supposed to bring refreshments," I say.

"Oh, pooh," Trixie says. "We're just glad you're here."

Padma offers everyone herbal tea. I've never cared for hot tea, but I accept a cup because I don't wish to be rude. Its sweetness surprises me.

"Under the circumstances, ladies," Padma says. "Daphne will not be joining us."

"Poor Daphne," Trixie says. "I don't know what I'd do if Rose . . ."

Rose gives Trixie's hand a reassuring pat. "I'm not shuffling off this mortal coil anytime soon."

"I heard whispers that Daphne poisoned Bill," Helena says.

"I wouldn't put it past the woman," Rose says.

"Do the police suspect foul play, Officer Nowak?" Padma asks.

"The crime lab found traces of plant-based toxins in Sinclair's system that shouldn't have been there."

"They did?" Padma asks.

"From what type of plants?" Rose asks.

"I'll know for certain when I receive the final toxicology report."

"Mother Nature is a force to be reckoned with," Padma says. "We must respect her power."

"Our chickens were poisoned with elderberries," Trixie says.

"I'll bet that was Daphne's doing, too." Rose says.

"Let's not leap to any conclusions," I say.

"Officer Nowak is right. Innocent until proven guilty is a fundamental tenet of your legal system." Padma rises. "My belladonna plants have blossomed. Would anyone care to see?"

We follow Padma outside and around behind her shop. A glass-enclosed greenhouse connects to a lush outdoor garden. She shows us three bushy plants that are about three to four feet tall and covered with bell-shaped, purplish-green flowers. The women admire how much the plants have grown since they last saw them.

"In the fall," Padma says, "the flowers transform into dark purple berries."

When we go back into the shop, Helena calls me aside.

"I'm worried Daphne may have stolen Padma's belladonna berries."

"Why do you say that?"

"The night we learned about the nightshade family, Padma showed us she had four bags of the frozen berries," Helena says. "Later, I spied Daphne digging through the freezer."

"Maybe she needed ice."

"Padma keeps an ice bucket on the table."

"Perhaps Daphne didn't notice."

"Earlier, I saw her fix a drink, and she used ice from the bucket. I didn't think anything about it at the time. But given everything that's transpired since then, I felt I should speak up."

"Did you see Daphne Sinclair take a bag of belladonna berries out of Padma's freezer?"

"No, but—"

"You were both sleeping with Oliver Crispin, weren't you?"

"You think I was jealous of Daphne? That's a laugh. She thought if she gave Ollie what he wanted, he would introduce her to his Hollywood agent."

"In that case, why would she poison him?"

"Ollie thought Daphne was a joke. He used to mock her behind her back. Maybe she found out."

"I am sorry to interrupt," Padma says. "But we are ready to get started now."

Before taking my seat, I pour myself a glass of water.

"Try Trixie's granola," Rose says. "She makes it using all organic ingredients."

I pop a cluster of almonds coated in oats and honey into my mouth. "I feel healthier already."

For the next half hour, Padma discusses the benefits of eating dandelions. The common weed aids digestion, detoxifies the liver and kidneys, and reduces inflammation. All parts of the plant can be cooked in soups and tossed salads. The flowers can even be fermented into wine. Who knew?

After the meeting, Padma calls me aside and says, "I do not wish to point fingers at anyone, officer. But given recent events, I fear Rose may have stolen my berries."

"Why would you say that?"

"At the meeting where I showed everyone my belladonna harvest, Rose brought fresh fruit sorbet for everyone, which she stored in my freezer. Now that Bill Sinclair has died, I cannot help but wonder if she took the berries."

"But you didn't actually see Rose take anything but her sorbet."

"That is correct, officer."

Trixie follows me out to my pickup after the meeting. "I went hiking up the peak of our mountain yesterday. On the way back, I passed behind the Sinclairs's house."

"You need to stay off their property."

"Daphne grows elderberries in her garden."

"Which she uses to brew elderberry syrup."

"One of her plants was covered in berries," Trixie says. "But the other was picked clean."

"Perhaps birds or some woodland creature ate the berries."

"Only from that one bush, Cal?"

I drive away confident one of the women who attends those meetings took the missing berries. But which one?

CHAPTER THIRTY-TWO

THURSDAY MORNING, I drive to Kingston for Ernest Drucker's trial. By the time I take my seat in the courtroom, the bailiff calls Drucker's case number. Drucker steps forward with his attorney, a slight, older gentleman with a bushy beard who's wearing a drab gray suit. Drucker acknowledges that he understands his charges and pleads guilty. The judge asked if anyone coerced Drucker into making that plea. Drucker shakes his head and mutters no. He looks defeated. Without even hearing my testimony, the judge sentences Drucker to three years of probation and orders him to pay restitution, the amount of which will be set at a future date.

On my way back to town, I pull into the parking lot of Greenfield's Produce Stand and buy a pint of fresh strawberries and a bunch of rhubarb. The clerk mentions they received their first batch of sour cherries today. I buy a pound of those as well. Mama Libby bakes the best cherry pies.

When I reach Mama Libby's house, Gladys Crabtree's AMC Pacer is parked in the driveway behind Moses's Chevy Impala. Between Gladys and her gossip and Moses and his war stories, I dread going inside.

Mama Libby must've heard me pull up because she opens the

door before I even knock. Relief washes over her face. "Come in, Cal! It's nice to see you."

"I brought you strawberries and rhubarb from Greenfield's. And a pound of the first sour cherries of the season."

"How nice of you."

"I'll set them on the kitchen counter."

Mama Libby hobbles back to her chair and props her foot up on a stool.

"I'm glad to see that you're staying off your feet," I say.

"Like I have a choice."

Gladys Crabtree sits on the edge of the couch with Mr. Squiggles perched on her lap.

"I didn't mean to upset you, Gladys," Moses says. "But I swear on my life, it's true. The North Vietnamese eat dogs."

"Nobody is going to eat you, Mr. Squiggles," Gladys says.

"Dogs are animals, Gladys," Mama Libby says. "Like cows, pigs, sheep, and deer. You eat those."

"That's different."

"How?"

"Are you going to eat Sparky?"

"Don't be silly," Mama Libby says.

"I don't have to listen to this."

Gladys takes her little dog and leaves.

"Thank you, Moses," Mama Libby says. "You're a natural Gladys repellent."

"What does that mean?"

"Take it as a compliment, old man."

While I'm here, I feed Sparky and give her fresh water. She wolfs down a few bites and races around inside her kennel, barking at the sparrows hopping across the lawn. Mama Libby assures me she will be fine. Moses promises he will keep an eye on her. Figuring there's nothing more I can do here, I take off.

———

AT THE STATION, Officer Lecoq sits behind his desk, filling out paperwork. I pull up a chair.

"What do you need, Nowak?"

"Your expertise."

"How so?"

"You're a whiz with computers, right?"

Officer Lecoq grins sheepishly. "Yeah, well . . ."

"Could you investigate Bill Sinclair's past and his marriage to Daphne? And see what you can find out about Rose and Trixie, too. Can you do that for me?"

"Give me a few hours."

"Don't share what you find out with anyone until you speak to me. Not even the chief. Understand?"

"I don't know—"

"Never mind. I'll handle this on my own."

"Fine. I'll keep my mouth shut . . . for now."

Chief Jimenez calls me into her office and asks for an update. I share what went down at the meeting last night. "More circumstantial evidence, Nowak." She frowns. "We're short-staffed as it is. We can't afford to waste any more time chasing theories. We need to turn this case over to the sheriff and let his detectives handle the investigation."

"So you admit we have a case?"

"If Bill Sinclair was murdered, we do."

"Give me twenty-four hours. If I don't bring you solid evidence by then, I'll back off. I swear."

"It would be a hell of a coincidence if the stolen belladonna berries and the toxicology reports weren't connected."

"I expect to hear from my source at the lab any moment now."

"Keep me posted."

Sergeant Reeves tosses me the keys to the squad car and clocks out. I hop behind the wheel and find a Jukebox Junction paper bag wadded up on the floor—again. I roll down the windows and air out the smell of stale grease. When I brake at the light, I smash a French fry that had gotten stuck under the pedal. I drive through the car wash and scrub the squad car inside and out.

After leaving the car wash, I drop by the hardware store. Demetrius's smile swiftly fades when he sees me.

Gladys Crabtree approaches. "Which one of these deadbolt locks would you recommend, officer?"

"Ask the store's owner." I nod toward Demetrius. "He's the expert."

"I should've known better than to ask a cop in this town for help."

"You can't go wrong with either of those locks," Demetrius says.

"There's a vagrant prowling around my house, but the police aren't doing a damn thing." Gladys shoots me a side-eyed glance. "They're too busy accusing law-abiding citizens of speeding so they can fill their quotas."

"Will there be anything else, ma'am?" Demetrius asks.

"Just the lock," Gladys says. She tosses a twenty-dollar bill onto the counter. "If I die in my sleep, you can blame the ineptitude of the Nyes Landing police force."

"I live right next door, Mrs. Crabtree," I say. I may regret this, but I give her my card. "If you see or hear the prowler again, call me."

Gladys Crabtree snatches my card, takes her change, and leaves.

"That woman would drive the devil to drink."

"You didn't lose your temper with her," Demetrius says. "I'm proud of you."

"I know I've been distracted lately."

"You're on a case. I get that. But I still miss you."

"How about I come over tonight and we make up for lost time? I'll bring dinner."

"This is Trevor Speedman's last night in town. I told him I'd meet him for a drink at the Roadhouse."

"I'm surprised he wants to go back there after what happened."

"He's not going to let the assholes scare him away."

"What time?"

"Seven o'clock."

I don't like Demetrius hanging out with Trevor.

"Can I tag along?"

"I would've invited you, but I assumed you'd be working."

"Speaking of which, I'm on patrol."

I kiss Demetrius goodbye and duck out the door in need of evidence. The clock is ticking. Vona is my best hope. I should speak with Daphne again, too, but I doubt she'll tell me anything new. Bottom line, two men died from drinking poisonous syrup that came from that house.

While I'm cruising through the neighborhood streets on the north side of town, I spot two adolescent boys lying face down in the street. The taller one has his arm stretched down the storm drain. The slighter boy clutches two baseball gloves. I pull over and ask them what they're doing.

"Our baseball rolled down the drain," the taller boy says. "My fingers aren't long enough to reach it."

"Let me try," I say.

I roll up my sleeve and lie on my stomach. With some effort, I squeeze my hand through the grate, stretch my arm out down, and clasp my fingers around the ball. Pulling my arm out proves a struggle, but I manage. I dust off the ball and toss it to its young owners.

"Thanks, officer," the taller boy says.

"Yeah, officer," his slighter friend says. "Thanks!"

The boys dash off down the sidewalk in the direction of the park.

As I drive around the corner, I spot a large dog chasing a

smaller dog. I pull over and am prepared to leap out and rescue the little dog when a bristled orange tabby cat dashes out of nowhere and attacks the larger dog. The larger dog emits a shrill yelp and races away. The tabby cat curls up beside the smaller dog. It appears my assistance isn't needed here.

When my shift ends, I clock out and go home, hang up my uniform, and take a shower. I trust Demetrius more than I trust myself, but I will be glad when Trevor Speedman goes home to California. I put on the nice blue dress shirt that Demetrius gave me for my last birthday in April and the pair of chinos Annie bought me because she was tired of seeing me wear jeans everywhere. Splashing on a few drops of aftershave, I comb my fingers through my hair. I won't be winning any beauty contests, but I'm presentable.

CHAPTER THIRTY-THREE

When I arrive at the Roadhouse, I find Demetrius and Trevor on the dance floor. Trevor may be wrapped in bandages, but he's not letting his injuries slow him down. I belly up to the bar and order my usual.

"If I were you, I'd keep an eye on Trevor," Tanner says when he brings my beer and shot. "He's in rare form tonight."

"I trust Demetrius," I say.

"Could've fooled me."

"I Want It That Way" blasts from the jukebox.

"I love this song!" Trevor gyrates around Demetrius.

"In for a dime, in for a dollar," I say.

I knock back my shot and cut in on Trevor.

"Hey, babe," Demetrius says. "I didn't see you come in."

"I just got here."

"I'm glad you came."

"Me, too."

Trevor turns his attention to another guy. Relief washes over me. I lock eyes with Demetrius and get lost in the moment. The song finishes.

"I could use a drink," Demetrius says. He leads me over to the bar and orders a draft beer. Grabbing a stack of cocktail napkins, he mops the sweat from his brow. "That was fun."

Two burly guys get into a scuffle. They knock over a chair and wrestle around on the floor. Patrons back away from their skirmish. I rise, prepared to intervene. The pair hug and make up, saving me the hassle.

My mother's friend, Charlie, ambles through the door and straddles a stool at the end of the bar. I go over and say hello.

"Have you made any progress on your mother's case?"

"The crime lab retested some fingerprints and hair strands but didn't turn up any matches."

"That's too bad. Dede deserves justice."

"My father may be living in Troy."

"I thought I spotted Marty at a gas station in that area a few years back. But the guy drove away before I got a good look at his face." Charlie sips his beer. "Are you planning on tracking him down?"

"He abandoned us. I can't forgive that."

"Your father didn't abandon you kids. He left your mom. Dede was my best friend, but she could be a handful." Charlie calls Tanner over and orders a shot of tequila, which he knocks back. "Marty put up with a lot from Dede."

"He walked out on his family."

"You should think about giving your dad a second chance."

Chief Jimenez ambles through the door. Sergeant Reeves and Officer Washington follow her inside.

"I can't believe you talked me into going to a gay bar," Sergeant Reeves says.

"Relax, Reeves," Chief Jimenez says. "You're not as hot as you think."

"I don't hear the ladies complaining."

"Because you're out the door too fast."

"I've been dating Roxie for a month now."

"I'm not into girl-on-girl action, but the drinks in this joint are cheap," Officer Washington says. "And I don't have to worry about guys like Prince Charmless here hitting on me."

"In your dreams," Officer Reeves says.

"I would eat you alive, Reeves. Now tell the man what you want to drink. He doesn't have all night."

Trevor Speedman joins us at the bar.

"Sergeant Reeves, I had no idea you were a friend of Dorothy's."

"Huh?"

"Back off, Trevor," I say. "Reeves isn't gay."

"Too bad," Trevor says. "I've got a weakness for men in uniform."

I don't believe I've ever seen Reeves blush before.

Chief Jimenez orders a round for the team.

"That Gladys Crabtree is a menace," Officer Washington says.

"What did Gladys do now?" Chief Jimenez asks.

"She turned left on a red light and damn near ran me over."

"One of these days, that woman is going to hurt someone."

Marta arrives. She gives the chief a kiss and commences complaining about her co-workers at the salon where she styles hair. The chief leans in and asks me if I've made any progress on the case. I shake my head.

Several guys buy Sergeant Reeves drinks. He basks in the attention, until he realizes what they expect in return. Officer Washington laughs at the dumbfounded expression on his goofy mug.

A tall woman with broad shoulders and kinky ginger curls asks Officer Washington if she would like to dance. Washington accepts but adds the caveat that she's not gay.

"The Boy is Mine" plays on the jukebox. I take Demetrius by the hand and lead him onto the dance floor. He spins me around. I do my best not to step on his feet.

Chief Jimenez and Marta finish their drinks and take off.

Demetrius asks if I'm hungry.

"Starving."

"Maestro's Pizza is open until ten o'clock. We could grab a pie and go back to my place."

"Sounds like a plan."

———

DEMETRIUS and I curl up on his couch and watch a nature program about the secret lives of elephants while we devour a large sausage and mushroom pizza. Flower crouches on the floor. His droopy eyes rove between the pizza box and our plates. He drools and licks his chops.

"Flower looks so sad," I say.

"No human food."

"One little bite won't kill him."

"No."

"Sorry, Flower. Your mean old dad said no."

"Eat that last slice of pizza," Demetrius says. "I'm full."

The elephant herd on the television encircles one of their fallen comrades and stomps their feet. Their trunks unfurl, and they roar. Their enormous eyes tear. They're mourning, something I never realized elephants did.

There's a knock at the door. I sit up.

"Are you expecting someone?

Demetrius shakes his head. I grab my weapon, sidle up to the door, and peek out the window.

"Seriously?"

"Who's there?" Demetrius asks.

I open the door and take a step back.

"I'm sorry to bother you guys," Trevor says. "But I messed up."

"What did you do?" Demetrius asks.

"I feel so stupid. When I booked my bungalow, I gave the owner the wrong date for my departure. Long story short. I don't have anywhere to sleep tonight."

Trevor Speedman is like herpes. He never goes away.

"You're welcome to the couch," Demetrius says.

"How can I ever thank you?" Trevor says with more than a hint of innuendo in his tone.

"What time is your flight?" I ask.

"One o'clock tomorrow afternoon."

"Let me grab you a pillow and some blankets," Demetrius says.

"The night is young," Trevor says.

"Some of us have to work in the morning," I say.

"Party pooper."

"Here you go," Demetrius says.

"Do you have any booze?"

"Would you like a beer?"

"If that's all you've got."

Demetrius tosses Trevor a can from the refrigerator, and he and I turn in for the night.

Lying in bed, my thoughts race between wondering how I'm going to solve this case and whether I should look up my father. Demetrius's snoring soothes me. He brushes against my back. I roll over and recoil.

"What the hell are you doing, Trevor?"

"You know what they say," Trevor says. "Two's company, three's a party."

My eyes rove over Trevor's body.

Demetrius wakes up. "What's going on?" He leaps out of bed, snapping me out of my momentary lapse in judgment. "Trevor, get back on the couch. Now!"

"And stay there," I add.

"You two are so uptight," Trevor says. He adjusts his member inside his briefs and swaggers out the door. There was a time not so long ago that I would've tapped that so fast. Sometimes I don't recognize myself anymore.

Demetrius locks the door. Our eyes meet. We crack up laughing.

CHAPTER THIRTY-FOUR

FRIDAY MORNING, I relieve Officer Lecoq. He shares a printout of the information he's unearthed on Bill Sinclair. The eldest son of a wealthy family, Sinclair grew up in Darien, Connecticut, and attended Yale University and later New York University for graduate school. A financial wizard, by the age of thirty he was managing one of the most successful hedge funds in the world. He's faced several lawsuits over the years but never suffered a major legal loss. The only blemish on his record seems to have been an unsubstantiated accusation of sexual misconduct his senior year at Yale.

"I've got a buddy in Ohio who's a cop," Officer Lecoq says. "We met at the Ohio National Poultry Show a few years back. He's asking around about Rose Ryland. Patricia Sylvester was born and raised in Buffalo.

"Good work, Lecoq." I pass him the Sinclairs's attorney's business card. "Maybe give this guy a call. See what you can learn."

"Will do."

"And while you're at it, see if you can find anything on Vona, the Sinclairs's housekeeper."

Suki shouts that I have a call on line two. She refuses to use the intercom. I press the blinking button and answer.

"I have the results on that syrup you brought me," Kaden says. "My tests revealed lethal levels of atropine, scopolamine, and hyoscyamine, which aren't found in elderberries."

It's clear now that Bill Sinclair and Oliver Crispin were poisoned. I grab the keys to the squad car and take off.

On my drive up the mountainside, I encounter a familiar Ford Escort parked in front of Rose and Trixie's farm with its hood raised. Rose leans over the engine, inspecting a loose hose, while Vona paces the front lawn, fretting she's going to be late for work.

"What seems to be the problem here?" I ask.

"I'm not sure yet," Rose says. She wipes her greasy hands on a rag. "Could be a faulty fuel pump or a clogged fuel line. Or these filthy spark plugs. Let me wipe them off, and then we'll see if she turns over."

Papa Frank taught me how to change spark plugs and oil filters, but I don't have a clue how to replace a faulty fuel pump or clean the fuel line.

"You're quite the mechanic, Rose."

"I paid my way through nursing school by working in an automotive repair shop."

"Is that where you met Trixie?"

"Heaven's no." Trixie strides up and wipes her hands on her overalls. "I was living with my now ex-husband in Buffalo at that time."

"You were married?"

"Nine of the longest months of my life."

I am reminded how little I know about the people in this town. I've only been home for a year now. In many ways, I'm still on the outside looking in.

"Trixie and I met at a fundraiser for the Catskill Forest Preserve," Rose says.

"You're not from around here?"

"I was a military brat," Rose says. "My dad got transferred a lot. But I lived in Ohio for years before moving back east."

"Why New York?"

"I thought the people here would be more open-minded," Rose says. "But there are assholes everywhere."

"You should check the battery cables," Trixie says.

"I did," Rose says.

I whisper to Vona, "You and I need to talk."

"I haven't done anything wrong."

"The crime lab found lethal amounts of atropine, scopolamine, and hyoscyamine in the elderberry syrup you brewed. Doctors found those same toxins in Mr. Sinclair's system. Toxins that are not found in elderberries."

"What does that have to do with me?"

"You brewed the syrup we tested."

"Like Mrs. Sinclair told me to do."

"Did you steal a bag of belladonna berries from Padma Patel?"

"I have never set foot in that woman's shop."

"She is missing a bag of belladonna berries. Belladonna contains atropine, scopolamine, and hyoscyamine, the toxins found in the syrup you brewed."

"Mrs. Sinclair told me to use the berries in her freezer, and that's what I did."

"Bill Sinclair died after drinking the toxic syrup you brewed. A jury might consider that manslaughter."

"I followed Mrs. Sinclair's instructions. Boiled two bags of berries from the freezer in water. Added honey and a slice of fresh ginger root. Simmered the mixture for forty-five minutes. Let it cool. Strained into their bottles. Same as I always do."

"You'd brewed elderberry syrup for Mrs. Sinclair before?"

"Whenever she slipped out of the house for a little afternoon delight with that arrogant jerk of an actor, she would ask me to do the cooking."

"So you knew Mrs. Sinclair was having an affair with Oliver Crispin?"

"She didn't exactly hide her infidelity," Vona says. "That's how Mr. Sinclair caught her."

"What happened when he found out?"

"He yelled and stomped his feet so hard the walls shook and the china in the hutch rattled. He said he should've known better than to marry an actress because they're all sluts and whores. Mrs. Sinclair swore the affair meant nothing. I heard a heavy thud, like maybe she'd fallen."

"Did you check on her?"

"Mr. Sinclair would've . . . I have my kids to think about."

"Here's your problem," Rose says. "Your ground strap slipped loose. Give me a minute." She tightens the part back into position. "Give her a go now."

Vona slides behind the wheel and turns the key in the ignition. The engine rumbles to life.

"You better get going," Rose says. "You don't want to piss off Daphne."

Vona casts a furtive glance in my direction and drives away.

"What is this?" Rose crouches and picks up what at first glance appears to be a grape. But upon closer examination, it is a smashed berry.

"It looks like an elderberry," Rose says.

"It must've fallen off of Vona's shoe."

"She may have stepped on the berry while she was pacing around our yard," Trixie says.

"I suppose," Rose says.

Could Vona have poisoned Rose and Trixie's flock? A smashed berry on the ground doesn't give me just cause to search her vehicle. I'm grasping at straws.

Daphne's older sister answers the door when I arrive and passes me another business card for the Sinclairs's attorney.

"It's urgent that I speak with Mrs. Sinclair."

"My sister is resting."

"Wake her up."

"I beg your pardon?"

"We have evidence that Mr. Sinclair was poisoned."

"My sister—"

"That's okay, Phoebe. If someone poisoned Bill, I want to help in any way I can."

"I hate to bother you," I say, "but time is of the essence."

Daphne gestures for me to follow her into the living room. She tightens the belt of her bathrobe and fluffs her tangled curls. She looks a mess.

"Would you like a drink?"

"I'm on duty."

"That doesn't answer my question." Daphne pours two bourbons, hands me one, and plops down on the couch.

"Perhaps we could speak in private," I say.

"Anything you have to say, officer, you can—"

"Take a walk, Phoebe," Daphne says.

Phoebe glares at me and marches out of the room.

Daphne takes a long gulp of bourbon and says, "What is this about poison?

"Mom's coming tonight!" A young woman bounds into the living room. "I'm sorry, I didn't realize—"

"Officer Nowak is investigating Bill's death, Chloe."

"Bill died of a heart attack, right?"

"He may have been poisoned," I say.

Daphne's eyes well with tears. My heart aches for her.

"Chloe, go watch television."

"Okay."

Chloe shrugs her shoulders and skips out the door.

"My little sister can be a pain, but I'm glad she came. And Phoebe means well. I'm grateful she's here."

"The lab tested that bottle of elderberry syrup you gave me."

"And?"

Daphne leans forward. She seems eager to hear the results. I don't spot the hint of a tell that she already knows the answer.

"It contained more than elderberries."

"I don't understand."

"Padma Patel is missing a bag of belladonna berries. Witnesses saw you searching through her freezer."

"We often keep frozen treats in there."

"You said you were looking for ice."

"Well, that explains it."

"There was ice on the table."

"What are you suggesting, Cal?"

"I'm going to ask you a question, Daphne, and I need you to be honest with me."

"I don't have anything to hide."

"Did you steal a bag of belladonna berries from Padma Patel?"

"Why would I—?"

"The elderberry syrup Vona brewed contained lethal levels of the toxins found in belladonna."

"How can that be?"

"I was hoping you could tell me."

"You think I—?"

"You had access to the belladonna berries. You were having an affair with Oliver Crispin. He promised he would introduce you to his Hollywood agent. The way I figure it, you needed your husband's money so you could run away together."

"My husband left me this house and a modest monthly allowance. Most of his estate goes to the Star of Hope Foundation for orphaned children in India."

"Why India?"

"I never asked."

"Why not?"

"I wasn't sure I wanted to know the answer."

"Call me if you think of anything else I should know."

My spidey sense tells me Daphne is being truthful, which leaves me even more confused than I was before I paid her a visit.

On the drive back to town, Officer Lecoq radios and tells me to meet him at the diner. Ten minutes later, I slide into a corner booth and order a cup of black coffee. Lecoq orders an iced tea. He dumps three packets of sugar into the glass and stirs so vigorously he sloshes a few dribbles over the rim.

"What have you got for me?" I ask.

"My buddy in Ohio called me back," Officer Lecoq says. "You are not going to believe this." He leans in and whispers, "Rose Ryland cared for an elderly man who died under suspicious circumstances. The medical examiner ultimately concluded the cause of death to be an accidental morphine overdose. But the detectives my buddy spoke with think she deliberately offed the old guy."

"Are you freaking serious? What happened?"

"The old guy overdosed while under her care."

Rose and I need to have a chat.

"There's more. I searched through the student records at Yale University. In 1958, a girl accused William Jessup Sinclair of sexual assault. The Sinclair family made a substantial contribution to the school and the board of directors dismissed the case."

I would say I'm surprised, but men of Bill Sinclair's stature often abuse their power.

"What became of the girl?"

"She dropped out of school."

"Damn fine work, Lecoq."

Officer Lecoq's ears flush. "I'm pretty good at researching stuff, I suppose." He idly stirs his drink.

"You're sharper than most of the guys I worked with at the NYPD, Lecoq. And I'm not just blowing smoke up your ass."

"I left a message for the Sinclairs's attorney." Officer Lecoq shakes ice from his glass into his mouth. "I'll see what I can dig up on the housekeeper tonight."

At the station, I toss Sergeant Reeves the keys to the squad car. He tells me to have a seat.

"The chief filled me in. We don't have much time before we're going to have to hand this case over to the sheriff and his boys."

"I'm making progress."

"What can I do to help? Don't look at me like I'm crazy. I don't want the county taking over our investigation."

"Our investigation?"

"If you say someone murdered Sinclair, Nowak, that's good enough for me. Now let's nail the bastard."

CHAPTER THIRTY-FIVE

SATURDAY MORNING, the chief calls me into her office. "The clock is ticking, Nowak. What have you found?"

"When Bill Sinclair died, he had lethal amounts of the toxins found in belladonna in his system. The elderberry syrup I confiscated from the Sinclairs's bar contained the same toxins. Best guess, Padma Patel's missing berries ended up in that bottle." I lean back in my chair. "But how? That's the question. Daphne had the means, motive, and opportunity, but her grief seems sincere, unlike her acting."

Chief Jimenez chuckles.

"Rose Ryland and Trixie Sylvester had access to the berries, and they are engaged in an ongoing feud with the Sinclairs. Helena Potter could have taken the berries, but I can't think why she would want Bill Sinclair dead. And she was sleeping with Oliver Crispin."

"That gringo got around."

"The Sinclairs's housekeeper, Vona, brewed the toxic syrup using the frozen berries that Daphne told her to use."

"But no one saw Daphne take the berries?"

"If they did, they're not saying."

"We need proof."

"Rose Ryland used to be a home health aide when she lived in Ohio. An elderly man under her care died under suspicious circumstances. A judge acquitted her, but the detectives who worked the case believe she gave the old man the wrong dose on purpose."

"Good work, Nowak."

"Lecoq did the computer research."

"I didn't approve that."

"He wanted to ask you first, but I suggested that wasn't necessary."

"You did what?"

"And I told him not to tell you."

"The mayor wants me to hand this case off to the sheriff," Chief Jimenez says. She leans forward. "I had to grovel before that awful woman to buy you another day."

"It won't happen again."

"Yeah, right." Chief Jimenez shakes her head. "You're dismissed." On my way out the door, she adds, "Bungle this investigation, Nowak, and I won't be able to save your job."

The medical examiner ruled Crispin's death an overdose. I could've walked away from the case then, but I didn't, and now that Bill Sinclair has been poisoned, there's no turning back. The details of the case are sketchy at best, and the clock is ticking. What have I gotten myself into?

Sergeant Reeves invites me to ride along. I'm beat, but I'm not going to sleep tonight with my career hanging in the balance. I climb inside the squad car. We pull into the drive-thru at the Jukebox Junction and order cheeseburgers with fries and jumbo-sized black coffees. I normally hate when Reeves eats in the car because he never cleans up after himself, but I've got more important things to worry about tonight.

Folk music fans crowd the restaurants and shops along Main Street. Musicians performing in this weekend's festival sign autographs on the sidewalks outside.

Suki radios that Daphne Sinclair spotted a prowler on her property again. Sergeant Reeves hits the gas. We speed through town with our lights flashing, cruise up the mountainside past Rose and Trixie's place, and screech to a halt in front of the Sinclair mansion.

Daphne answers the door and invites us inside. "My sisters went into town for groceries." She leads us into the living room. Sergeant Reeves plops down in a plush white armchair. I elect to stand.

"Those witches down the mountain keep bothering me," Daphne says.

"Are you talking about Rose and Trixie?" I ask.

"The tall, bony-ass lesbian walks across the property all the time."

"Trixie is your prowler?"

"She's spying on me."

"Why would she do that?" Sergeant Reeves asks.

"She and her partner think Bill and I poisoned their livestock."

"Did you?"

"Are you seriously asking me that question?"

"Well?"

"I would never hurt an animal."

"Your husband was accused of sexual assault when he was a student at Yale," I say. "Did you know that?"

"What does that have to do with anything?"

"So, you did know."

"This desperate girl falsely accused Bill of rape after he'd dumped her."

"Is that what he told you?"

"He said she was the sort of girl who went to college to catch a rich husband."

"Did he now?"

"If you're not going to help me, I'd appreciate it if you'd leave."

"We'll have a word with Rose and Trixie," I say.

"You'll believe whatever they say."

"Did you poison their chickens?"

"I've already answered that question, Cal. Now, I'd appreciate it if you and Oakley would get out of my house."

"We'll be going, Daphne," Sergeant Reeves says. "You take care now."

On our way down the mountain, we stop by Rose and Trixie's farm. Rose invites us inside and serves us freshly squeezed limeades. "If you're wondering why your drinks are cloudy, I muddled some sour cherries in the bottom of your glasses."

Sergeant Reeves takes a sip. "Dang, that's good!"

"Raccoons dug through our garbage cans last night," Trixie says when she joins us. She dries her hands on a dish towel. "I've been cleaning up the mess the varmints left behind."

Pests in the country, like raccoons and skunks, may be annoying, but at least they're cute. In the city, I battled rats and roaches. Those are nasty creatures.

"Last week, a bear made off with one of Jude Hewes's trash cans."

"We chain our cans to the rack and lock down the lids," Rose says. "But the darn nuisances always figure their way inside."

"We just came from the Sinclairs's house," I say.

"How is Daphne holding up?" Rose asks.

"Hard to say."

"We received a report of a prowler on the Sinclairs's property again," Sergeant Reeves says.

"That woman is a piece of work," Rose says.

"Did either of you walk across the Sinclairs's property this morning?" I ask.

"I hiked up to the peak," Trixie says.

"That doesn't answer my question."

"I might have cut across their backyard."

"Why would you do that?" I ask.

"That's where the path runs."

"Don't make us arrest you for trespassing, Trixie," Sergeant Reeves says.

"Fine. I'll walk around their lot."

On the drive back to town, Sergeant Reeves asks me what's going on between Rose and Trixie and the Sinclairs. I share what I know about their ongoing feud.

"Have you made any progress on the investigation into Bill Sinclair's murder?"

"Daphne seems to be our most obvious suspect," I say. "But Vona brewed the poisonous syrup."

"That's a problem for her."

Suzi radios that there's been another incident at the Roadhouse.

"Hold on, Nowak!" Sergeant Reeves makes a U-turn, tires squealing, and speeds toward the scene. We arrive to find Luke and Jordan visibly shaken and ask the preppy couple what happened.

"A bunch of rednecks almost ran us over," Luke says.

"They came this close to hitting Luke," Jordan says. He indicates an inch or so with his fingers.

Gunner brings Luke and Jordan bottles of water.

"Appreciate the gesture, man," Luke says. He takes a gulp and wipes his mouth on his sleeve. "I'm still shaking." He holds out his hand. His manicured fingers tremble.

"Me, too," Jordan says.

"What sort of vehicle were these guys driving?" Sergeant Reeves asks.

"A tricked-out pickup truck," Luke says. "Bright lights. A big steel bar running up the side and over the cab."

"Make? Model?"

"We don't know one brand of pickup from another."

"It was big and white."

"Did you catch the license plate?"

Luke looks at Jordan. Jordan shakes his head.

"It all happened so fast," Luke says.

"Did you see the driver?" I ask.

"Little white guy with stringy hair."

"Wayne Gerber and his thugs," I say. "It's not the first time."

"Won't likely be the last, either," Gunner says. "Why don't you guys come inside and have a drink on the house?"

"We're too shaken up," Luke says.

"I'm sorry you had to go through this experience, fellas," Sergeant Reeves says. "Our little town is usually more welcoming."

"We're going to catch these guys," I say.

Gunner walks Luke and Jordan to their car, and the preppy couple drives away.

"Have a drink on me, boys," Gunner says.

"I'm on duty," Sergeant Reeves says. "But I'll take one of those bottles of water if you don't mind.

Sergeant Reeves and I follow Gunner into the Roadhouse. Four young guys shoot darts. Two older women make out in a corner booth.

Gunner passes me and Sergeant Reeves bottles of water. My phone rings. I recognize Demetrius's number and am about to answer when tires screech through the parking lot outside. Reeves and I rush out the door. Wayne Gerber's turbocharged Chevy Baja speeds away. Gerber and his redneck buddies whoop and holler homophobic slurs, which pisses me off. As they veer out onto the road, they clip the bumper of a passing car.

"Let's go, Nowak."

Sergeant Reeves leaps inside the squad car. I hop inside the passenger seat and haven't even closed my door yet when the sergeant floors the accelerator. We fishtail out of the parking lot. The taillights of the Chevy Baja flicker through the trees ahead, which overhang either side of the road. We wind our way through a series of curves in the road. Reeves is a better driver than me, although I'd never tell him that.

Gerber drifts into the oncoming traffic lane and speeds past a semi-truck. He swerves back into the right lane, narrowly avoiding a head-on collision with another pickup. The semi-truck pulls over onto the shoulder. We speed past. I radio Suki and apprise her of our location. Gerber brakes behind a slow-moving van. Oncoming traffic prevents him from passing on the left, so he veers onto the shoulder and narrowly escapes landing in the ravine.

Once the left lane clears, Sergeant Reeves floors the accelerator. The speedometer on the squad car crests a hundred miles per hour and continues to climb. We round the next bend. Gerber veers into the left lane. Reeves stays on his tail. Gerber turns sharply across the right lane and exits toward Ellenville.

"Shit!" Sergeant Reeves exclaims. He drifts onto the exit ramp, bouncing over the curb, and merges onto the highway. I radio Suki we're traveling south on the highway now. The road ahead winds through the woods. The taillights of the Chevy Baja fade and reappear. A semi-truck approaches from the opposite direction. Its horn blares. Gerber veers into the right lane and loses control. The Chevy Baja goes airborne and crashes into a ditch.

Sergeant Reeves pulls over, leaps out, and draws his weapon. "Show me your hands! Hands! Now!" He advances. I follow his lead.

Gerber sticks his hands out the driver's side window. His passengers crawl out their side and flee. My mouth goes dry at the thought of pursuing the pair into the dark woods, but I have a job to do. I whip out my flashlight and give chase. The obese passenger trips over his pants, which keep slipping down, and lands on his face in the dirt.

Sergeant Reeves shouts from behind me, "Hands behind your back! Now!" He tells me to cuff the guy, which I do. "Take this idiot away," he says, and he runs after the other guy. I haul our prisoner onto his feet, pull up his pants, and march his ass back to the squad car.

Wayne Gerber sits handcuffed in the backseat. I shove his buddy in beside him.

"What were you thinking, you fool?" Sergeant Reeves drags a grungy little guy out of the woods. "Get over here." The guy whines that he hasn't done anything wrong. Reeves shoves him into the squad car beside his buddies.

A state trooper pulls over. We fill him in. Another trooper arrives. We surrender jurisdiction and let them handle the paperwork. By the time we transfer our prisoners, it's three o'clock in the morning, and I can barely keep my eyes open.

CHAPTER THIRTY-SIX

ANNIE SHAKES MY SHOULDERS. I sit up in bed and rub my eyes. "What's up?"

"Sorry to wake you," Annie says. "But you have a phone call."

I leap out of bed. Annie passes me the cordless receiver. I grunt hello.

"Nowak?"

"What's up, Lecoq?"

"I tried your mobile phone, but you didn't answer."

"Sorry about that."

I glance at my cellular phone screen. I have seven voicemails.

"Padma Patel does not own the Sacred Root Apothecary."

"What?"

"I couldn't find any information on Padma Patel, so I pulled a copy of the lease on her shop, and it's signed by Maya Kumar."

"Who's that?"

"I'm not sure. But the girl who accused Bill Sinclair of sexual assault at Yale, who seems to have vanished after she left school, was named Mayra Kumar."

"Mayra, not Maya?"

"That's right. Wait until you see what else I've found. I'll show you when you get to the station."

"I'm on my way."

As I dash out the door, Annie shoves a cup of coffee into my hand and tells me to be careful. I check my voicemail. Demetrius called five times last night. He's worried about me, and I know why. I should've called. Someone left a garbled message from an unknown number. My last message came from Lecoq this morning.

When I reach the station, I find Lecoq seated behind his desk, staring at his computer screen. He gestures for me to have a look. I peer over his shoulder.

"You found Padma?"

"That's not Padma," Officer Lecoq says. "That's a photograph of Mayra Kumar from her senior year at Yale University."

"You're shitting me." The image on the screen is the spitting image of a young Padma Patel. "Find out whatever you can about this Mayra Kumar."

Vona walks through the door. Her eyes flit around the station. I ask what brings her by.

"I left you a message earlier, but you didn't call me back."

That must've been the garbled voicemail I received.

"I'm listening now."

"I didn't poison Mr. Sinclair," Vona says. She glances over her shoulder and whispers, "But I wouldn't be surprised if Mrs. Sinclair did."

"Why do you say that?"

"Mr. Sinclair was a bad man."

"How so?"

"Like I told you before, he hit Mrs. Sinclair a lot. Called her stupid. Said all her talent was in her tits. Mean stuff like that."

"Why didn't you come forward before now?"

Vona blanches.

"Because Mr. Sinclair held a gun to my head and said he'd kill me and my kids if I told anyone what I'd seen." Vona is trembling. "He would have, too. I don't doubt that for a moment. But that evil son-of-a-bitch is dead now. He can't hurt me or anyone else."

"You brewed the syrup that killed Bill Sinclair."

"With the berries Mrs. Sinclair told me to use. Which I'll bet she stole from Miss Patel."

"Do you have any evidence of that?"

"All I know is I used the berries from the freezer that Mrs. Sinclair told me to use."

"Walk me through everything you did that morning."

"I dropped my kids off at my sister's house, like I do every day. Probably got to work around eight o'clock. Soon after I arrived, Padma Patel brought Mrs. Sinclair a bottle of frankincense and told her if she sniffed the oil or placed a few drops under her nose, it would relieve her anxiety."

Perhaps Daphne befriended Padma Patel so she could find a natural means of slowly poisoning her husband. No one would have suspected foul play had Crispin not foolishly drunk a large dose of the syrup and died a miserable death.

"Padma Patel offered to water Mrs. Sinclair's garden. Mrs. Sinclair thanked the woman and rushed out the door, a bundle of nerves because her show opened that night."

"What did you do after she left?"

"Made breakfast for Mr. Sinclair—two soft-boiled eggs with dry toast."

No wonder the man stayed so fit, for all the good it did him in the end.

"That same morning, Mr. Sinclair got into a fight with that tall lesbian who lives down the mountain."

"Patricia Sylvester?"

"I don't know her name."

"What did they argue about?"

"Her trespassing on his property."

I'm not surprised.

"Is that when you brewed the syrup?"

"I washed the breakfast dishes first, made the Sinclairs's bed, and cleaned the bathrooms, upstairs and down. Then, I brewed the syrup."

"Did you try the batch you made?"

"No way. That shit tastes nasty."

"Anything else?"

"The other lesbian—the short, tough one—she came over before I left to take the syrup to Mrs. Sinclair at the theater, and she and Mr. Sinclair screamed at each other. She told him he'd better leave her wife alone, or he was going to be sorry." Vona snickers. "What a joke, right? Two women can't get married."

"What did Mr. Sinclair do?"

"He told her to get the hell off his property."

"What did she do?"

"She left."

"Anything else?"

Vona shakes her head. "I should go. Mrs. Sinclair docks my pay when I'm late." She rushes out the door.

I grab the keys to the squad car and hit the road.

———

A DISHEVELED DAPHNE answers the door and invites me inside. Her bloodshot eyes look swollen from crying. She offers me coffee, which I accept, and I follow her into the living room. We sit on the couch and sip our brew, which tastes hot and strong.

"I'll cut to the chase," I say. "Someone poisoned your husband with the elderberry syrup your housekeeper brewed. She says you gave her the berries."

"I froze a few bags of the berries I harvested last fall."

"The crime lab found belladonna in the syrup. How could that be?"

"I don't have a clue," Daphne says.

"You and your husband had a contentious relationship."

"We had our disagreements. What couple doesn't?"

"From what I heard, these disagreements often became loud and violent."

"Vona has a big mouth." Daphne sets her cup and saucer on the table beside her. "My husband had his faults, Cal. Show me a man who doesn't. But he treated me like a queen . . . before I messed things up."

"You were spotted rummaging through Padma Patel's freezer."

"I did not steal those berries."

"Mrs. Sinclair, I finished changing the beds," Vona says. "I'm going to do the laundry now." She sees me and flushes. "I didn't realize you had company. I'm sorry." She rushes out of the room.

"You should be interrogating Vona. She brewed the syrup that killed my husband."

"Why would Vona want to poison your husband?"

"Ask her."

"I did," I say. "One of you is lying."

"Quit wasting time and find out who poisoned my husband."

"I may be looking at her."

"Am I under arrest?"

"Not yet."

"Then get out of my house."

Daphne shows me the door.

———

AFTER KNOCKING on Rose and Trixie's door several times and receiving no answer, I wall around behind their farmhouse. They aren't there either, but I surprise a family of raccoons digging through the garbage cans. The startled creatures hiss at me and scurry off into the woods, leaving trash strewn around the ground.

As I set the garbage cans back in their rack, I spot an empty plastic food storage bag under the corner of the house that's stained purple. I lean closer and notice the words "belladonna berries" written across the label. I retrieve a pair of gloves and the digital camera from the squad car, snap wide shots of the location that capture the address on the mailbox, and shoot close-ups of the evidence before confiscating the bag.

Trixie and Rose pull into the driveway in their catering van. Trixie climbs out from behind the wheel and shouts, "You looking for us, Cal?" She gathers an armload of grocery bags from the cargo hold. "Come inside."

"You both attended the meeting where Padma showed you her belladonna plant, right?"

"Yes," Rose says. "Why do you ask?"

"Trixie, did you see Daphne take the belladonna berries out of Padma's freezer?"

"No."

"But you were there that night?"

"Yes. Why?"

"It's not important. Thank you for your time."

Trixie knows Daphne grows elderberries in her garden. She attended the meeting where Padma Patel discussed the nightshade family of plants and showed everyone where she kept the belladonna berries. Trixie has trespassed on the Sinclairs's property numerous times. Perhaps she stole the belladonna berries and planted them in the Sinclairs's freezer. Why else would the empty bag be found in her trash?

At the Sacred Roots Apothecary, Padma Patel greets me with a smile. "Officer Nowak, what brings you by?"

"Do you recognize this?" I set the food storage bag I confiscated on the counter.

"Is this your missing bag?"

"Where did you—?"

"Is it yours?"

Padma nods.

"Are you certain?"

"See how the double L's connect with that curve? That's my handwriting."

"Who do you think took your berries?"

"Like I told you, Rose used the freezer for her sorbet. But I didn't see her take anything that wasn't hers."

"Helena mentioned seeing Daphne digging through the freezer."

"She may have been searching for ice."

"Don't you keep a bucket on the refreshments table?"

"Daphne gets confused when she drinks."

"You were drinking that night?"

"Daphne brought a couple of bottles of chardonnay that everyone shared. I only took a sip. I am not much of a drinker."

"Besides discussing natural remedies and such, you gossip about your lives, right?"

"We are women, after all."

"Did Daphne ever discuss her marriage?"

"Of course. Rose and Trixie sometimes talked about their relationship too. I do not have a husband yet. But I will one day, and then I will complain."

"Did Daphne ever disclose that her husband hit her?"

"I noticed she had bruises on her face a few times, but I am not a person who pries into the personal lives of other people."

"Did you know Daphne when you lived in the city?"

"We only met after I moved to Nyes Landing."

"What brought you here?"

"A change of pace from the rat race of the city."

"Who do you think took your berries?"

"I cannot imagine any of my friends stealing from me. But I suppose any one of them could have taken the berries."

That is no help. If Vona is telling the truth about the abuse she witnessed in the Sinclair home, then Daphne may have wanted her husband dead. Rose and Trixie have a beef with the Sinclairs, and I found the food storage bag on their property. It seems more and more probable that Crispin was never the target and died because of his own foolishness.

"You look tired, Officer Nowak."

Padma fetches a small brown vial off a shelf along the wall. She unscrews the lid and wafts the scent under my nose. I inhale a camphorous whiff. My eyes water.

"Eucalyptus oil. Sniff the bottle or dab a few drops on your neck or chest when you are feeling mentally or physically exhausted." Padma passes me the vial and a bottle of pills. "And take two of these a few minutes before bedtime."

"What are they?"

"Melatonin," Padma says. "A natural hormone for regulating sleep cycles."

Feeling refreshed and energized, I leave determined to find out how Padma's belladonna berries ended up in the elderberry syrup Vona brewed.

CHAPTER THIRTY-SEVEN

WHEN I REACH Rose and Trixie's farmhouse, I find the couple weeding their garden. They rise and brush the dirt off their hands.

"What brings you back so soon, Cal?" Rose asks.

I hold up an evidence bag containing the empty storage bag labeled "belladonna berries."

"Would you mind telling me why I found this near your garbage cans?"

"A food storage bag?" Rose says. "We must go through hundreds of those every month."

"Do you write 'belladonna berries' on them?"

Rose and Trixie take a closer look.

"I've never seen that before," Trixie says.

"Padma Patel confirmed the bag came from her freezer."

"I should've kept my mouth shut," Rose mutters under her breath.

"I beg your pardon?"

"I had a brush with the law in Ohio," Rose says. "I shared that information with the other women in the group."

"Was this when you were working as a home health care aide?"

Rose nods.

"You were accused of malpractice, right?"

"I did not kill that man," Rose says. "But I suppose I aided and abetted. He was in so much pain from the cancer that was eating him up from the inside out."

"What did you do?"

"Before I retired to my room that night, I left the bottle of morphine tablets and a glass of his favorite scotch whiskey on his night table. He took his own life that night. I lost my license for gross negligence."

"How do you explain this bag being in your trash?"

"I can't," Rose says. She slouches in defeat. "Am I under arrest?"

"Not yet."

"Then I'd appreciate it if you'd leave."

I return to the Sinclairs's house. Vona answers the door on my first ring of the bell.

"Mrs. Sinclair is not to be disturbed."

"I need to ask you a question."

Vona slips outside onto the porch and eases the door shut behind her.

"I've told you everything I know."

"Did you ever see Trixie or Rose set foot inside the Sinclairs's house?"

"Mrs. Sinclair invited the lesbians over for tea once as a peace offering, but that backfired."

"How so?"

"The meeting descended into a screaming match before the lesbos stormed out."

"I gather you don't like Trixie and Rose."

"I don't approve of their lifestyle."

"But that didn't stop you from taking advantage of their hospitality when your car broke down."

"They offered. What was I supposed to do?"

"Some people might look down on your lifestyle."

"What does that mean?"

"Aren't you on public assistance?"

"For my children, sure."

"Thank you for your time."

—————

THE MOMENT I step through the door of the station, Chief Jimenez shouts, "Nowak! My office. Pronto!" I dash down the hallway. "Close the door," she says. I do so. "Sit." I slide onto the chair before her desk. She leans back and folds her arms across her chest. "The mayor stopped by earlier. She's pressuring me to call the sheriff."

"Officer Lecoq and I have made progress," I say, and I share what we know.

"More circumstantial evidence."

"I just need to connect the dots."

"Is that all?"

"Don't call the sheriff."

"I already did. He's fly fishing today. But tomorrow, you must hand off the case."

Chief Jimenez's phone rings. "Mayor Miller, to what do I owe the pleasure?" The chief dismisses me with a wave of her hand.

If we don't wrap up this case today, I'm toast. What am I missing here?

Officer Lecoq calls me over to his desk.

"I found Maya Kumar." He jiggles his mouse. His computer screen lights up. An image of Padma Patel appears on the screen.

"Shit," I say.

I grab the keys to the squad car and rush out the door.

—————

WHEN I ARRIVE at the Sacred Root Apothecary, Padma Patel is assisting two women. I feign interest in a shelf of decorative candles. Padma shows the women the door and faces me.

"Have you caught the thief who stole my berries?"

"Are you sure they were stolen?"

"They are missing, are they not?"

"You haven't lived here long, have you?"

"I moved here and opened my shop last year."

"What brought you to Nyes Landing?"

"A change of pace."

"From where?"

"The city."

"Is that where you're from?"

"I grew up in India," Padma says. "But I earned my business degree from New York University."

"Bill Sinclair attended NYU for graduate school," I say.

The vein in Padma's temple twitches.

"Before that, he attended Yale University."

Another twinge from Padma.

"If you'll excuse me, officer, I have work to do."

"Have you always been interested in nature?"

"My mother died soon after I was born. My great-aunt raised me. She taught me Ayurveda, an ancient system of medicine that focuses on herbal remedies."

My heart goes out to Padma.

"How well do you know the Sinclairs?"

"I met Daphne the day I opened my shop. She came in seeking remedies for her husband's aging heart."

"So, you knew Bill Sinclair?"

"As Daphne's husband, yes."

"I appreciate your help."

As soon as I get back to the squad car, I radio Suki. She patches me through to Officer Lecoq.

"Find out what became of Mayra Kumar after she dropped out of school."

"I'm one step ahead of you, Nowak. Mayra Kumar returned home to India. After that, she vanished."

"Check death records."

"Will do."

I grow lightheaded, and no wonder. I haven't eaten all day. I stop by the Gas & Go and fill the tank of the squad car. Before I pay the clerk, I microwave a beef and green chili burrito and pour myself a large cup of black coffee. I wolf down half the burrito on my way out the door and take several gulps of coffee before climbing behind the wheel.

I stop by the hardware store and catch Demetrius locking up for the day. "I'm sorry I missed your call last night." I say. "Wayne Gerber and his thugs scared the bejesus out of Luke and Jordan. The good news is, we busted the goons."

"Good for you."

"If I don't close this case today, the chief is going to hand off jurisdiction to the sheriff and his team."

"Maybe that's for the best," Demetrius says.

"Do you sell pocket-sized tape recorders?"

"I carry two models."

Demetrius takes two recorders packaged in stiff plastic off the shelf behind the register and sets them on the counter.

"What's the difference?" I ask.

"The Sony model costs seven dollars more than the generic brand."

"Sell me the Sony," I say, not wishing to take any chances.

"Take it," Demetrius says. "But you owe me a date night after you close this case."

"I don't deserve you."

"We've established that."

Rose and Trixie eye me with suspicion when I drive up. I leap out and say, "I come in peace." They hear me out and allow me to search around the trash cans behind their house. I find what I'm looking for, process the scene, and rush back to the station.

Sergeant Reeves runs the fingerprints found on the two food storage bags through the system. As I'd hoped, we get a match. I call Kaden. He agrees to test the bags for toxins immediately. I'm back on the road when my radio crackles to life.

"Nowak? It's Lecoq. You are not going to believe this. After Maya Kumar graduated with her master's degree from New York University, she went to work for Sinclair Investments."

———

I PULL up before the Sacred Root Apothecary a little before six o'clock. Padma Patel's brow furrows when I walk through the door.

"Maya Kumar, I need to ask you some questions."

Padma looks like I slapped her in the face. She gathers her wits and smiles. "I beg your pardon?"

"You graduated from New York University in 1996 and went to work for Sinclair Enterprises."

For the first time, Padma Patel, or Maya Kumar, rather, loses her composure. Her dark eyes narrow. She clenches her fists. I step backward and prepare to draw my weapon if she's armed.

"How did you—?"

"When you learned the Sinclairs had bought a house here, you leased this shop."

"A mere coincidence."

"You befriended Daphne and convinced her of the benefits of elderberry syrup."

"Daphne came to me for help. That's not a crime."

"A jury might consider intentionally substituting belladonna berries for elderberries homicide."

"Bill Sinclair raped my mother," Maya Kumar says. "Did you know that?"

"Not according to the school's records."

"Of course not. The powers that be at Yale did not wish to alienate the Sinclairs and their money."

"What became of your mother?" I ask, hoping I can get her to open up. Talkative suspects often betray their intentions.

"When she returned home pregnant with me, her family turned her away." Tears spill down Maya Kumar's cheeks. "After I was born, she doused herself in petrol and set herself on fire. She survived for three days before succumbing to her wounds."

Maya Kumar has spent her life plotting revenge against the man she considers responsible for her mother's death. If anyone understands that level of rage, it's me. But I can't let her get away with killing a man.

"You poisoned Bill Sinclair."

"Where is your evidence, officer?"

"You identified the bag marked belladonna berries as belonging to you. I found another bag containing trace amounts of elderberries near where I discovered that bag. We found your fingerprints on both bags."

"Of course you found my fingerprints on the bag of belladonna berries. They came from my freezer. Whoever stole them must've taken another storage bag of mine."

"Or you fed the elderberries to Rose and Trixie's chickens and left the bags there hoping they'd get blamed."

"That's an interesting theory, officer."

"The prosecution will paint your mother as a desperate young woman who lied because a wealthy young man rejected her."

"But that is not true!"

"Bill Sinclair was an important man."

"Bill Sinclair was a monster! He deserved to die for what he did to my mother."

"So, you took matters into your own hands."

"I did what your elite American justice system failed to do."

"You must've plotted your revenge for years."

"I would've gotten away with it had that fool of an actor not drunk the belladonna syrup."

"Maya Kumar, you're under arrest for murder."

"It's your word against mine, officer."

I hold up the recorder Demetrius gave me.

"You taped our conversation without my permission. That's entrapment."

"New York is a one-party consent state, and I consented to be recorded."

Maya Kumar rushes toward the door. I block her path. She knocks over a rack of greeting cards and dashes behind the counter. I leap over the mess and scramble after her. She blows a pinch of dark purple dust in my face. I stagger backward. My vision blurs. My head grows light. I sit down on the floor before I fall on my ass.

For the moment, I forget where I am. A door opens and shuts. Or does it? I can't be certain of anything right now. I crawl into the bathroom and rinse my eyes over the sink. My mouth is so dry. I gulp water straight from the faucet.

Sirens sound outside. I stumble out the front door of the shop and find Sergeant Reeves and Officer Lecoq wrestling handcuffs around the wrists of a raving Padma Patel. I rush to assist my fellow officers. My knees cave, and I black out.

CHAPTER THIRTY-EIGHT

CHIEF JIMENEZ SITS behind her desk, listening to the recording I captured of my conversation with Maya Kumar. My head aches, but I'm no longer disoriented from the powdered belladonna Kumar threw in my face. Had I ingested the toxic dust instead of merely inhaling a few whiffs, I'd be hospitalized right now.

"You trusted your instincts, Nowak, and they did not let you down."

Knowing I've done the right thing by pursuing justice even after the case was closed makes me reconsider my decision to join the local force last year. If I'd returned to my post in the city and eaten crow for a while, I'd have my detective badge by now.

"I called the sheriff."

"This is my investigation."

"Maya Kumar is an Indian citizen. We don't have the resources to manage a case with international implications."

"That's bullshit."

"That's reality. You will turn over your evidence to the county. Is that clear?"

"Yes, ma'am."

"I realize you've been putting in major overtime and

appreciate your hard work. Our force may be small, but we're mighty." Chief Jimenez holds up a manila folder of resumes. "I intend to hire three new officers before the Fourth of July weekend."

"If the fireworks display in Turtle Park attracts the size of crowds it drew last year, we're going to need the extra force."

"Go home and rest, Nowak. You can fill out your reports tomorrow," Chief Jimenez says. "I'll wait for the sheriff and oversee the transfer of our suspect."

———

WHEN I REACH HOME, I find Demetrius's pickup parked in our driveway. He's been more than patient with me while I've worked this case. I owe him a night to remember. He rises from the couch when I step through the door.

"I should get home before Flower pees on my bearskin rug."

"Don't rush off on my account."

"Not everything is about you, Cal." Demetrius hugs Annie and whispers, "I'll call you."

"I'll see you later," I say.

"You know where I live."

Demetrius dashes out the door. Does he expect me to chase him and beg forgiveness? Or should I give him his space? When he gets moody like this, I'm never certain how I'm supposed to respond.

"You look like crap, Cal," Annie says. "Go change your clothes."

"You're not going to believe the day I've had."

"Are you hungry?"

"Starving."

"I baked a lasagna. I'll fix you a plate."

I shuffle into my room, strip off my uniform, and step into the shower. The knotted muscles in my shoulders unfurl under the steaming hot spray. I shave and trim my beard, slip on a black tee shirt with a pair of clean blue jeans, and join Annie on the couch. She passes me a plate of gooey lasagna.

"I've hardly seen you these past few days."

"I've been a little busy," I say.

"Are you still chasing your theory about Bill Sinclair being poisoned?"

"It's not a theory. Maya Kumar confessed."

"Who's Maya Kumar?"

"That's Padma Patel's real name."

"You're kidding me."

I share as much information as I can without compromising the case.

"That sounds like a movie."

"I know, right?"

"I am amazed by how far some people will go for revenge," Annie says. "I watched this true crime documentary the other night, and some of the choices those inmates made boggled my mind. This one woman hacked her husband to death with a meat cleaver because he flirted with the cashier at the grocery store. Can you believe that?"

"You wouldn't sleep at night if you'd seen the things I have."

"You love your job, don't you?"

"When I'm on duty, I feel like I'm making the world a little bit safer."

"A badge makes for a cold bedfellow."

"What does that mean?"

"You're a smart boy. You'll figure it out." Annie takes a sip of her wine. "Hopefully, before it's too late."

"What did Demetrius say?"

"Talk to him."

"I will."

I rinse my plate and put it in the dishwasher, grab my keys and wallet, and dash out the door.

———

FLOWER LEAPS on me when I step through the door. I crouch and pet the wriggling dog. He gives me kisses, which is more than I can say for Demetrius, who sits on the couch, watching a nature program on the television. A cheetah on the screen corners and kills a baby warthog. That may be the natural order, but I can't help but feel sorry for the warthog. The poor creature never had a chance. I take a seat on the couch and place my hand on Demetrius's thigh.

"I know I've been distracted—"

"I fell in love with a cop."

"You're upset."

"I'm not mad at you for doing your job if that's what you think."

"I'll make this up to you."

Demetrius turns off the television and opens the front door. Flower bounds outside. A crisp breeze rustles the leaves in the trees. A waxing moon and hundreds of stars light up the night sky. He takes my hand, and together we watch Flower race around the yard, sniffing the ground.

Once we're back inside, Demetrius shuts Flower in his room for the night and crawls into bed with me. Our mouths lock in a passionate kiss, and our hands rove over one another's bodies. His hardness presses against my thigh. I roll over, and we make love for the first time in days. Neither of us lasts long. We collapse in a sweaty heap. He whispers in my ear, "I love you," and for the first time I don't hesitate to say the words back.

Long after Demetrius drifts asleep, I lie awake, stewing over the fact that I must hand over all my evidence tomorrow. I'm seriously starting to question what I'm doing with my life.

At some point, I must've drifted off because Demetrius brings me coffee in bed. I check the time on his digital alarm clock—

7:46 A.M. It's been a while since I've slept this late. I sit up and give him a kiss.

"I should be bringing you coffee in bed."

"We need to talk."

"Uh-oh."

"You don't understand what it's like for me, lying awake all night when you're on patrol, fearing the worst."

"I'm sorry."

"All I can do is pray you're not lying in a pool of blood on the side of the road somewhere with a bullet lodged in your brain or your heart."

"I'm not used to—"

"Being in a relationship," Demetrius says. "How much longer are you going to use that excuse?"

"It's not an excuse."

"We've been dating for over a year now."

"Okay, fine. I'm an asshole. Is that what you want me to say?"

"Let's not fight."

"Who's fighting?"

"Don't yell at me."

"I'm not yelling!"

"Forget I said anything."

Demetrius goes into the bathroom. Seconds later, I hear the water running. I crawl out of bed and find him seated in the tub with the shower running. He's crying. I enfold him in my arms. He squirms free and rinses his face under the steamy spray.

"Did I do something wrong?" I ask. "I mean, more than usual."

"I'm fine."

"You're not fine. Talk to me. Please."

"Twenty-two years ago today, the doctors took my mother off life support."

"Oh, Demi, I'm sorry."

I enfold Demetrius in my arms and feel his heartbeat against my chest.

"I'm grateful I had her in my life for as long as I did." Demetrius wipes his eyes. "I'm sorry. I didn't expect this day would hit me so hard."

"I've got you."

Demetrius pulls back and looks me in the eye. "I'm glad you're here."

"I'm the lucky one," I say. "Ask anyone."

"Hold me a little longer."

We cling to one another in silence. I've slept with dozens of guys over the years, and no one has ever made me feel this way. I'm addicted to Demetrius's kisses. His touch. His smile. He makes me dream things I never thought possible.

CHAPTER THIRTY-NINE

BY THE TIME I reach the station, it's almost noon. I find Chief Jimenez seated behind her desk, sorting through stacks of paperwork. She informs me the sheriff and his deputies booked Maya Kumar into the county jail.

"The sheriff has assigned a detective who will close the case. Lecoq has already handed over his computer records. I need you to share everything you have."

"If it weren't for me, there'd be no case."

"No one will forget that. Least of all me. But the county is better prepared to get justice. Isn't that what you want?"

"Of course. It's just—"

"You're a cop, Nowak. You did good work. That should be enough for you."

If I'd stayed in the city and kept my nose clean, I might be cracking major cases now instead of patrolling a sleepy mountain town, telling downstaters where they can find the best burger, and tucking parking tickets under their windshield wipers.

"Nowak!" Sergeant Reeves shouts. "We've got a domestic at that rundown trailer park north of town. Armed and dangerous. I need backup."

"Go!" Chief Jimenez says. "Washington is on patrol if you need her. And I can be there in a flash."

I follow Sergeant Reeves out the door. We leap inside the squad car and speed toward the scene.

"Can I ask you something personal, Nowak?"

"I wish you wouldn't."

"You're gay, right?"

"Are you finally coming out of the closet?"

"You wish."

"Not a chance."

"I'm being serious."

"What do you want to know?"

"How do I tell Roxie her blowjobs suck? Or don't...suck...you know what I mean?"

"If the sex is bad, I don't return for seconds."

"You think I should break up with her?"

"You're an idiot, Reeves. You've found a woman who'll put up with your crap. Even if you never get laid again in your life, you should be thanking your lucky stars."

As we approach the trailer in question, we spot a shoeless hulk of a man wearing a stained undershirt and sweatpants pacing around the yard, shaking his fists and shouting. His fat toes poke through the holes in his dirty socks.

"Bitch, let me inside! This is my frigging trailer!"

"Another crackhead," Sergeant Reeves mutters. He pulls over and parks the squad car several yards from the scene.

"That guy's high on methamphetamine," I say. "Not crack."

"How do you know?"

"Look at the way he's scratching and picking at his skin. His meth high's worn off, and he's tweaking badly."

"Nowak, you're smarter than you look."

"I wish I could say the same for you, Reeves."

Our suspect grabs an ax from the bed of his broken-down pickup and takes wild swings at the trailer.

"Call for backup," Sergeant Reeves says. He steps out of the squad car. "And cover me, while I try to talk some sense into this fool." I follow orders. Reeves steps forward and freezes. "And Nowak, if you must discharge your weapon, try not to hit me, okay?"

"You're confusing me with Lecoq."

Officer Lecoq may be a whiz at computers, but we've gone to the gun range together, and his shots miss center mass more often than not.

"Open up, woman!" Our tweaking suspect pounds on the door. "Or I'll burn this trailer to the ground with you inside!"

"Talk to me, buddy," Sergeant Reeves says. He cautiously advances a few steps. "What's happening here?"

"This doesn't concern you, Five-O."

"Whatever is going on, we'll work it out."

Sergeant Reeves remains chill under pressure, which I admire. I stand ready to discharge my weapon, but I hope I don't need to pull the trigger.

"Nobody can fix this mess."

"What mess, buddy?" Sergeant Reeves says, his voice soft and soothing, like he's addressing a child. "Talk to me."

Our suspect lowers the ax and whines, "I've screwed up my life." He punches the trailer door. "What is wrong with me?"

"Easy, buddy. You're tripping. That's all. Let us help you."

"Nobody can help me."

"Who's inside the trailer?"

"My old lady and our baby."

"Are you all right in there, ma'am?" Sergeant Reeves shouts.

"I'm fine," a feeble female voice that sounds familiar says. "Huey smoked the last of his meth two nights ago, and now he's accusing me of stealing his drugs."

It's as I suspected. Huey is crashing hard.

"Bitch, you better open up!"

Huey pounds on the trailer door. The woman inside shrieks.

"You aren't taking my baby, woman!"

"Is that what this is about, Huey? You don't want . . . what's your name, ma'am?" Sergeant Reeves asks without taking his eyes off Huey.

"Jewel," the woman calls out.

I knew I recognized that voice. I didn't realize Kit's younger sister, Jewel, lived out here.

"You don't want Jewel to take your baby away?" Sergeant Reeves asks.

"I'll shoot the bitch dead before I'll let her take my kid."

Huey kicks a clay flowerpot across the yard. It shatters. He raises his axe overhead.

"Stay out of my business, Five-O!"

Sergeant Reeves steps back and says, "Threatening a police officer is a bad idea, buddy. Now drop the axe." Huey fails to comply. The sergeant adds, "I don't want to shoot you, but I will."

"Go on! I deserve to die."

"Your baby needs a daddy, Huey," Sergeant Reeves says. "Now, lower that axe, and let's figure things out."

Huey spots me. His bloodshot eyes widen. "I see you, too, Five-O. If you so much as twitch, I'll charge." Perspiration streams down the big goon's ugly mug and soaks his filthy undershirt. I'm sweating bullets myself, but for different reasons.

Sirens sound in the distance. Their blare grows louder. Officer Washington arrives on the scene, tires screeching. She leaps out, ducks behind her car door, and draws her weapon.

"Hold your fire!" Sergeant Reeves shouts. "Nobody needs to get hurt here." He backs away and confers with Officer Washington for a few seconds. Washington creeps around behind the squad car and waddles my way in a crouch. I ask what's up. She shares the sergeant's plan of action.

"Let's talk about this, Huey," Sergeant Reeves says. He cautiously approaches our unhinged suspect.

Officer Washington and I creep around the edge of the woods

in the opposite direction and position ourselves to the rear of Huey. He paces around the yard, arguing with whatever paranoid delusions cloud his chemically altered brain.

Sergeant Reeves inches a few more steps forward and gives a slight nod. Officer Washington flies through the air like a linebacker and tackles Huey. The sergeant and I leap into the fray and disarm our suspect.

Officer Washington straddles Huey around the waist and grabs his elbows. "Give me your hands, Huey." Huey clasps his fists. Washington wrestles his left arm free and shouts, "Cuffs! Who has cuffs? Quick!"

Grabbing my handcuffs, I secure Huey's wrist. Reeves and Washington wrench the big guy's right arm out from underneath him. I secure that wrist as well. The sergeant produces a hobble, and we restrain our suspect's legs. Working in tandem from both sides of the squad car, we slide the guy into the back seat on his stomach and slam the doors shut.

Officer Washington leans against the hood of the squad car and wipes the sweat from her brow with a bandana. "I don't need to go to the gym after that."

"The meth head's lucky he didn't get shot," I say.

"I've only discharged my weapon once in the line of duty," Sergeant Reeves says. "And that was enough."

Sergeant Reeves doesn't have to say when that was because Officer Washington and I were both there when we apprehended the former chief of police who shot and killed Kit and abducted little Evan Langford.

I knock on the trailer door. Jewel peeks outside. She clutches her baby in her arms.

"We've arrested Huey."

"What happens now?"

Sergeant Reeves explains the process. I pass Jewel my business card and tell her to call if she needs anything.

CHAPTER FORTY

AFTER GRABBING a late lunch at the diner, I return to the station and wait for Detective Murphy from the sheriff's office. The little guy arrives a half hour late and blames his tardiness on the traffic. With his sharp features and twitchy nose, he reminds me of a rat. He grabs a tissue from the box on the desk and sneezes.

"Allergies."

"Shall we get started?" I ask, eager to get this meeting over with.

"You wouldn't happen to have a bottle of water, would you? My throat's so dry."

"There's a cooler down the hall."

Detective Murphy fills a cup of water and settles across the table from me. "Show me what you have," he says. His nonchalance rubs me the wrong way. I slide my files across the table. He flips through the pages and says, "Let me hear the recording."

I play the tape through twice.

"Tell Officer Lecoq I'll call him if I have any questions."

"If you need me to testify—"

"I'll handle things from here."

Detective Murphy struts out the door with my evidence. I want to punch my fist through a wall. Instead, I go for a run. I should never have left the city.

When I return to the station drenched in sweat, Officer Washington tosses me the keys to the squad car and clocks out for the day. I go on patrol, speeding through the red light at the intersection because I can. Taking a deep breath, I slow my roll.

As I pass the Nyes Landing Diner, I spot Mama Libby and Moses wandering through the parking lot with their eyes focused on the ground. I pull over and ask what they're doing.

"I dropped my purse on my way into the diner," Mama Libby says. "My wallet must've fallen out."

"You should call your bank," I say.

"He's right," Moses says. "One time, I left my wallet at the grocery store, and someone picked it up and spent two hundred dollars of my hard-earned money before I figured out what had happened."

"When I got out of the car," Mama Libby says, retracing her steps, "my sleeve caught on the door handle and my purse spilled on the ground." She bends down.

"Let me help." Crouching, I feel around under the car and find the wallet behind the front wheel. "Here you go."

"You're a lifesaver, Cal," Mama Libby says. "Why don't you join us?"

"I'm on patrol."

"How about dinner tomorrow night, then?"

"What can I bring?"

"Demetrius."

"If he's free."

"If you ask, he'll be free. We'll see you tomorrow night. Seven o'clock."

Mama Libby takes Moses's arm, and the pair shuffle across the parking lot toward the diner.

Annie calls on my cellular phone.

"Are you busy, Cal?"

"I'm on patrol, but the streets are quiet. Why? Do you need something?"

"A ride home. My car was making a strange rattling noise this morning, so I dropped it off with Howie at the garage."

Annie stands on the sidewalk out front when I pull up before the elementary school. She hops inside the car and thanks me for rescuing her.

"You're welcome to borrow my pickup."

"Mom's coming over."

"How's Nadine?"

"Depressed."

"Why?"

"Stanley got offered a job in Kansas City."

"If he asked her, do you think she'd go with him?"

"Who knows with my mom?"

Demetrius has built a life here. I could never ask him to move to the city with me. That wouldn't be fair. I hope I'm not faced with choosing between my relationship and my career because I don't know what I'll do.

When I drop Annie off at the house, I spot Gladys Crabtree watering her front lawn. She eyes me suspiciously. I smile and wave before driving away. She's an old woman all alone in the world. I must be more patient with her.

———

AFTER MY SHIFT, I call Demetrius and vent about losing my case. He invites me over. When I pull up, he's tossing a football around the yard with Flower. I park and leap out.

A mischievous grin lights up Demetrius's face. "Go long!" He hurls the football my way. I sprint across the grass with my arms outstretched and snatch the ball out of the air before momentum takes me down in a graceless somersault. Laughter bubbles up as I spring back to my feet and toss the ball back to him.

For a while, we fall into an easy rhythm—throw, catch, repeat. Flower bounds back and forth between us, wagging his tail. My grip slips, and I throw the ball too high. It sails over Demetrius and lands in the woods. Flower dashes into the underbrush and returns with the ball clutched in his mouth. Demetrius wipes off the slobber and fakes a pass, then lunges and tackles me. We tumble onto the grass in a tangle of limbs and laughter.

Pinned beneath Demetrius, I catch my breath. He leans in close. His dark eyes soften. "I'm sorry you had to hand off your evidence," he says. "That sucks." And then he kisses me.

"I didn't realize how much I missed my dream of becoming a detective until this case came along."

An awkward silence filled with the weight of unspoken words settles over us. After a while, Demetrius asks, "Are you sorry you moved back home?"

"I'm not sorry I met you."

Demetrius helps me onto my feet, and we go inside. Flower laps up water from his bowl. Demetrius kicks off his sneakers and asks if I'm hungry.

"Starving," I say, shucking off my boots. "I haven't eaten since lunch."

"I made venison stew from that eight-point buck I shot last fall."

"Smells delicious."

"Let me fix you a bowl."

How did a guy like me, who detests the great outdoors, end up dating a man who hikes, hunts, and fishes?

"Why do you put up with me?"

"You're my cross to bear." Demetrius sets a steaming bowl of venison stew before me. "Eat before you get any grumpier."

As I shovel stew into my mouth, the glassy eyes of the bearskin rug stare my way.

"Don't you ever tire of that bear watching your every move?"

"That bear would've eaten my brothers and me if my grandfather hadn't shot him dead."

I wolf down my venison stew, even though it's so hot it burns the roof of my mouth.

"Before you lick the bowl, there's a whole pot on the stove."

"I'm ready for dessert," I say, pulling Demetrius down on the couch. We kiss and snuggle for a few minutes before retiring to the bedroom.

CHAPTER FORTY-ONE

Tuesday afternoon, I'm seated at my desk at the station, filling out an incident report on a fender bender I responded to earlier, when Detective Murphy calls and questions my handling of the evidence from the theater. I remind him that the medical examiner ruled Crispin's death as an overdose.

"I don't doubt your credibility, Officer Nowak."

"You could've fooled me."

"You didn't risk your badge pursuing this case only to let it get dismissed in court, did you?"

I shake my head and, realizing he can't see me, grunt, "No."

"Then help me get justice."

"How?"

"Tell me what made you suspect poisoning that night at the theater."

"I've dealt with my fair share of overdoses when I was with the NYPD. I've never seen anyone turn that shade of red. His skin was so hot it burned my fingers. And dry as a bone. With every other overdose I've witnessed, the victim has been drenched in sweat."

"Interesting."

"If you need me to testify, I'm happy to take the stand."

"I doubt that will be necessary," Detective Murphy says. "I'll let you know if I have any further questions." He hangs up. His dismissive attitude pisses me off.

———

DEMETRIUS IS DRESSED and ready when I arrive. He climbs into the passenger seat of my pickup and gives me a kiss.

"What's in the bag?" I ask as if I didn't know. He makes the same thing for every party.

"My artichoke dip."

I chuckle.

"We can't show up empty-handed."

Traffic is light even by Nyes Landing standards. We reach Mama Libby's house in minutes and park behind Moses's Impala.

"We're here!" I shout when we walk through the door.

"In the kitchen, boys!"

Demetrius hands Mama Libby his dip. She thanks him with a kiss on the cheek.

Through the kitchen window, I spot Moses shuffling downstairs from his apartment over the garage, clutching a bottle of wine in his frail arms.

"I think I have a leak under my sink," Mama Libby says.

"I'll take a look," Demetrius says.

"If I don't get called in to work tomorrow," I say. "I'll come by and mow your lawn."

"You boys spoil me."

"After all you've done for me, it's the least I can do."

"How's your case going?"

"Don't ask."

"What's wrong, son?"

I tell her what happened without revealing any of the sensitive details.

"That little jerk has the nerve to question my police work!"

"You don't need to yell," Mama Libby says. "My hearing is fine."

"Sorry about that. If I hadn't stayed on the case, though, we might never have discovered those men were poisoned. I should've stayed in the city and cleaned up my record. I'd have made detective by now."

"Or you'd be dead," Mama Libby says.

"Who died?" Moses asks.

"Moses, get your hearing checked," Mama Libby says. "I'm tired of reminding you."

Demetrius and I set the table. Mama Libby says grace, and we dig in. The vegetable risotto is so good that I almost forget it's meatless . . . almost.

"I picked up this rosé from the liquor store," Moses says. "It was on sale. I hope it's not too sweet." He pours four glasses and passes them around. "When I was in Nam, I tried the most delicious rice wine. It had—"

"Eat your risotto, Moses," Mama Libby says, "before it gets cold."

I'm not much of a wine drinker, but Mama Libby and Demetrius agree the rosé pairs well with the risotto, whatever that means.

Moses launches into a story about how the Vietnamese brew rice wine, which I tune out because I'm obsessing over having to hand over all my evidence to the county. The longer I fume, the more convinced I become that I made a mistake by leaving the city. I should check in with my old partner, Ahn Tran, and find out how things are going at my old precinct.

After dinner, Demetrius and I load the dishwasher. Demetrius crawls under the sink and inspects the pipes. "I need plumber's tape. I might have some in my pickup. Oh, wait. You drove."

"Show me the leak, and I'll fix it when I stop by tomorrow."

Demetrius tells Mama Libby not to run the dishwasher until the leak is patched. We visit until Moses goes home and say goodnight ourselves.

CHAPTER FORTY-TWO

WEDNESDAY MORNING, I grab a cup of black coffee and a microwave breakfast burrito from the Gas & Go and finish my last bite as I pull into Mama Libby's driveway.

Mama Libby greets me at the door. "I can't believe they actually gave you a day off."

"I may still get called in."

"You need rest."

"I'm here to fix your sink."

"I just brewed a pot of coffee. Help yourself."

I pour a cup, take a few sips, and crawl under the sink.

"I'm worried about Moses," Mama Libby says.

"Why?" I ask.

I turn off the water valve and turn on the faucet so any water remaining in the pipe can drain out.

"He's getting forgetful. More than usual."

"How so?"

I dry the pipe with a dish towel and remove the fitting with an adjustable wrench.

"This morning, he wandered off into the woods and thought he was back in Vietnam. It scared me."

I wrap plumber's tape around the threads, replace the fitting, and turn on the water. The pipes rumble, and water spews from the faucet.

"All fixed."

"You want me to make you some breakfast? I can fry you up some eggs and ham if you'd like."

"I ate earlier."

"What should we do about Moses?"

"Who is this 'we' you speak of?"

"Don't get smart with me, boy."

"I don't know what to tell you."

"Are you sure I can't fix you something to eat?"

"Maybe after I mow your lawn."

"You don't need to do that," Mama Libby says. "It's your day off."

"When I finish, a ham sandwich would be nice."

The sun shines bright through the few stray clouds in the sky. I shuck off my tee shirt and soak up its warm rays. A cool breeze wafts over my skin. I open the garage door and check the tank on the lawnmower. It's half full, and the gas can is empty. In case I run out of fuel before I finish, I mow the front lawn first, which is on a steep hill, so I get a good workout. When I cut the grass in the backyard, Sparky races up and down inside her dog run, barking at the top of her lungs. The lawnmower sputters and dies a few feet from the end of my last row. I rinse off the blades, put away the machine, and toss the gas can into my pickup so I can fill it later.

Before going inside, I play with Sparky. The energetic dog leaps on me and licks my face. She's a smart girl. If she were younger and more trainable, she'd make a good police dog.

"Wash up," Mama Libby says when I go inside. "I set out a fresh towel for you in the bathroom. You have clothes you left in the chest of drawers in your old room that you can change into."

My high school bedroom, where I stayed several weeks last

year when I returned home and helped Mama Libby recover from a broken wrist, holds many memories.

"By the time you're dressed, your sandwich will be ready. Do you want mustard or mayonnaise?

"Mustard, please. And cheese, if you have any."

"Have I got cheese? Do you want cheddar, Swiss, or provolone?"

"Cheddar, please."

I go upstairs and shower off the dirt and grass. The showerhead leaks. I'll pick up a new one from Demetrius and install it the next time I come over.

"Leave your dirty clothes," Mama Libby says. "I'm about to do laundry. I'll throw them in with my load."

"You don't need to do my laundry."

"Don't argue with me, young man." Mama Libby hands me my plate. "Eat your sandwich." I grab a bag of potato chips off the counter and take a seat at the table. She pours a cup of coffee and joins me.

"When Frank and I first got married, he worked at the lumber mill day and night because we needed the money. But we eventually realized that our time together meant more than anything we could buy. He cut back his hours, and when we found we couldn't conceive, we became certified foster parents with the state and took in children who needed a safe haven for a while."

"Why are you telling me this?"

"Relationships take work."

"You think I don't know that?"

"Would you like more lemonade?"

"I know Demetrius and I haven't spent much time together lately, but this case—"

"There's always going to be another case."

"If I'd stayed in the city, I'd have—"

"May I remind you, young man, that you were on administrative leave when you came home last year?"

There is no point in arguing with Mama Libby.

"I should get going."

I give Mama Libby a kiss on the cheek.

"Get some rest," Mama Libby says, "and a haircut."

"Yes, ma'am."

As I pull out of the driveway, my cellular phone rings.

"Officer Nowak, it's Detective Murphy from the sheriff's office."

"What do you want?"

"I thought you might like to know that the district attorney's pursuing charges of second-degree murder and criminal use of a chemical weapon against Maya Kumar, aka Padma Patel."

"What about Crispin?"

"Reopening that case might muddy the waters."

"So you boys only dole out justice when it's not too much hassle."

"That's not what I meant. It's just—"

I hang up the phone and pound my fists against the steering wheel since I can't punch Murphy. Oliver Crispin may have been a hot mess, but he didn't die of an overdose and deserves for his name to be cleared. To blow off some steam, I take a drive through the mountains, and before I know it, I'm at the cemetery. The grass over my mother's grave needs trimming. I must call the groundskeeper. I throw away the flowers from my last visit, which are so dry they fall apart, and replace them with some wildflowers I pick near the creek.

"I'm not sure coming home was such a good idea, Mom," I say. "I spend my days writing parking tickets and giving directions to lost downstaters. The one real case I've caught since I joined the local force got snatched away from me."

Mom can't answer me, but I feel her presence, and that comforts me. After sitting quietly with her for a few minutes, I know what I must do.

An hour's drive later, I turn down a side street in Troy, New

York, and slow to a crawl so I can read the addresses spray-painted on the curb. I reach the house where my father may reside. A tall, paunchy guy in his late fifties wearing a golf shirt and Bermuda shorts finishes mowing the lawn. He pulls a bandana from his back pocket and dabs the sweat from his brow. A heavyset woman brings him a glass of water, which he gulps down. She must be his new wife. I wonder if he has new kids, too. I speed away before he sees me. I should never have come here.

My phone rings. Thinking it's Murphy calling again, I snap, "What now?"

"Somebody woke up on the wrong side of the bed, as my abuela always said whenever one of us grandkids gave her attitude."

"Sorry, chief. I just—"

"We need to talk."

My heart skips a beat. What have I done now?

"What's up?"

"I'd rather discuss matters face-to-face."

I fret all the way to the station and find the chief in her office.

"Sit, Nowak."

I slide into the chair across from her and notice she has my file open on her desk.

"Are you happy here, Nowak?"

Of all the times for her to ask me that question.

"It's been a bit of an adjustment," I say, hoping that will satisfy her.

"As you know, the city council has approved funds to expand the department."

I nod.

"I need to know if you're planning on sticking around."

Her question catches me off guard.

"I heard you might return to the city."

"Who told you that?"

"Believe it or not, Nowak, there are people in this town who care about you."

"Fine. Don't tell me."

"I know you're disappointed," Chief Jimenez says.

"It's just—"

"I wouldn't have asked you to hand off the case if we weren't so short-staffed." Chief Jimenez leans forward. "You're a pain in my ass, Nowak. But you're a good cop."

"I never imagined I'd be spending my life arresting drunks and ticketing downstaters for parking violations. I was on track to make detective at the NYPD."

"I've seen your test scores," Chief Jimenez says. "They're impressive. So are your recommendation letters."

"I'm not sure if the NYPD will take me back, but I need to find out."

"They will," Chief Jimenez says.

"How would you know?"

"I spoke with your former captain."

"Why would you do that?"

"He'll take you back, but he can't promise you'll make detective."

"Are you trying to get rid of me?"

"Before I propose naming you as Nyes Landing's first detective, I need to know you're going to stay put."

I did not see that coming.

"Not full-time, of course. We don't have enough major crimes. You'll still have to work patrol shifts. But you'll take the lead on any cases we catch."

I'm speechless.

"I have the budget to hire three new officers and lease a couple more squad cars."

"I don't know—"

"I need your answer by the end of the week."

CHAPTER FORTY-THREE

AFTER DRIVING around town aimlessly for an hour, I reach the elementary school as the bell rings. Shrieking kids stream out the double doors and line up for their buses. Annie stands on the grass, listening to an irate woman who I assume is the mother of the little freckle-faced girl with the strawberry-blond pigtails standing beside her. Annie spots me and waves. I wave back. The irate woman drags her little girl away in a huff.

"What's up?" Annie asks without taking her eyes off the rowdy swarm of children.

"Are you busy after work?"

"Helena and I are going to the new *Matrix* movie in Kingston tonight."

"Demetrius and I were supposed to see that last Sunday, but I had to work."

"You two should come with us."

"We'll see," I say. "Can we talk?"

"Give me ten minutes."

When Annie finishes loading the last of her students into their bus, we drive to the Nyes Landing Diner. Kiki brings us menus and takes our drink order—a yogurt smoothie made with fresh local strawberries for Annie and a shot of whiskey and a beer for me. We share an order of cheese fries.

"How was school?" I ask.

"The usual. But we're not here to talk about my day. What's going on?"

"As you know, I had to hand over all my evidence to the sheriff's office."

"You're disappointed, and you have every right to be."

I chug my shot of whiskey and slam down the glass.

"I'm pissed off, that's what I am!"

"Whoa!" Annie recoils.

"I'm sorry for yelling."

"Don't do anything stupid."

"Like move back to the city, you mean?"

"No . . . wait . . . what?"

"I was thinking about seeing if I could get my old job back."

"Are you serious?"

"But I don't know now."

I tell Annie how my meeting with the chief went.

"Do you want my advice?"

"I do and I don't."

"Your dream is to make detective, right?"

I nod.

"Now's your chance."

"I don't know—"

"What did Demetrius say?"

"I haven't told him yet."

"Oh, my God, Cal, what is wrong with you?"

"What do you...oh...I should've talked to him first."

"There may be hope for you after all." Annie throws a French fry at me. "Go on, get out of here."

WHEN I ARRIVE at the hardware store, I find Demetrius helping a woman choose window blinds. Several other customers await his attention. I catch his eye and ask if we can talk when he gets off work. He eyes me suspiciously and nods. I tell him I'll meet him at his cabin and go.

Flower rushes outside as soon as I open the door and runs around the lawn, sniffing for the perfect spot to do his business. He chases a squirrel. The squirrel runs into the woods. Flower gives up the chase. I scratch his chin and agree the woods are a scary place. We go inside, and I give him a piece of beef jerky. He curls up on the bearskin rug and gnaws on his treat. I pour myself a whiskey, plop down on the couch, and grab the remote control. So many channels on the television, yet I can't find anything I want to watch.

"What a day," Demetrius says when he steps through the door. "Are you hungry?" He rushes past me into the kitchen. "Let me see what I can rustle up for dinner."

"I had an interesting meeting with the chief today."

"How about pork chops?" Demetrius asks. "I can fire up the grill. I've got some fresh corn on the cob."

"Chief Jimenez spoke with my former captain at the NYPD."

"There's beer in the fridge," Demetrius says. "Help yourself."

I open a bottle and take a long pull.

"He told her that he would welcome me back if I wanted to return."

Demetrius freezes.

"Are you breaking up with me, Cal?"

"What? No."

"Then, where is this conversation going?"

"The chief offered me my detective's badge. I'd be the first in the town's history."

"That's what you've always wanted, isn't it? To make detective."

"I'd still have to patrol the streets, of course. We don't have enough crime to justify a full-time detective."

I hug Demetrius from behind and rest my chin on his shoulder.

"What are we doing here, Cal?"

"What do you mean?"

"Is this life enough for you?" Demetrius's eyes tear. He averts his gaze. "Am I enough?" I enfold him in my arms. He rests his head against my chest and whispers, "I love you."

"I love you, too."

A peaceful feeling settles over me. Maybe this is what home feels like.

ABOUT THE AUTHOR

S.F. Williams is a member of the Alliance of Independent Authors (ALLi), the Mystery Writers of America (MWA), and the NYC Writers Critique Group. He has a diverse portfolio that ranges from published short stories and poetry to reflections on fatherhood as a single gay man, but his roots lie in the theater. Williams holds a BFA from the University of Oklahoma and membership in the Actor's Equity Association, and he has acted in, directed, produced, and written over a hundred productions for the stage.

Williams's novels, characterized by their fast-paced narratives and resilient protagonists, reflect the diverse tapestry of our world.

facebook.com/sfwilliamsauthor
x.com/sfwauthor
instagram.com/sfwauthor

MAKE AN AUTHOR'S DAY!

If you enjoy *A Fatal Affair*, please consider leaving a review on Goodreads, Amazon, or the bookstore platform of your choice. Even a sentence or two would be a tremendous help and most appreciated.

Sign up for my newsletter at https://sfwilliamsauthor.com and I will notify you about upcoming book releases and giveaways.

If you think your followers might enjoy *A Fatal Affair*, please spread the word on your social media platforms. You can find me at @sfwauthor on Facebook, Instagram, and X.